Beyond

A Collection of Metaphysical Short Stories

RON TEACHWORTH

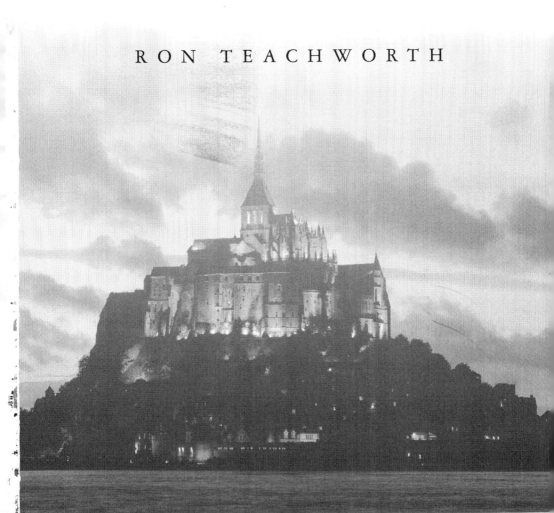

To Carrie :

All the Best ,

R

To Jilia

"Michigan artist, Ron Teachworth, has turned his talents from visual art to Literary art. He has written two incredibly charming YA books, a novel and a collection of short stories. Ron has an incredible command of setting. His novel is set in Florence, Italy, and his short stories take place in Scotland, France, Canada, New Mexico, Tennessee, Michigan and beyond. His protagonists are equally comfortable as young men or women. There's plenty of adventure at hand, the writing is beautiful yet accessible, and all the pieces are linked by religious/spiritual and even metaphysical motifs. The work has that classic, enduring quality that you recognize instantly."

Kimberly Kafka, Author

Table of Contents

Fireflies

The flat valley provided a perfect corridor for the Southwest Electric Power Company to locate the high-tension power lines that reached as far as the eye could see. Four sets of spiderlike steel structures supported eight braided cables strung less than a hundred feet above the ground. They originated at the Mindo coal-powered electric plant just north of Taos, and passed near the small town of Chimayo, and beyond to Albuquerque and on into Texas.

Transformer substations were located about every mile, units that reconstituted and amplified the electromagnetic fields, ensuring a constant flow of six thousand volts per cable. The most efficient mechanisms known to man, these cables conducted ten thousand microwatts of electric power per square centimeter. If the air was still and the humidity just right, their vibration emitted a low bass frequency that sounded like a B-flat chord on the cello.

"I get a penalty shot for that," Tamia said, getting up and dusting off her jeans. "You know you can't trip me, even if it was an accident. Look at my knee." She pointed at a two-inch tear in her jeans where blood was visible on the exposed skin.

Tamia's long black hair was braided and pinned high on her head, covered by a baseball cap. Her red long-sleeve cotton shirt fit tightly, revealing early signs of puberty. She held the soccer ball in her hands and looked at the makeshift goal: a piece of inch-thick yellow nylon rope stretched tightly between two legs of the power line towers. Two vertical pieces of rope were located twenty feet apart and staked down in the sand, marking the outline of the rectangular goal. The players moved to the sidelines and watched Tamia place the ball on a clean spot of gravel, making ready for her penalty shot.

The goaltender, Miko, a young Navajo boy, was tall for his age, and his long black hair was pulled back in a ponytail. His Converse tennis shoes were faded, his black T-shirt clung to his thin frame, and he wore a wristband decorated with bands of colored beads. He walked forward about ten feet, hoping to cut off her angle. He crouched down and, without expression, looked directly into Tamia's eyes. She would not get this shot by him.

Tamia was the best striker in the neighborhood, and when they chose teams, she was one of the first selected. The rule was they played until 6:00 p.m., and whoever was ahead was the winner. It was five minutes before six, and the teams were tied 2–2. This shot could determine the winner, at least for now, for this game, where boys and girls played as equals. After setting the ball down, she backed up twenty feet so as to get a hard run at the ball. By now, several adults had joined the crowd on the sidelines. Tamia took off and kicked the ball on the right side with all her might. The white soccer ball lifted on a straight trajectory and then suddenly started to curve left. By the time Miko noticed, he had leaped left with arms extended, but it was not enough. Tamia's shot soared through the upper left corner of the makeshift goal to a roar from her teammates as they rushed to her side. The goal was the tiebreaker, and on this cool autumn afternoon, it was Tamia's team who had won.

This gathering of young middle school students was a mixture of Navajo, Pueblo, and Mexican families living side by side in a complex of government-subsidized housing on the outer edge of Chimayo. The pastel-colored units were framed in wood, with an exterior made of plaster sheathing. The forty or so mostly two-bedroom homes were heated by natural gas and totaled no more than six hundred square feet of living space. Many of the families had left the reservation for jobs and the hope of a better education for their children.

Onida, Tamia's sister, ran up to her breathless with excitement.

"Great shot! Your team won because of you!"

"Did you see the curve I put on that shot?"

Onida grabbed her sister's hand as they started walking back toward the subdivision. The two sisters were very close. Their mother, Catori, was a full-blood Navajo who had grown up on the reservation, but when she married, had left to be with her American Mexican husband who was an electrician for the city of Taos. Catori had gone to school at the community college in Taos and had earned her certification as an early preschool teacher.

Their marriage had just begun, with one young child and one on the way, when he was called one night during a violent thunderstorm to repair the large transformer that normally provided power to the northern part of the city. They were in the process of replacing the unit when lightning struck nearby and electrocuted both workers. Grief-stricken at the loss of her husband, Catori moved back to the reservation, where she delivered Onida at the reservation clinic two months later.

The support of her family was helpful, and needed, until recently, when she took a position at Chimayo Elementary and Middle School as their first preschool teacher. The reservation was only a couple of hours away by car, and she had an aunt who lived nearby. Catori and her daughters managed the small house, a busy schedule, and all the chores.

Suddenly, Onida pulled back on Tamia's hand and pointed to a bird lying still on the ground. They knelt to look at the bird without touching it. Tamia picked up a stick and rolled the large blackbird on its back.

"It's a grackle," she said, "and it's odd, there are no signs of violence or disturbance."

Tamia looked over the gravel plain at the spotted population of small yucca plants, and the horizon peppered with rock buttes. Then she looked straight upward and realized they were kneeling directly under the power lines.

"Maybe it was the electrical wires. Sometimes they perch on the cables and get shocked because there's a leak in the coating."

"You mean it was electrocuted?" Onida asked.

"It's possible. I'll ask our science teacher."

"Should we bury it?"

Tamia shook her head. "Nature has its own way. It will provide food for other animals." She stood up and looked at the massive network of power lines. *Those lines seem awful low,* she thought.

The girls caught up with friends and scooted on home, worried they would be late for dinner. They took a shortcut through a couple of yards, hopped a fence, and snuck in the back door, hoping their mother wouldn't notice the time.

Catori said, "It's past six thirty, and dinner is almost ready. Wash up and set the table. Onida, make some juice. Tamia, make us a small salad." Catori was extremely organized, and had to be, but it was a skill that came naturally to her. The girls washed their hands in the kitchen sink and started on their tasks.

"Mom, Tamia scored a penalty shot and won the soccer game for her team."

"That's good. I hope she does as well on her science test tomorrow. Have you studied?"

"Of course I studied, and I'm going to study some more tonight. Let's eat. I'm starved."

Catori placed the food on the table, Onida set down a pitcher of lemonade, and Tamia finished the salad by adding a few slices of tomatoes. Their mom had warmed up some slices of lamb from Sunday's dinner, and made some fried corn cakes.

Catori crossed herself and lowered her head. "Onida, it's your turn."

"Father, bless this food, and forgive us our sins. Bless my sister, Tamia, for her penalty shot. In the name of the Father, Son, and Holy Spirit, amen. Let's eat."

"What happened to your knee?" Catori asked Tamia.

"I got tripped on the soccer field, ripped my jeans, and it scratched my skin…It should be all right."

"That's why she got the penalty shot. Then she put the shot past Miko, the goaltender. It was unbelievable, Mom. Tamia was something."

"Sew up the tear in your jeans. There's a needle and thread in the round tin on my dresser. Is Miko the boy who lives down the street?"

Tamia's mouth was full, but she wanted to say something before Onida chimed in. Quickly swallowing, she coughed and said, "Yeah. He's one of the smarter kids in my class, but he didn't expect the shot to bend like it did."

"His father is on the Chimayo police force, and his mother cooks at the elementary school."

"Miko's nice, but we're always competing. We usually get the highest grades in math. Sports too. He plays basketball and listens to some strange music. The Kinks. Whoever heard of the Kinks?"

They always ate dinner together. It was the time each of them could share what was going on in their lives and talk about what was coming up in the future. Catori kept the house very neat, and everyone helped with the cleaning and chores. There were assignments. Once dinner was over, Onida cleared the table, and Tamia washed the dishes while her sister swept the floor and wiped the table. When the dishes dried, they both put everything back in its place. Because she usually cooked, Catori took her coffee into the living room and watched the evening news. They depended on each other for everything, and that's how it worked. After dinner, the girls did their homework. Only after they finished could they watch TV.

* * *

The girls' adobe school was only four blocks from Polercio Plaza and housed students K–8. Dating back a hundred years, the original building was a private Catholic school operated by the archdiocese, but the local school board had purchased the old buildings and, after a complete remodeling, added two new large wings, a gymnasium, and a media center. All the students living within a mile of school were required to walk to school, enabling the school district to operate only four buses for those living on farms and in the foothills.

With backpacks in tow, the girls always scrambled to get out the door, knowing exactly how long it took to walk to school and make their first class. Onida grabbed the last piece of toast and started running to catch up with her sister, when she heard her mother.

"Don't forget your instrument!"

Onida swung around and grabbed her clarinet case and used it to push open the screen door. "Bye, Mom, I'll be home late. Orchestra practice after school."

Catori watched as her daughters matched up with their friends in a string of students walking west toward the school. The house was suddenly quiet. She looked at the coffee table and saw the needle and thread sitting next to the round tin. A photograph of her late husband was on the end table, intentionally placed as a reminder to the girls of their father. His chiseled features, dark eyes, thick black hair, and gracious smile reminded her of Tamia. She found herself going back to that night when the storm raged on, so violent she screamed when an airborne garbage can hit the back corner of their house. Right after that, the phone had rung; it was her husband's partner calling. They were to meet at the way station and assess the damage as soon as possible. The display on their clock was black. The only light in the room came from a continuous display of lightning flashing through the windows. As he had rushed to get dressed and searched in the dark for his boots, Tamia came in and got in bed with Catori.

"Where are you going, Daddy?" asked Tamia.

"Don't worry, I'll be back soon." Now dressed, he kissed them both. "I love you guys."

Catori played the scene over and over like a video loop. It was the last time she saw her husband alive.

* * *

"OK, put your books underneath your chairs and clear the tops of your desks, and yes, you're taking a short quiz."

Mr. Terry Lemke was in his late thirties, had a brush cut, and always wore a white lab coat. He was responsible for teaching the seventh- and eighth-grade science curriculum and one class of pre-algebra. His glasses were thicker than most, and the heavy black rims contrasted against his light skin. He was strict, gave more homework than was necessary, but he liked kids, and that was evident by his lame jokes.

He passed out single sheets of paper with a place for the student's name in the upper right-hand corner, and two multiple-choice questions.

"Since we have been studying electrical power, here are a couple of review questions to help you prepare for the test on Friday. The first question, what is the standard unit of measurement used for measuring force: watt, kilogram, Newton, or mile? And the second question, what is the term we use that describes the flow of an electric charge: ohm, ampere, voltage, or current? Take five minutes."

The class was stunned, and their eyes glazed over while searching to remember, was this covered in class, or was this from the textbook? At least it was a multiple-choice quiz and they could play the odds, but for most, it was a much harder quiz than they'd had before.

After collecting the quizzes, Mr. Lemke asked for a show of hands reflecting their answers. First question: watt, six hands went up; kilogram, ten hands went up; Newton, two hands; and mile, no hands. Second question: ohm, four hands; ampere, four hands; voltage, two hands; and current, ten hands went up. Mr. Lemke walked to the board and wrote down two names: Miko, Tamia.

"Did anyone notice the two hands up correctly on both questions?"

The bell rang, and Miko looked across the room at Tamia, remembering the bend she put on that shot. *Damn*, he thought.

* * *

Catori sat at her desk watching the last preschooler leave the room for recess. She hadn't slept well and felt as though she could really use a cup of coffee. The teachers' lounge was just down the hall, and maybe a hot cup of espresso roast would pick her up. The teachers' lounge was a place the staff could use their planning time to work on lesson plans, catch up on school gossip, or just take a break from the constant barrage of questions that came from their students.

Catori greeted the other teachers before grabbing a clean cup from the dish rack and pouring herself a cup. The aroma from the freshly brewed coffee was heavenly. She plopped herself down on the institutional couch, exhaled, and stared at the dust under the green chairs, thinking she should remember to talk to the custodial staff about that.

Amanda Medina laid down the local paper after a PA message called her to the office. Catori glanced down at the front page that displayed a full-color football photo from last Friday's big game, next to a headline on water rights. Across the bottom of the front page, she read a head-line: Leukemia Cases Alarm Residents. She picked up the paper and read the story, which pointed to a relationship between the corridor of high-tension power lines and cases of leukemia in children. The article outlined a report that had just been released by the National Academy of Sciences in partnership with the National Cancer Institute.

The published report in *The New England Journal of Medicine*, "Residential Exposure to Electromagnetic Fields and Acute Lymphoblastic Leukemia in Children," investigated 638 children living in and around the Southwest Electric Power line corridor. The study showed that there was a 70 percent increase in childhood leukemia found in those living 200 meters from an overhead transmission line. The article was supported by independent research conducted by the World Health Organization. It provided data that showed there were clusters of cases that existed along the edge of the corridor, which declined as families lived farther east, and dropped off substantially in areas farther away. *This is not good*, she thought.

Catori glanced at the clock and realized she had lost track of time and the bell was about to ring. She folded the paper and put it under her arm. As she walked back to her room, she recalled her neighbor telling her about a young boy in their neighborhood who was being treated in Albuquerque for leukemia. The combination of radiation and chemotherapy treatment seemed to help, and his family was encouraged by the gradual remission of the illness. The coffee was helpful, but offset by the disturbing article, creating an uneasy feeling of anxiety. *We're only blocks away from the corridor.*

The screen door slammed, and Onida shouted, "What's for dinner, Mom?" She threw her backpack on the couch, set up her music stand, opened the case, and started playing her clarinet. A half hour of music practice had to be completed before she could go outside with her friends.

Catori peeled some potatoes and listened to the clarinet scales. As she glanced out the kitchen window, she saw Tamia walking west toward the corridor. "Onida, do you play under those power lines?" she called out. Her only answer was the clarinet.

Without any direction from Catori, both girls started the pre-dinner drill, and by six o'clock, they were all sitting down to potato pancakes, asparagus, and sausage. Catori quickly asked about their day, and then started reading aloud from the article she'd found in the teacher's lounge.

"What do you think?" she said, but was interrupted by the phone ringing. It was a friend of Tamia's asking her if she wanted to study. "Call her back," Catori said. "I want to talk to you about these power lines. I'm really worried about you both playing out there."

"We found a dead bird," Onida said. "Right under the wires."

Tamia looked at her sister and spoke harshly. "We're not sure what killed that bird. It could have been many things, not necessarily the wires."

Catori thought for a minute. "Until there is some testing here in the corridor, I do not want you playing out there. Understood?"

There was silence. The girls could tell their mother was upset and meant what she said. It was getting cool outside, and there wasn't much reason to be over there anyway, so the girls acknowledged their mother, and said nothing.

* * *

The meeting was organized by the school principal and held during their science class in his conference room. There were six eighth graders and two seventh graders, dismissed by their teachers and sent down to the office. They all assumed they had done something wrong, only to find out they had been selected by their science teacher to participate in a statewide competition. The principal, Dr. James Nawara, closed the door and sat down.

"The Department of Education has created a statewide competition for science students. They are offering summer camp scholarships to those who participate, and cash awards for the winners. Your science teachers have submitted your names as some of the most outstand-ing students we have here…and I hope you choose to participate." He passed out the handout that contained all the rules and regulations for the competition. "There are a variety of topics, ranging from effects on the environment to global warming. You have about six weeks to produce a project with findings. I suggest you work in teams of two, and we have allotted fifty dollars per team for materials. Once you have decided, fill out the application and bring it into the office…Are there any questions?"

The students were in awe and dared not ask a question. To be selected to represent their school was for them an honor, and besides, this sounded like fun. All the eighth graders naturally assumed they were superior to the two seventh graders, and Tamia wanted to prove them wrong.

Returning to class, Tamia spoke to Miko in the hall. "Hey Miko, what do you think? I would like to show these eighth graders we can compete."

"Well, if you do science like you play soccer, we shouldn't have a problem."

Mr. Lemke was giving his science class their homework assignment when Miko and Tamia got back to class. He asked them to stay after the bell and fill him in on the meeting with the principal.

"How did it go?" he asked.

Tamia put the handout on his desk. "Here's the handout about the competition."

"So will the two of you team up for a project?"

"Sure," said Miko. "This girl is dynamite. We just need an idea."

They could tell by his expression that Mr. Lemke was excited. "I'll help in any way I can. If you need to use the equipment here in the lab or anything, just let me know."

* * *

The gymnasium was filling so quickly it looked as if they may need extra chairs.

It was the fall concert, and there were performances by the band students as well as the small orchestra in which Onida was second- chair clarinet. Catori was running late due to a phone call from her mother, and had to drop Onida off and then find parking. By the time they got there, the only seats they could get were near the back.

Tamia noticed Miko and his mother in the audience, remembering his younger brother was in 4ᵗʰ fourth grade. The final performance was the Oorchestra, made up of students from grades five through eight. Miko's brother, Fala, played violin and had a solo in the closing number, Canon in D. The audience gave the final performance a standing ovation as the members of the orchestra took their bows. Catori was so proud of her daughter. She struggled with some of her academic subjects, especially her math assignments, so her participation in the orchestra helped with her self-esteem. Catori had brought her a flower, and gave it to her when she walked out from behind the black curtain carrying her clarinet case.

"You were wonderful, honey. We're so proud of you." Catori noticed Tamia wander over to where Miko was standing.

Tamia said, "Your brother really plays well for his age." She paused, feeling awkward now. "Do you have any ideas for the project?"

Miko responded in his usual shy, laid-back way. "No, not really. You?"

"My mother read me a newspaper article about the effects of electromagnetic fields. It was about exposure in the corridor from the power lines. You hear anything about that?"

Miko shook his head. "No, but I'll do a search."

"Maybe we get some mice and set up two groups, one exposed and one not, and try to measure the effects," Tamia said as she noticed her mother waving her over, wanting to leave. "I gotta go, but let's talk tomorrow."

They quickly parted, and Tamia navigated back to where her mother and sister waited near the rear door. She put her arm around her sister. "Great show, sis."

* * *

Dr. Nawara was rushing to a meeting when he saw Mr. Lemke in the hallway and waved him over. He was trying to contain the contents of a large folder as he spoke rapid-fire at the science teacher.

"I would like to give a report to the board on the science projects we're submitting to the Department of Ed. Can you have it on my desk end of the week?"

Mr. Lemke swallowed hard. "Yes, sir. Any special format?"

"Just give me copies of their proposals, OK?" And off he went, leaving Lemke late for his next class.

Mr. Lemke was a stickler for punctuality, so when he walked in late, the class gave him a look he refused to acknowledge. Instead, he took attendance quickly and began his lecture, which consisted of an explanation of the concepts from the assigned reading offset with an occasional joke. The lecture that day was shortened because of an assembly, so Lemke started to wrap things up.

"Test next Friday, and I need to see Tamia and Miko before you leave. Oh yeah, did you hear about the kid who ate his homework? The teacher told him it was a piece of cake."

The bell drowned the sound of a collective class groan.

Lemke turned to Tamia and Miko. "I need your science project proposals by Thursday. Can you do it?"

"Sure," said Tamia without hesitation. "We have an idea involving electricity."

Miko played along, not really sure about the details.

"Great. See you tomorrow."

* * *

Meadow, cactus, and wildflowers mixed together at the foothills near the edge of the corridor. Tamia and Miko had arranged to meet after dinner at the end of the block and talk about the science project. The light was getting low as they walked out to the power lines. It was the place where they played and had grown up, but now there were doubts about its safety.

Tamia was doing most of the talking, while Miko kept his thoughts to himself. He hid his difficulty in reading, something they call dyslexia, and compensated by being very observant. He rarely spoke up during his classes.

The sand was still warm from the afternoon sun, and at a distance, they could see the warm air flowing upward, causing the cables to emit that sound they had come to describe as the "hum." As the sun started to set, it caught the tops of the buttes and made them look as though they were wearing light hats. Rising from the tall grass, there were tiny blurs of light that flashed a lamplight glow of orange. Fireflies. Rhythmically pulsing, these small beetles floated harmlessly above the meadow, calling to mates and warning predators.

"Look at the fireflies," said Miko. "It must be just the right time of year for a hatch. Maybe we should do a study on them?"

Tamia shook her head dismissively. "My sister and I used to try and catch them and put them in a glass jar. We were too short then. Didn't have much luck." She shoved some paper at him. "Here's the newspaper my mom gave me with the article about the power lines. Let me know what you think."

Miko folded the newspaper and put it in his pocket. "I'll read it later. Have you thought about how to design the project?"

"I did some reading. You set up two groups and create a protocol, an electromagnetic field over one, and not the other, then measure the results, to see if there are any effects. Something like that. We just need to write up something that follows his outline, and we can figure out the details later."

"Fine with me. I'm not too crazy about mice. When I was little, we used to have mice in the house, and my mother was afraid of them. I think the fear transferred to me. But, I can build the containers and do the wiring if you'll handle the mice."

Tamia smiled. "Deal. I'll write something up tonight to give to Mr. Lemke."

* * *

The next morning, a thunderstorm hit Chimayo, and the school was awash in rain gear and umbrellas. The office was jammed with students running late, and the parking lot was backed up with parents who were dropping their kids off. By midday, Mr. Lemke had given the principal the proposal from his class. He'd only had time to give it a cursory

13

look, but it clearly was a project that would measure the effects of electromagnetic fields on mice, something he found interesting. It was rough, but there was enough information he could use to share with the board. It was all very rushed, but Lemke knew there would be time to go over the details of the proposal with Tamia and Miko later.

Dr. Nawara walked into the conference room and sat at the end of the table, next to Dr. Lisa Wilkinson, the president of the board of education. She was a full professor at the University of New Mexico, Taos, and lived on a hundred-acre farm north of Chimayo. The seven members of the board were mostly businessmen and community leaders from the town who were elected for four-year terms. The only other woman was Mary Barrett, the local pediatrician. The sidebar talks came to an abrupt end as she spoke.

"Good afternoon, everyone. I guess we had a little rain this morning, which we could certainly use. I have asked Dr. Nawara to give us an overview of the projects we're submitting to the state science competition."

"Thank you, Dr. Wilkinson...members of the board. Here are the six proposals written up by selected students from our science classes. Three are from eighth-grade teams, and one is from a seventh-grade team. The eighth-grade projects are different types of plant studies, and the seventh-grade project is on electricity. Please take this home and read them over. Call me if you have any questions."

George Ruffin was the vice president, who had lost in a close runoff race to Wilkinson for board president, and was an executive for Southwest Electric, the utility responsible for the power line corridor that ran through Chimayo. He was often described as a bull in a china shop. His family had lived in Chimayo for several generations, and he had inherited a large farm west of the town that he leased out for grazing. Approaching his sixtieth birthday, he was overweight and losing his hearing, or so it seemed if the decibel level of his voice was any indication, something he put to good use when trying to intimidate such as he was now.

"What in the hell is this electricity project about?" he bellowed. "These kids don't know anything about EMFs, and neither do these left-wing journalists. The EPA has tested those lines, and they are safe. Period."

Dr. Mary Barrett was a small young woman who had just returned home from her internship in Boston, at Massachusetts General Hospital, where she had studied internal medicine. Her specialty in pediatrics was from Harvard Medical School, where she graduated in the top of her class. She returned to Chimayo because it was close to her parents' home in Santa Fe, where she was raised. She responded.

"You sound a little defensive, George. If there has been testing, then the kids won't find anything. At least they're not checking the antibiotic levels in your beef cattle." She wished she could capture the look on his face at that moment.

Lisa Wilkinson did not want a battle, not here, and not now. She had been board president for only two months, and there were more important differences that needed mending.

"We will defer to Dr. Nawara and his judgment on the projects we submit. Let's take these handouts home and read them over. Let me know if there are any other questions."

Lisa glanced at Mary with a "Thanks…You got him all riled up" look. Lisa and Mary were close friends both on the board and in the community. Lisa was the first woman to hold the office of president, and she needed all the help she could get.

Before she left, she caught Jim in the hall. "Consider another project," she said, leaving no room for a response.

He watched her open her umbrella and jump into a waiting car. *Now what do I do?* he thought.

* * *

Catori was reading the paper when Tamia came in from school and told her about what happened in Sscience that day.

"Mr. Lemke said we should find a more appropriate topic for our project. I asked him for an explanation, and he said the principal told him he thought the project was too advanced. Miko asked him why, but I think, secretly, he would rather study fireflies. What's going on, Mom?"

Catori needed a few moments to process her daughter's question. She was very intuitive and wondered if there was something more to it than "criteria." She took her time thinking. She thought she smelled a rat, but she worked for Mr. Nawara and was grateful for her job. Still, when she gave her answer, she opted for tact.

"Maybe fireflies would be fun. They're a weird little phenomenon that is beyond most people's understanding. Maybe you could subject them to something or figure out why they blink. Probably better to keep Lemke and the principal happy. You do remember I work there, right?"

"Yeah, you're right. Who cares if we all get fried by the power lines?"

Tamia grabbed the phone and went to her bedroom as Onida came into the house and headed straight to the kitchen. As always, she was starved and had to have a snack that would get her to dinner. Her mother told her there were apples in the fridge, which satisfied her for now. Tamia came out of the bedroom and sat on the couch.

"Well?" said Catori.

"Well, what? Oh, the phone call. Yeah, he was thrilled. Fireflies it is, as long as they haven't all been cooked by the power lines."

Onida walked into the living room. "I'm not sure that apple will do it. I'm still hungry."

"You're growing like a weed," Catori said, then turned to Tamia. "Maybe you should study the growth spurts in fifth graders."

Mr. Lemke was ecstatic when Tamia handed him the project outline that described a protocol to study the nature of fireflies. This whole affair was something he was not used to. He had made a decision to go into teaching, not politics. He could not wait to give it to Dr. Nawara, and before the end of the day, the three-page outline was faxed to all the board members. All was well in the small educational universe of Chimayo.

* * *

Miko and Tamia worked hard to collect the beetles in the meadow, and by the end of the week, they had six canning jars full of fireflies. At first they tried to capture the flying insect at dusk, when they started to fly, part of their mating procedure. But soon they realized if they looked on the grass stalk an hour or two before sunset, the beetles were there and nearly asleep, waiting for their witching hour. This became the time for their gathering and made the process much easier. In Miko's garage, they did their experiments and recorded their data.

The female firefly lays a clutch of fifty eggs in the soil, and it takes three weeks for the eggs to hatch into voracious larvae that go through a series of molts, where they are commonly known as glowworms. The larvae emerge in late summer. Most of their time is spent finding a mate, copulating, and then laying their eggs. Then the cycle repeats. Their study revealed that the insects emerge and loosely congregate for several weeks in a synchronous nocturnal display traditionally called "the light show." In the southern part of the United States, they are called "lightning bugs."

Their report described the time of the year, time of day, and length of display. They recorded air temperature and humidity. Their research work determined the firefly has not been found below seven hundred meters elevation. They could even draw correlations to the phases of the moon.

Miko and Tamia were immersed in science, and the time they spent together was extraordinary. They grew closer as friends, until one night, Miko came up behind Tamia and kissed her on the back of her head. She froze, lacking the experience to respond.

Finally she said, "This has gone better than I expected, thanks to you." For the first time, something changed in Tamia's body, and she felt her face flush.

Miko put his arms around her and said, "You're the one with all the brains, and besides, you're so beautiful."

"Miko!" yelled his father through the screen door from the kitchen. "It's getting late. Tia's mother called. I'll run her home in the car."

When Tamia got home, she explained once again why she was working late, but now they were finished. Everything was documented and put together in time to submit to the Department of Education, along with the other projects. It had been four long weeks, but the deadline loomed, and everything needed to be packed up, postmarked, and shipped.

Tamia closed her bedroom door and lay down, listening to her sister and mother laugh at something on TV. She felt different. Her mind was flooded with pictures of Miko and her. *What's going on?* she wondered.

The next morning she showered and, for the first time, put on a skirt and blouse, along with some blush and a touch of lipstick. Her braids, which were always pinned on the top of her head, were undone, and her hair lay past her shoulders. When she emerged from the bathroom, the changes did not go unnoticed.

"Wow, who is this girl?" Catori asked. "*Bonita*. Look, Onida, Tamia is wearing a skirt. And a little makeup."

Tamia had prepared herself for this and responded, "It's seventh-grade dress-up day. Didn't you hear?"

Catori was smart enough to get off the subject, but she sensed a loss, and it was bittersweet. "We're running late, so you both can ride with me."

* * *

The halls were jammed with students when Tamia got to her locker and pulled out her books for her morning classes. She knew the project had been delivered to the school by Miko's mom in their station wagon, so she thought it was a good reason to stop by his locker and ask if everything went OK. Her heart started pounding. She felt nervous. All this was new. She tucked in her blouse, looked for a second in her locker mirror, and pulled down on her skirt before heading for Miko's locker in the south hall.

As she turned the corner, she saw Miko talking with a cheerleader. The attractive Navajo girl smiled as they exchanged animated remarks. Tamia did an immediate about-face and rushed off to first-hour class, fidgeting now in a skirt that was not comfortable to begin with. Later, in science class, Miko was not there. Mr. Lemke acknowledged the delivery of the project and seemed happy. He approached Tamia after class.

"Everything is in order, and your project looks great. I wish you both luck in the competition."

"Have you seen Miko?" asked Tamia.

"I think he had an early dismissal. He'll probably be here tomorrow. So now it's just waiting to hear the results. It shouldn't be more than two weeks. I'll let you know as soon as I hear something." With that, Lemke hurried off in his usual way toward the lab, one shoe untied, and his keys still on his desk.

The day at school whisked by, and Tamia could not wait to get home. She hurried down to the preschool wing to catch her mom before she left for home.

Catori was behind her desk working when Tamia came in. She looked at her daughter and held her breath. She could see something was wrong. Tamia couldn't talk. She started to cry.

"What is it, Tia?" her mother asked.

Tamia just shook her head from side to side without saying a word. Catori got up from her desk immediately and rushed to hold her daughter. She couldn't remember the last time she saw Tamia cry. *What has happened?* she thought.

Catori held her daughter for a short time before she asked, "What happened?"

Tamia wiped her eyes and swallowed, and then said nervously, "I went to say hello to Miko this morning, and he...he was talking to another girl...a cheerleader."

The sentence was intermixed with gulps of air and tears. Catori held her daughter. It was if it had happened to her. She remembered her first boyfriend and the pain that she suffered because of his behavior. She searched for the right words, something that would comfort her daughter, but instead, she held her close and kissed her on the head. In the car on the way home, she offered some thoughts.

"You really don't know what the conversation was about. It may not mean anything."

Tamia looked out the side window of the car at the distant mountain range, her face a blank. She couldn't wait to get home, get into bed, and pull up the covers.

Catori realized that less was more, and anything more was only a reminder of what had happened. They drove the rest of the way in silence.

When they got to the house, Tamia rushed inside. Catori remained in the car and rested her head on the steering wheel. What more could she do? She could hear Onida's voice in the distance as she walked home with her friends. She stayed in the car until Onida got close and then opened door.

"Hey girl. How are you?"

"Great! What's for dinner?"

"Not sure yet, but listen, Tamia's not feeling good. It's better if we don't bother her, OK?"

Saturday morning, Catori kept the girls busy with chores until she had time to ask Tamia if she wanted to learn how to make the traditional Navajo corn cake. Onida was off to join her friend's family in Chimayo, so Catori and Tamia spent the afternoon getting what they needed from the store, grinding the corn into a meal, and then forming it into a round cake. All the time, Catori played a CD that her mother had given her that was recorded on the reservation.

Eventually, she told Tamia there was a Navajo Blessingway Ceremony known as the Kinaalda. The cakes they had prepared were called *alkaan* and represented the sun. She told her daughter that the ritual demands that the universe be kept in perfect order and that nature is to be valued. While the corn cake baked in the oven, she washed Tamia's hair and gave her a light massage. Without speaking, Catori communicated this rite-of-passage ritual that had been practiced for thousands of years. For Tamia, it was a comforting distraction.

* * *

"Let's go...We'll be late," said Catori to her daughters. The Sanctuario de Chimayo was a Catholic chapel near the plaza, and their routine was to attend the five o'clock Mass. Kneeling a few rows ahead, Catori saw Celia, Miko's mother. After Mass, as they walked out, she asked her about the family.

"Miko has a really bad case of the flu, and we're all afraid we'll get it. I need to get back and make him some soup."

"I didn't know Miko was sick," said Tamia in a soft voice.

"He came home from school early on Friday. You should call him. It might make him feel better."

It took Miko several days to return to school, and by then, the school midterms occupied everyone's time. He made a point to walk over to Tamia in science and say hello.

"What's up?"

"I heard you were sick?"

"I couldn't get out of bed for a while, but I'm better now. Any news about the project?"

"Mr. Lemke said we might hear something this week. You must be behind in your schoolwork?" said Tamia, trying to act normal.

"I tried calling you, but the line was always busy," he said. "You talk on the phone too much."

Mr. Lemke was waving them to their seats.

"I'll talk to you later," Miko whispered.

Tamia's stomach growled, and her mind drifted back, as it had many times over the past week, to the scene in the hall. All she could gather about the girl was her name was Jena Truyillo, an eighth-grade girl who was new to the school this year. So much for being connected. Miko was himself, and it felt good to see him.

* * *

Dr. Nawara was on the phone when his secretary came in with the usual bundle of mail. She had already done her best to weed out the advertisements and vendor promotions. He continued his conversation as he fumbled through the letters until he came to a large white envelope from the New Mexico Department of Education.

He immediately ended the call and opened the letter, then asked his secretary to send for Mr. Lemke as soon as possible. As soon as his class ended, Lemke made his way to the front office, where he was quickly ushered into Nawara's office.

Nawara launched right into the contents of the letter. "One of our eighth-grade projects received a third place for plant discovery, but the seventh-grade project won first place on insect research. It came in first place among a hundred and twenty-five entries from all over the state. Congratulations."

Lemke was stunned. He took off his glasses and wiped the perspiration from his brow. "These kids really deserve it," he said quietly. "What's next?"

"I'll verify the letter. Then we'll call the kids into the office and let them know. I need to notify the board. They'll want to recognize the kids at the next meeting, and you as well. It's a reflection on your teaching skills. This is a big deal. Congratulations!"

Mr. Lemke's head was spinning. He headed for the men's room. This would be a new experience for everyone.

* * *

The lunchroom was chaotic. Tamia was eating lunch with her friends when Miko sat down next to her.

"Can we walk out on the patio for a minute?"

It was not unusual for the two of them to talk, given the intense time they'd spent together on the project. Tamia got rid of her lunch trash and followed Miko through the glass doors, onto a large tiled terrace furnished with benches and tables.

"I haven't heard anything about the project. I would have told you if I had," Tamia said coolly.

"Can't I just *talk* to you?" Miko said, looking hurt.

"I thought you had your cheerleader for that," Tamia said, trying to keep her voice calm.

"Jena?" Mika said. "She's my cousin. My mother asked me to be nice to her. She's new and all."

Tamia bent down and retied her sneaker in an effort to cover the tears that had come, unbidden. Finally, she stood up. "She's your cousin?"

"Yeah. My uncle's kid. I don't even know her very well. Do you want me to introduce you?"

Tamia stammered, "No...well, sure, if you want, but..."

Miko took a step closer to her. "Tamia, can we forget about Jena for a minute? I wanted to know you if you would go to the dance with me Friday."

This time she didn't try to hide the tears in her eyes.

Miko held out his hand. "Is that a yes?"

Tamia nodded.

"Just one promise, though. No more of those curve shots like you did in soccer. OK?"

She smiled and nodded again, still unable to make her throat work.

* * *

They each received messages in the following class to report to the principal's office. When they arrived, Mr. Lemke was already there. This had to be about the competition.

Dr. Nawara started right in. "Two of our teams have won awards. The eighth-grade team took third place in plant discovery, and the seventh-grade team..."—he paused to look first at Miko, and then at Tamia—"you took first place in research. This is an outstanding achievement! Congratulations!" Nawara shook hands with all the students.

Mr. Lemke thanked the students for their hard work. "You'll all be getting scholarships to the state summer camp, and for first prize, there are cash awards. Congratulations!"

Afterward, Tamia and Miko headed straight for the preschool wing, where Catori was in the middle of a lesson with her students. They burst in without bothering to knock.

Tamia shouted, "Mom, we won first place in the science competition."

Catori dropped her booklet and ran to Tamia and held her. "I'm so happy for you both! Congratulations."

Tamia wriggled out of her mother's embrace. "We have to go tell Miko's mom before she leaves. Isn't it great, Mom?"

When they caught up with Miko's mom in the cafeteria, she was equally thrilled and almost crushed them both in a hug.

By the end of the day, word had spread around school like a wildfire, and the local newspaper reporters were there interviewing the students and taking pictures. Dr. Nawara had faxed all the board members a copy of the letter from the Department of Education. The local television satellite truck pulled up in time to run a story on the evening news. This was something that everyone in Chimayo could be proud of, and Lisa Wilkinson was using the coverage to make the school district look as good as possible. When interviewed, she made sure everyone knew there would be recognition at the upcoming board meeting.

* * *

The board of education meetings were held in the evening, once a month, in the high school gymnasium. Catori and her daughters were getting ready, arguing over bathroom rights. Tami decided to wear a skirt and blouse, while Onida stayed with her favorite jeans and a T-shirt from their trip to the Grand Canyon.

"How did you get picked to talk at the meeting?" Catori asked Tamia.

"Miko didn't want to, and neither did the eighth graders. So I volunteered. I wrote out my speech and showed it to Mr. Lemke. He liked it."

The parking lot was full. Extra chairs were set up to accommodate the crowd that had gathered, including local reporters, for a board meeting that would recognize the science students. It seemed as if the opening introductions and remarks would never end. Finally, Dr. Nawara introduced Tamia.Tamia was more nervous than she could imagine. Not only was the setting so formal, but also behind her sat almost everyone she knew. She grasped her written remarks in her hand, took a deep breath, and proceeded to the podium. *Just like a penalty shot,* she thought.

"Thank you, Dr. Nawara, Dr. Wilkinson, members of the board. On behalf of all of us, thank you for this recognition. We are overwhelmed by this event and winning in the state competition. I think this has to do with our craving to learn science. My mother taught me that the Navajo consider the outdoors, the mountains, the prairie, and the meadow as their home. When we first began this project, we proposed to study the power line corridor and the electromagnetic fields that have become so controversial. Maybe now, at the science summer camp, we will get our chance to do that."

The board members exchanged nervous looks, except for George, who tried to ignore the remark, his large body squirming in his seat.

Dr. Nawara leaned into Mr. Lemke's ear. "I thought you vetted this speech?"

Mr. Lemke held up his hands in surprise. Dr. Wilkinson exchanged a smile and an eyebrow lift with Dr. Barrett. Tamia continued.

"But when Miko and I took a walk out into the meadow one evening, we saw the fireflies. It was a light show beyond imagining. We wanted to understand what was happening." She went on to outline their technical work before concluding, "The Navajo believe the world to be an orderly place filled with interconnected objects all existing in a state of balance and harmony. It's the same with science. So thank you, Miko, for suggesting we study the firefly, and thank you, Mom…for *everything*."

The audience broke into spontaneous applause, and everyone stood up, including the members of the board. The reporters flashed their cameras, and Catori wiped away her tears.

On the way out, the parking lot was lit softly by a canopy of bright stars. Miko came running and caught up with Tamia before she and her family reached their car. Catori and Onida continued walking as car headlights flooded the parking lot.

"Is it OK if I pick you up at six for the dance Friday?" he said. "My father will drive us."

Distracted, Tamia didn't answer.

"The dance…is it this Friday night?" She reached into her coat and pulled out a small piece of wrinkled paper. Tilting it toward the headlights, she said, "I wanted to read you something. It's for you."

Fireflies in the Garden

Here come real stars to fill the upper skies,
And here on Earth come emulating flies,
That though they never equal stars in size,
(And they were never really stars at heart)
Achieve at times a very starlike start.
Only, of course, they can't sustain the part.

"Did you write that?" asked Miko.

"No. That's Robert Frost."

Catori honked the horn, and Onida yelled out the window, "Tia… let's go!"

"Gotta go. And the dance, yeah, that would be so great."

Finding Edith Allen

T he sleek silver Trailways bus rolled slowly into the makeshift bus station, came to a stop, and released the air pressure from its brakes. It was a late-night stop just outside Marion, Indiana, the only stop on a twelve-hour trip from Detroit to Union City, Tennessee. There was just enough time to refuel and change drivers. Most of the passengers were asleep.

From her seat at the very back of the bus, Helen Scott watched sleepily as a new driver in a beige cotton uniform climbed into the bus lit only by blue-green fluorescent station lights that filtered into the bus windows. He slid behind the wheel, then opened his silver thermos and poured coffee into the cap. The aisle between the seats was cluttered with children's toys, strollers, and bags that wouldn't fit into the small carry-on racks above the seats.

Because Helen had been one of the last persons to purchase a ticket, she ended up sitting in the back of the bus with a small group of black passengers. This would be her first trip alone, and although she had just turned twenty-three and it was 1954, young women didn't usually travel alone. She was a little nervous. As she tried to get comfortable against the side of the bus, she remembered her mother had told her to get some sleep as the bus traveled through the night.

Before Helen nodded off again, she could feel the motion of the bus accelerate up the ramp to US 25 South, and didn't wake again until several hours later, when the bus came to a stop just off the main street in downtown Union City.

Helen's eyes opened slowly to early morning light. The sun was low and cast shadows across the extra-wide avenue that ran north and south through the small, sleepy town. Union City was the county seat of Obion County, tucked up in the northwest corner of the state. The early morning light made the town glow like a postcard, but not many people were out and about at 6:30 a.m.

She pulled herself together and gradually made her way down the aisle. As she approached the driver, he emptied the last bit of coffee from his silver thermos into the plastic cap and looked over his check-list. Helen stopped to ask him if he knew where the restroom was in the station. She noticed an oval patch over his shirt pocket spelling the name Bud.

Helen made her way into the tiny ticket office and read the sign above the restrooms: Whites Only. Coming from Detroit, this kind of blatant racism was something she had only read about. After she'd washed her hands and fixed herself up in the bathroom, she felt better. She pushed open the door on her way out and accidentally bumped into the cleaning woman who was pulling a mop and pail on small wheels.

"Excuse me," said Helen.

"Yes, ma'am. Excuse me."

Union City was a small town surrounded mostly by farms that raised soybeans, tobacco, corn, and wheat. The early Scottish and Irish settlers had come from the Carolinas and Virginia. Locals who didn't farm worked at the Brown Shoe Factory, the Canvas Duck Decoy Company, or the new meat processing plant on the edge of Reelfoot Lake. The monument at the center of town had been erected in 1869 and was dedicated to all the unknown Confederate soldiers who lost their lives in the war. The county courthouse, built by the Public Works Administration, dominated the town architecture, and the Capitol Theater, the Central School, and the Union City Armory eclipsed a small park.

Across from the bus depot, Helen stopped and looked into the windows of Turner's Dixie Gun Works, the largest supplier of antique guns and parts. She spotted a restaurant, Dewey's, that was just opening for business. A young girl inside was pulling up the window shades. Several farmers were milling around out front, chewing the fat and waiting for the door to open. *I need a cup of coffee*, Helen thought.

Helen sat down on a stool at the dairy bar and rested her suitcase close her feet.

"Morning, miss. Coffee?"

"Please, thank you," said Helen, looking around at the clientele who were dressed in jean bib overalls and flannel plaid shirts. The small restaurant had four booths along the wall, a couple of tables, and a dairy bar that seated six. Behind the counter, on the back wall, was the largest Confederate flag Helen had ever seen, with deer head trophies on each side. The young waitress brought a cup of coffee and set it down in front of her.

Stella was fresh out of high school, and working at the restaurant was her first real job. Her family owned a twenty-acre farm where they raised dairy cattle and hogs. She had grown up helping with the farm and going to school, where she loved her drama class. Stella hoped she could save some money over the summer and go to the new beauty school in Paducah, Kentucky. Her aunt Ruth had a small hair shop in town and promised her a job if she went to school and got trained.

Helen looked at Stella dressed in a light-green chiffon uniform, a white apron, and a half hat stuck in her pinned-up hair. She had the gift of gab, a pencil behind her ear, and charm that warmed the customers' hearts.

"Reckon you been on the bus all night. Where y'all from?"

"I'm from...I just got in from Detroit. It was a long trip."

Helen caught herself because she was not sure where she was *from*. Her parents had told her from an early age that she was adopted at birth, and they knew there would come a day when she would want to visit Tennessee.

Her birth records indicated she was born at Memorial Hospital in Obion County, Tennessee, June 10, 1936. Her adoptive mother had helped her find as much information as possible. Fortunately, her brother-in-law was a law clerk who helped them navigate the system. Together, they had spent weeks reading page after page from the Childhood Welfare League of America, where they found the birth mother's name listed as Edith Allen. That was really all the information she had, so she was on a quest to find out more.

It wasn't as if she didn't have good parents. George and Mary Scott were loving and supportive parents who had been unable to have children of their own. To them, Helen was a gift from God. Over the years, they provided her with a safe and secure home. She was given a private school Catholic education on the west side of Detroit. Her adoptive father, George, was a bricklayer and worked in a city where the building trades were expanding by leaps and bounds. Mary, her adoptive mother, worked part-time as a nurse after Helen started school. Her parents had siblings who lived in and around Detroit, providing Helen with a large extended family. She did well in school and was considered well-adjusted. She had asked her adoptive mother: How could a mother abandon her child? Is she married to my father? Are there siblings? Growing up, Helen had dreams that often involved a woman giving up her baby just after birth. Mostly, she wondered about where she was born and whether her natural mother was alive.

The young waitress was talking to her. "Hi, I'm Stella."

"I'm Helen Scott."

"And you said you're from Detroit, right?"

"Yes. Have you been there?"

"I've never been there, but I'm a big Tigers fan. They're my team. Do you like baseball?"

"I love it," Helen said. "Have you heard of Al Kaline? He's the toast of Detroit. He hit three fifty-seven last year, and he might take us to the pennant. Do you have a team here?"

"Just a minor-league team, the Greyhounds. They're a farm club for the Brooklyn Dodgers, but the bleacher seats are only two bucks. My daddy's a big baseball fan. He likes the Cincinnati Reds, but my brother and I, we like the Tigers. We watch the games on the TVs at

Reelfoot Appliance, through the display window. Have you been to Briggs Stadium? It looks so big on TV."

"A couple of times."

Helen went on to describe it to her as best as she could before Stella went off to pick up some orders. Helen sipped the last of her coffee. She figured she could start her quest with Stella since the girl was a lifelong local. Still, she was a little nervous about asking her outright.

When the girl finally returned to Helen to ask if she wanted more coffee, Helen asked, "Say, Stella, do you know a woman named Edith Allen? She would be in her late forties. I think she lives somewhere here in Union City."

Stella set the coffeepot down after pouring Helen a refill. "No, I don't think so." Stella leaned over the counter and said loudly, "Hey, anyone here know Edith Allen?"

The farmers continued reading their newspapers, mostly the sections on commodities and pork bellies. If they did know something, they weren't interested in responding.

"You might check the library," Stella said to Helen. "Ask for Miss Holly Miller. She knows everything and everyone."

"Stella!" yelled the short-order cook. "Your eggs are up. Quit your jawbonin', girl. These people here are hungry."

"Excuse me, Miss Helen. I gotta get these people their breakfast."

Helen looked in the mirror that was mounted high on the wall behind the counter. She could see the booths behind her filled with locals drinking coffee. There were two young Jim-Bob boys with brush cuts, jeans, and white T-shirts. She could hear them talking about wanting to catch some bream using bobbers and split shot. Then the conversation changed to playing pool with some local girls. She noticed the first thing they did when they sat down was take a couple of aspirins with their orange juice. The two farmers directly behind her had faces that were tanned dark up to where their hats came down on their forehead. From there up, their skin was pure white, and small locks of hair were trimmed tight to their heads. Helen observed their thick, weathered hands as they shoveled hotcakes into their mouths, exposing their missing teeth. *It's a different world*, she thought.

"Can I get you anything, Miss Helen?" asked Stella.

"Do you know where I can get an inexpensive room? Just for a few nights?"

Stella tore a blank receipt off her pad and wrote something on the back of it. "Couple of blocks from here. Miss Rita Hutson has some rooms, and I think she makes breakfast for her guests. Good luck, and let's hope those Tigers have a good season."

* * *

The Hutson House was four blocks from the restaurant, just off the park, and a perfect location for Helen. As she walked up the large porch steps, she could see a small sign next to the door: Rooms and Breakfast. Helen set down her suitcase and rapped the door knocker a few times. As she stood waiting, she looked at the large suspended swing seat in the center of the extended porch, and flower boxes on the railing filled with geraniums. A large white cat lay sleeping on the swing, looking at her with cautious eyes. The door opened, and a short woman dressed in a plain print dress pushed open the screen door holding a dust broom.

"Can I help you, child?"

"I'm looking for a room, just for a few days."

"Well you come on in and let's see what we can do for you. I've got two rooms available, one upstairs and one down here. Upstairs has its own bath. Down here, you would need to use the bath down the hallway. It's ten dollars a night, and that includes breakfast."

"I'll take the downstairs room for three nights."

"Well all right. Come over here and sign in while I get you a key. What's your name?"

"My name is Helen Scott. You must be Rita. I came from the coffee shop, and Stella gave me your name and address."

"Oh, that's Gwyneth's child. She's a character. She says she wants to fix hair, but I doubt she'll do that. She's too scattered for that kind of thing."

"You sure have a pretty place here. Are there many people staying over?"

"There are only two rooms occupied, the Beulah sisters are up from Memphis visiting their mother, and Miss Dixie Wilkes is a local elementary school teacher. She's living here while she looks for something permanent. I prefer just renting to women, but I can't say that, you know. There's laws about that, I guess. Just fill out this form, and here is your key. Lights out at ten, and I serve breakfast starting at seven a.m., and I like to finish up by nine. Does that all sound good?"

Helen opened her purse and handed Rita some bills. "That all sounds good to me, and thank you, ma'am."

Helen closed the bedroom door and started unpacking her things. She took out her paperwork, then lay down on the soft featherbed and admired the fancy curtains. The double-hung window was opened slightly, letting in a warm breeze that lifted the lace cotton cloth. Sunlight lit half the room.

It had been a long trip, but Helen felt settled. She took a deep breath and closed her eyes, thinking she'd feel better if she took a short nap.

The dream placed her at a baseball field for a big playoff night game. In the stands, she could hear the public address system announcing Bud Windfield, the star outfielder for the Union City Greyhounds, and he was coming up to bat. Helen could see the scoreboard: top of the ninth inning, and the score was tied 2–2. A familiar-looking woman stood in the stands, cheering loudly. As the batter came to a full count, Bud made a monster of a swing and hit a fastball so far it went over the power lines in left center field and won the game.

The dream sequence skipped to a parking lot where Bud and the woman from the stands were getting into the backseat of a 1932 Chrysler Imperial. Slowly the car windows fogged up until the scene shifted to a farm where she could see the same woman now working in a garden. She was thin and plain, with straight brown hair and fine features. Two small barrettes held back her bangs. Her face was young and framed with wire-rimmed glasses. The woman had stopped what she was doing in the garden to talk to an older man, presumably the woman's father. They were arguing about something. The woman looked frightened. When Helen tried to intervene in the argument, she woke up.

* * *

Memorial Hospital was a ten-block walk from Rita's rooming house and provided medical care for all of Obion County. What started out as a small clinic in the early 1920s had expanded over ten years to include nearly fifty beds. The hospital was quiet, with only a few people sitting in the waiting room. It seemed like a clean local hospital. *I guess this is where I was born*, Helen thought.

In the lobby, she noticed a small bank of pay phones and remembered she had promised to give her mother a call as soon as she arrived and got settled.

Once she'd spoken with her mother and reassured her she was safe and staying in a nice place, Helen proceeded down a long hall, following a sign that read: Records. After producing the right identification for the records clerk, Helen was given a folder that she held in her shaking hands for a while before opening it finally.

The only information in the record was that a live birth had taken place on June 10, 1933, at 4:23 a.m. Edith Allen had given birth to a healthy baby girl. The name of the newborn was left blank. The information only confirmed what she already knew. Helen traced the handwriting with her finger, thinking she might be able to glean some information. Her eyes welled up, and images swirled in her head. *Where are you, Edith Allen?* she wondered.

The woman working the desk offered little help, as people were now anxiously on line with requests.

"Ma'am, do have any other requests?" she asked with authority.

Helen clenched the paperwork in her hands and shook her head. Finally, she turned and headed back down the long, straight hallway toward the exit. She had expected to find more...an address or phone number. She needed to pull herself together psychologically and move forward.

* * *

For the next couple of days, Helen scoured the small town, visiting hotels, bakeries, and grocery stores, and talked with anyone who would listen. Finally, she remembered the advice from Stella and ended up at the library asking for Holly Miller.

Truvy, the young black girl working at the information desk, had to be just out of high school. Her braided pigtails were almost touching her shoulders as she sat on a stool reading a small pulp fiction paperback. Helen walked up to the information desk and asked for Holly Miller.

The young girl came out of her reading trance and hopped off her stool.

"Yes, ma'am, just one moment." She disappeared into an office behind the information desk. A moment later, Truvy poked her head out of the office and motioned to Helen with a wave of her arm. "Right this way."

Holly Miller was a short, heavyset woman in her late fifties, wearing a print dress that nearly reached the floor. Her graying hair looked like a tangled nest in need of a good brush. She had worked at the library longer than any other employee, and held the informal position of town historian. Her horn-rimmed glasses sat halfway down her nose, punctuating her friendly smile.

"Come in, child. How can I help you?"

"Thank you, Miss Miller."

"Please call me Holly. Everyone does. What are y'all lookin for?"

"I just came down from Detroit, and I am trying to find my birth mother. I think she lives here in Union City. I was born at Memorial Hospital in nineteen thirty-three to an Edith Allen and then put up for adoption. I'd like to find her if I can. Have you ever heard of her, or do you know her?"

Holly Miller had been down this road before. She was familiar with the bookkeeping at the hospital, and it was sloppy at best. After looking at a variety of county and state voter registrations, property owners' tax payments, jail records, student yearbooks, there was only one place left to look: cemetery records. Under the name Allen, she found a grave at Mt. Moriah Cemetery: Edith Allen. There was no other information.

Helen's heart sank, and she found herself faced with the reality that she had often considered, that her mother had passed away.

"Does that mean she's dead and buried there?" asked Helen, holding back her emotions.

"Well, I am sorry, child, but that's the only record I can find with that name. It means she is buried there, but it doesn't list a date. It is unusual. Most of the records usually have a birth and death date after the name. This just gives a name."

Helen looked at Holly Miller without seeing her. She knew she should say thank you and leave, but her legs felt so wobbly she sat down in the nearest chair instead. It did not seem possible she had come so far to find someone, only to find that she no longer even existed. On the one hand, she had resented this Edith Allen for abandoning her child, but she also realized that she did not know the circumstances. Helen had been born in the Great Depression, when people could not afford to have more children. Giving up a child in hopes it would have a better life with someone more able to pay for it was common practice.

Holly Miller was looking at her closely. "Are you all right, dear?"

Helen wiped her eyes and tried to paste a polite smile on her face. "Yes, ma'am, thank you. At least I have an answer." Helen rose as if to leave, then thought to ask, "Where is Mt. Moriah Cemetery?"

"It's about ten miles south, on the road to Troy. It is a very old and small cemetery. Mostly local farm folk buried there, maybe a few soldiers from the Civil War. I haven't been there in years, but if I recall, there is a small white chapel on the grounds. You can't miss it. It has a beautiful wrought-iron fence around the perimeter, and there is a sign over the entrance." Holly Miller put her hand on Helen's arm. "Honey, I'm sorry to disappoint you. You can take comfort in the fact that she's with God now."

Helen left the library and walked down the stairs into the warm sunlight that reached into the park. The sun was moving downward in the late afternoon. It gave a whole different feel to the place from when she first arrived. As she passed people on Main Street on the way back to the rooming house, she couldn't help thinking that she bore some resemblance to some of them. When she saw a man in his early fifties with long hair combed high and back, she couldn't help wondering, *Is that my father?*

She stopped in front of Dewey's Restaurant, wondering if Stella was there. Maybe her down-home cheer would give Helen a much-needed boost. Stella was working, and it was another hour before there would be some dinner folk coming in for a pulled pork sandwich special. As the screen door closed behind her, Helen heard Hank Williams twanging softly about "Lovesick Blues" on the jukebox. She sat down in the same seat at the dairy bar.

Stella was sitting at the bar, engrossed in a scandal sheet, when she heard Helen's familiar voice.

"Hi, Miss Helen. How y'all today? I thought y'all had forgotten about me."

"Not a chance," Helen said, grinning. "Boy, I could sure use a milkshake."

"You're in the right place. I make a hell of shake, lots of chocolate ice cream. Comin' right up."

Helen asked, "So what have you been up to?"

"Me? Just working and listenin' to Elvis. Do you know about him?"

"The singer? Oh yeah. I saw him on *The Ed Sullivan Show* moving those hips around. 'Love Me Tender'...right?"

"He's a knockout," Stella said with a glint in her eye. "Makes all the girls scream, including me! I just read right here that he is singing in Memphis next month."

"You gonna go see him?"

"Heck no. I couldn't afford tickets, much less get there."

"Well, maybe next year after you get that new job in the salon."

"That's right," Stella said. "What about you, Miss Helen. What you been up to?"

"I was just at the library talking to that Holly Miller you told me about. I found out my mother is buried at Mt. Moriah Cemetery."

"I am so sorry to hear that, Miss Helen."

"Do you know where it is?"

"Yeah, but I haven't been there."

"I would like to go there and see my mother's grave. Is there a bus or something that goes that way?"

"There's no bus goin' that way, but I could ask my brother, Jake. Maybe he'd run us out there in his pickup. It's not far, ten miles maybe."

"That would be so generous of you. And your brother."

"No problem," Stella said and winked. "I'll just tell him you're a big Tigers fan."

* * *

The plan was set. Stella called that evening to say she and Jake would come by in the morning to pick her up. After dinner, she walked into town and tried to soak up the local atmosphere as much as she could. She knew this might be the last time she visited Union City.

She walked past the Little League baseball field all lit up for a game. Families filled the bleachers and spilled out into the parking lot. Most of the young players were little towheaded boys whose voices had yet not changed. Helen looked at the players, coaches, umpires, and families, thinking, *Amazing, they're all white.* It was quite a contrast to all the school athletic fields in Detroit.

Helen was more of a baseball fan than she had let on to Stella. Briggs Stadium was ten minutes from their house, and her father, George, loved baseball. He would take her and her mother to the Saturday matinees, and sometimes they would stay for a doubleheader. She was well aware of the famous Jackie Robinson, and knew all the names on the Tigers' roster.

* * *

A few minutes before nine the following morning, Helen heard a horn honk out front. As she ran for the door, Rita handed her a bouquet of red roses that were still wet from the light rain that had begun to fall overnight. When Helen climbed into the 1949 red Ford pickup, Stella slid over next to her brother. He looked to be in his early twenties.

"Morning, Helen, this is my brother, Jake. Jake, this is my friend Helen. Jake just got back from Korea, and we're glad he came back in one piece."

Her brother was uncomfortable talking about the war, so he immediately changed the subject. "Stella tells me you're from Detroit and you follow the Tigers. That is very cool. Have you heard of Stroh's beer?"

"My father buys that beer at the ballpark. Do they sell it down here?" asked Helen.

"No, that's the problem. My basic training was at Fort Brady, and the local PX sold Stroh's. I fell in love with that beer, and I remember they said it was brewed in Detroit."

"They have a huge complex right down on the Detroit River. Some people say they use water from Lake Huron to brew that beer. I don't really know if that's true."

By the time they got into the countryside, the rain had stopped. The road was paved for the first three miles, then turned to gravel. The rolling hills were a continuous patchwork of farms where hogs and dairy cattle grazed together. There were large fields of Burley tobacco, and what seemed like miles of soybeans and wheat.

Stella talked a mile a minute and covered every romantic relationship she knew about in Obion County. Finally they pulled up on some high ground and saw a white chapel surrounded by old monuments, some of them crumbling and broken. Jake pulled up to the gate.

"Here we are. We'll wait here so you can look for your mother in peace. Take your time. She might be hard to find."

Helen got out of the truck, grateful for Stella and Jake's deference. She walked the rows, wondering if there was any rhyme or reason to the placement of the headstones.

It seemed as if the older stones were closer to the front, so she walked toward the back of the cemetery. Finally she saw it, a white marble stone set flush in the ground. "Edith Allen" was all it said. On closer observation, it looked as if there may have been a plate attached to the stone, but it had come off or been removed. *Maybe that's where there was more information*, she thought.

Helen sat down on the damp grass and cleaned away the debris and the light dusting of red clay soil that surrounded the weathered marble. She touched the stone with both hands. "Hello, Mama…it looks like I found you. This is Helen, your daughter, and I came a long way to see you." Helen laid the roses down and rested her head on the grave marker.

She stayed at the grave site for about a half hour, watching Jake and Stella playing catch not far from the cemetery gate. She finally made her way back to the truck.

As they pulled out, heading back to Union City, she continued to watch the cemetery until it was no longer in sight.

The ride back to town was quiet. Helen was internalizing her experience at the cemetery and gradually coming to accept that her natural mother had passed away. She still had many questions about having a father, or possible siblings, but from all her investigations, there was only one name: Edith Allen.

Allen was a common surname, but it was listed only four times in the phone directory for Union City. Helen had called and reached three of the numbers one day, asking for the whereabouts of Edith Allen without any luck. There was only one listing that rang and rang without an answer. She called again, later that afternoon, still without an answer. She thought maybe her mother was unmarried when she got pregnant and that she was an only child. The answers to many of her questions remained the same: unknown.

Jake pulled up in front of the rooming house and brought the pickup to a stop. Helen was so grateful for their help in taking her to the cemetery.

"Thank you both so much. This has been important to me, and I don't know how I would have made it to Mt. Moriah without your help. It's been great meeting you both."

Stella stepped out of the pickup and gave Helen a huge hug. "I hope I can visit Detroit sometime and catch a Tigers game. Take care of yourself, Helen."

"Thanks, Stella, and good luck with attending beauty school. I could use a good hairdo."

Stella pulled the truck door closed and waved good-bye to Helen as the pickup truck pulled away. Helen watched until it turned onto Eldon Street and disappeared into the neighborhood. *Good kids*, she thought.

She stood on the sidewalk and tried to scrape the stubborn red clay from the bottom of her shoes.

* * *

Helen got up early the next morning and brought her suitcase to the foyer. Rita had made a special breakfast: fried eggs, hotcakes, sausage, corn bread, and grits. Rita's rooming house had been the perfect place, and everyone there was so pleasant. They all exchanged information, and Helen made sure they all knew how much she appreciated their help with her situation.

By the time she reached the crowded bus station, there were people standing in line to get a ticket, waiting for their bus to leave, or picking someone up. Helen had purchased a round-trip ticket, so she sat down on a bench not far from the restrooms. Next to her was a mother working hard at managing three young children who seemed to want to go in different directions. The oldest boy, who was maybe seven years old, was acting out in an odd way. He was more expressive than a normal kid, and seemed to lack an understanding of where he was and how to act in public.

He came over to Helen and asked without making eye contact, "What's your name?" His expression was unusual, and as he walked around in a circle, he elevated himself with his toes.

"My name's Helen. What's yours?"

Still unable to look at her, he answered, "Jeremy."

Finally, this got the attention of his mother, who approached them with a toddler in tow. She gently took her son's arm.

"Jeremy, let's leave this nice woman alone."

"It's OK," said Helen. Sensing he was disabled, she asked, "How is he doing?"

"He's doing good. He's autistic and attends a special school. Thank you for asking."

The boy stood looking out of the bus station windows and finally blurted out loudly, "I'm hungry!" As soon as the mother let go of his arm, he walked quickly back over to Helen. "Hi. What's your name?"

"I think your mom wants you to join her. See? Here she comes."

"Jeremy, come with me, and let's get some lunch." And once again, she gently grasped his arm. He resisted, and pointed instead at the cleaning woman entering the restroom, then looked quickly at Helen before glancing away. "You look like her."

Quickly, the mother took her son by the hand, and before Helen had a moment to react, they were out the exit door and gone.

Helen sat on the bench wondering what the heck had just transpired. She glanced toward the restroom where the boy had seemed to be looking, but saw only two large yellow triangles sitting on a wet floor. The loudspeaker crackled just then, announcing the departure of her bus in five minutes. Helen figured she'd better use the restroom now while she could.

Inside she found the same cleaning woman as when she had arrived in Union City was mopping the floor. Her thin, straight brown hair was pulled back in a ponytail. Her wire-rimmed glasses reflected the bright fluorescent lights so that Helen could hardly see her eyes.

Helen closed herself into one of the stalls and sat there for a few extra minutes trying to collect her thoughts. For some reason, she was afraid to leave the small stall, but she shook it off and opened the door. In what seemed like slow motion, she observed the woman still mopping, and as they passed, she clearly noticed the name sewn into an oval patch above the shirt pocket. The dark green thread, set against a lighter background, spelled the name: Edith.

Play

Mila sat on a simple oak chair overlooking the courtyard as the sheer drapes lifted lightly in the breeze. From her second-story dorm room she could see young girls walking to class in plain gray uniforms, set against a rich and lush landscape with a water fountain having the Virgin Mary at its center. At the far end of the courtyard, Mila could see a group of sophomore girls practicing their soccer techniques. Several worked on their dribble, while some exchanged headers. As they juggled and passed the ball among themselves, Mila could almost see the invisible bond between them and the confidence they inspired in each other. It was something she admired. Their blue practice uniforms reminded her of a ball she and Jerome used to kick back and forth over what divided their backyards, a four-foot cyclone fence.

The door to the small two-person dorm room opened, and Rosalin entered. "Have you had your meeting yet?"

"No, it's in ten minutes. I was just thinking and trying to relax."

"Do you know who you're seeing?" asked Rose before taking off her sweater.

"The staff psychiatrist. Dr. Andrea Thomas, it says here." Mila pointed to the yellow slip of paper. "Do you know her?"

"No, but I'm sure she'll be helpful. The people who work here are really good at what they do."

Rosalin Guastella was a beautiful Italian girl from the east side of Detroit. Her parents wanted her to have a private school education, and Sacred Heart had the best reputation in the city. Her family owned an Italian restaurant, so they could afford the tuition and room and board. Rose had long black hair that framed a Mediterranean complexion. Between that and her green eyes, she always turned heads. Her family said there had been changes in Rose lately that had caused them to send her to the new school, but her mother insisted it was her rebellious and adolescent behavior. Her introverted manner made it an easy match for Mila. They connected from their first meeting, and Rose was really hoping Mila would be her new roommate.

The Sacred Heart Seminary was a conclave set behind tall brick walls that consumed an entire city block. Hamtramck was a Polish community within the city limits of Detroit that was predominately Roman Catholic. There were fourteen buildings in all, with a large Gothic cathedral at its center. The multistoried buildings housed a high school, a university for the preparation of priests, and a convent. The dorms, library, and dining areas were on the east side of campus. There were modest living quarters for the attending priests, including a small, but elegant house for the bishop. He was responsible for governing the large Archdiocese of Detroit. The exterior wall was constructed of common brick columns crafted by Italian masons using a herringbone motif. The building windows were made of beveled panes set in leaded glass. Each of the buildings had an array of thickly varnished oak trim, and exterior doors that were four inches thick.

Mila walked down the corridor toward the office and glanced out the windows at the men in blue uniforms pruning the hedges and trees. She listened to her footsteps and felt her stomach pushing upward as if she might vomit, but she fought it down. She hoped she was in a safe place. She entered the doctor's office hesitantly and found a nun sitting at a computer behind an office desk.

"You must be Mila. The doctor's waiting for you. You can go right in," said the young woman in a kind and pleasant way.

Mila opened the door into the inner sanctuary of Dr. Andrea Thomas, who sat behind a large and ornate oak desk. She was busy finishing up a phone call. Mila sat down in the soft leather chair and tried to calm herself.

"You must be Mila. I'm Dr. Thomas. It's nice to meet you. How are you feeling?"

"My stomach feels a little shaky."

"Can I get you a glass of water?"

"No, thank you."

"Do you have any idea why we're meeting?" asked Dr. Thomas. She put on her glasses and opened a manila file folder and flipped through the pages.

Dr. Andrea Thomas was the consulting psychiatrist for the seminary and was contracted by the archdiocese to provide counseling and evaluations when needed. She worked mostly with young men entering the priesthood, an occasional high school student, and, less often, a young woman who was being considered for the trial model program for servitude. Mila had been admitted directly from her hospital stay, and her file contained an admission sheet that had been signed by the bishop.

"I know my mother, and probably my grandmother, brought me here directly from the hospital. They didn't want me to go home after...after the incident."

"May I ask you some questions? If you're uncomfortable in answering, just say so."

"Sure," Mila said, tucking her hands under her legs. "I guess that's why I'm here."

"It says here you're fifteen and in the tenth grade. Is that right?"

Mila nodded and then said, "I saw a psychiatrist in the hospital and explained everything to him. Do I need to do that again?"

"I have your chart from Dr. Freiling here in my file, so I know what happened and why you were admitted to the hospital, but my job is to do some follow-up. Do you mind telling me what happened?"

Mila gazed out the window. Her sleep had been riddled with unpleasant dreams and flashbacks of the events leading up to her attempt at suicide. It was difficult for her to talk about what had happened. It brought everything back into her present consciousness, but she felt safe with Dr. Thomas, an attractive older woman with a kind and gentle voice. *This has to help*, Mila thought.

"Mila, do you want to tell me what happened?"

"My father started coming into my room at night after everyone was asleep. At first he would just talk to me. Then he tried touching me. He told me it was his responsibility to educate me about sex. It was horrible and made me sick. I didn't know what to do. Eventually I tried to tell my mother, but she slapped me in the face and told me I was crazy to say something like that. So, before it got worse, I locked myself in the bathroom and ate some Tylenol…a lot…a whole bottle. I remember hearing the ambulance sirens outside, and I could hear their voices. They pumped my stomach in the emergency room and made me drink something that tasted like charcoal. I was taken to the psychiatric floor, and I think I was there for about a week."

Dr. Thomas took her time to respond. She poured herself a glass of water and dropped her glasses, which were connected by an antique gold chain. Mila sat across from her desk with her face in her hands, wiping the moisture from her eyes.

"I am really sorry, Mila. You're right, it is a horrible thing. It's unimaginable. Did this happen over a period of days, or weeks, or months?"

"About three weeks. Three or four times."

"And may I ask, did he touch you sexually?"

"Not at first. On the fourth visit, I was sleeping on the floor, between the bed and the wall. I guess I was trying to hide or protect myself. He would always put his finger to his lips and whisper…shh…shh. He tried to touch my breasts, but I pulled away and made some noise. He left, but I knew he would come back, so I took the Tylenol before it got worse, as an escape, I guess. I didn't know what else to do."

Dr. Thomas got up and walked over to the large vertical windows that looked out over the campus. The sun was low, and the warm light cast shadows across the lawns and walkways. Finally she said, "Thank God you weren't physically assaulted. I am so sorry, Mila.

We don't really know what causes a parent to treat their child this way, but it is a pathological illness. It's rare, but it does happen." She paused again before continuing. "I think this is enough discussion for today. Please know you're safe here, and we will meet many times over the course of your stay with us. Try and get good sleep, exercise, and make a friend or two. Let me ask you, Mila, do you feel safe here?"

"I am staying in a dorm room with a very nice girl. We seem to have a lot in common, so yes, I feel safe. I think at some level, my mother brought me here to protect me, to make this all go away. She said she wants me to become a nun, and my grandparents are personal friends with the bishop, so they want to place me in a special program, but..."

"Do you want to become a nun?"

"I don't think so. I just want to be normal and go to school, like a normal kid. Friends, school, sports, boys...you know...all that stuff."

"That sounds good. Let's meet again tomorrow, OK? Same time, same place. Thank you, Mila, for sharing this with me. I know this must be hard. God bless you."

Mila got up from her comfortable chair and extended her hand to the doctor, but Dr. Thomas pulled her close and gave her a hug. By now, sunlight was streaming into the dark oak office and caught the edge of a cut-glass figure on the desktop, sending bits of light to the wall and ceiling. Mila closed the door behind her and said good-bye to the nun while she sat working at her computer. Within five minutes after Mila's exit, Dr. Thomas opened her office door.

"Get me the parish attorney on the phone, will you, Ellen?"

* * *

Mila remembered she was to stop by the principal's office and talk more about school and her stay. The terrazzo floor was polished, the lighting was subdued, and rich oil paintings of the saints adorned the office walls. The principal's office was a busy place with students coming and going. Mila filled out a request card and took a seat. It was nearly an hour before the secretary called her name. The secretary escorted her down a small hallway to an office at the end.

"Come in and sit down," said Mother Angelica, an older, heavyset nun dressed in the black-and-white habit. "You've seen Dr. Thomas, I take it?"

Mila avoided eye contact at first, not knowing what to expect. *What a contrast*, she thought. The office was utilitarian and plain. The tile floor was pristine. Mother Angelica sat behind a steel desk, and the only decoration was a crucifix on the wall behind her.

"Yes, ma'am, I just came from her office."

"I see. Your grandmother has requested that you be placed in a trial model program at the tenth-grade level here at our high school, and that you be considered for the convent. Did you know that?"

"Not exactly. I wasn't sure what had been arranged."

"Apparently your grandparents are friends with Bishop Sylvester, and they made the request through his office. You will finish out the school year as a tenth-grade student. During this time, you will continue to see Dr. Thomas on a regular basis, and I have assigned Sister Maria to be your counselor. She will help you acclimate to your classes and become better acquainted with our rules and procedures. Do you have any questions?"

"No...well, do I have to become a nun? And when will I see my family?"

"Don't worry about becoming a nun. There's plenty of time to sort that out. You're a little too young to be making that decision. I expect that is something your grandmother invented. We'll let her believe whatever she wants." Mother Angelica noticed the expression on the girl's face. "I know you've been through a lot, Mila, but you're safe here. Please feel free to see me whenever you want."

There was a soft knock at the door, and Sister Maria came in and introduced herself.

* * *

The phone rang on Dr. Thomas's desk, signaling that her secretary had reached the attorney on the phone.

"Hello, Ralph. How are you?"

"Busy. Just got back from court, a custody case. What can I do for you?"

"I'm working with a young girl, just fifteen, and her father made sexual advances towards her. According to the girl, and as far as I know, there was no sexual assault, but she made a serious attempt to take her life. She has been enrolled here at the school, probably for her protection. I just saw her for the first time this afternoon. Do I need to file a report with the authorities?"

"In this state, under code section seven twenty-two, mandatory reporting is required. Failure to report is a misdemeanor punishable by a hundred days in jail, and a five hundred–dollar fine. So the answer is a big yes. The judge will have power over testimony if prosecution is sought. In other words, he will determine what evidence will be allowed. You should file a ten thirty-three three short-form report with the state Family Independence Agency, and they will investigate. It's a CYA deal."

"Will they need to question her?"

"That's up to the prosecutor, but you might want to make a recommendation. And you can hold off for a while, say a week, and then file your report. Does that help?"

"Yes, I think so. I just don't want anyone questioning her right now, or even mentioning charges or court proceedings."

"Sometimes, if they visit the home and do an interview, it can put the fear of God in the father. End of story."

"Thanks, Ralph. If I have any questions, I'll give you a call. Have a good one."

* * *

Sister Maria gave Mila an hour-long tour of the campus and all the buildings. She stopped by the laundry, fitted her with a uniform, and gave her a handbook before sending her back to the dorm. Mila found Rose lying on her bed reading her English homework.

"How did it go?" asked Rose.

"It went well. Everyone has been so nice. What are you reading?"

"Mark Twain's *The Adventures of Huckleberry Finn*, for my American Lit class. Will you be staying?"

"I think so, at least for the rest of the year." Mila lay back on her bed, her arms crossed under head. "What's it like here?"

"Technically it's coed, but the classes are segregated, you know, all girls together in classes, and all boys together in their classes. Everyone has a religious studies class, usually first period, and the teachers are a mix of nuns and regular teachers. Like my history class, Mr. Rodriguez has been here forever, and math is taught by Mrs. Poterek. The rest are pretty much nuns that live in the convent. I think you'll like it, and the kids are really nice for the most part. Some of the freshman boys are immature and a little goofy, but watch out for senior boys. Some of them are too hot to handle. Woo-hoo! Do you have your schedule?"

"Yeah. Sister Maria is my counselor, and she gave me this." Mila handed Rose a computer-generated form. "What do you think?" Rose scanned the sheet. "You're in my history class third hour, we both have religious studies first period, and we have American Literature last period. So we've got three out of six classes together."

Mila smiled and felt more relaxed. That would make getting used to the school easier.

* * *

Mila slipped into the school routine easily with the help of Rosalin and Sister Maria. She became especially fond of Dr. Thomas and always looked forward to her appointments right after school. Sometimes the sessions were difficult. She sat in her office one afternoon as Dr. Thomas looked over Mila's hospital chart again.

Finally the doctor looked up and asked, "Have you thought much about your father since you left the hospital?"

"I think about why he did what he did, why he would want to abuse me. I wonder if he loved me."

"Men that do such things are extremely confused. Some would say they have an illness. It could have had something to do with his child-hood or his culture. He may have been abused when he was young. There is something we call cross-transference, which is an unconscious redirection of feelings from one person to another. He might have a dysfunctional relationship with your mother. There are many factors."

"Is there treatment?"

"Treatment is needed for you. That's where I come in. You need to acknowledge these recent events, learn how to grieve your loss, and regain trust, not just in your father, but in all people." Dr. Thomas paused and placed the folder back into her desk.

"What will happen to my father?"

"For one thing, what he did is criminal. He may be interviewed and face prosecution. We will have to wait and see what the authorities decide. There also could be coexisting problems, like substance abuse or even a psychiatric disorder."

Dr. Thomas started to realize Mila was a very solid and resilient girl. She sought out her new roommate for support, and had managed to avoid abusive physical contact with her father. Mila seemed to draw on her spirituality and realize there is a healing process.

Their discussion carried on longer than the usual forty-five minutes, until Dr. Thomas finally said, "Mila, our time is up. I think this has been good, and I would like to give you an assignment: next time we meet, talk to me about something pleasurable."

* * *

The dorm cafeteria was a sea of students at dinner because of some guests visiting from Poland. Mila searched for Rose and finally spotted her in the long dinner line. When she got her attention, she motioned with hand signals that she wanted to make sure they sat together. Rose saved her a spot as Mila made her way down the crowded aisle.

"How are you doing?"

"Other than a snap quiz in math, I'm good. What's up?"

"I had a pretty intense session with Dr. Thomas."

Rose frowned. "Your father?"

Mila nodded. "For next time, she asked me to prepare to talk about something good, something that makes me happy."

"You mean like your best roomie?" Rose said with a goofy grin on her face.

"Don't laugh," Mila said. "I did suggest you, but Dr. Thomas said it should be something before I came here."

"Like what?"

Mila looked at her plate and shoved chunks of potato around with her fork. "Did I ever tell you about my friend Jerome?"

"Oooooh. Boyfriend action. Do tell."

Mila blushed. "He's just a friend from since I was, like, nine years old. We started first playing by accident. His ball came into my yard, and I was out playing in the dirt. I had created a few houses and a wooden block for a car. He pulled a piece of gum out of his pocket and offered me some, and then he stayed and asked me if he could play. He built this cool bridge out of sticks and cardboard. One thing led to another."

"How cool. I just played dolls with my sister. Ever heard of Barbie? And Ken. What a dork." Rose rolled her eyes. "But seriously, sounds like this Jerome character would be the perfect thing to talk about."

Mila knew Rose was right. It would be easy, and even fun, to talk about Jerome.

The next day was a blur, and although Mila tried hard to concentrate in class, she was preoccupied with thoughts about her after-school session with Dr. Thomas. She arrived a few minutes early and had to wait, until finally the door opened and the doctor stuck her head around the doorjamb.

"Come in, Mila. Have you thought about your assignment?"

Mila was much more herself now and had spent time thinking about what she was going to say. "I want to tell you about Jerome."

"Well, you had mentioned him before. He's your neighbor, right?"

"Yeah, Jerome lives right behind our house, and we jump the fence to visit with each other. We usually play together in the yard, or in the dirt."

"Really? Tell me about it."

"Jerome and I like to create and build these towns, cities, or farm communities that we make up, I guess. We build roads, bridges, buildings, farms, sometimes rivers, and imagine people who live there. We collect stones, sticks, bricks, and logs. Jerome has some small cars and trucks that he collects and we use, but we create different voices for different characters. I am always the female characters, and he plays the parts for the men. Each character has a different voice.

"We play for hours. Sometimes we get totally lost in play and forget about dinner, and my mother has to call me home. Our subdivision is made up of small tract homes that are divided by a cyclone fence. Many families didn't get around to putting grass in the backyard, leaving it dirt, sand, and gravel. So we use each other's backyard as mini-universes. We gave them names. Jerome's yard was Prairie Hills, and my yard is called Green Acres, because there is some grass growing wild. It's hard to describe how much fun it is."

Dr. Thomas sat listening intently and then asked, "How long have you been playing together?"

"We first started playing when Jerome was seven, shortly after his family moved in, and I was nine years old. We had other kinds of play, sometimes word games, pick-up sticks, and catch over the fence with an old blue rubber ball. One time we played catch over the fence with water balloons. Occasionally we would just ride our bikes, but when we did, Jerome would always make it a made-up adventure. Our bikes became police motorcycles. I think we started playing together because we were the only two kids in the neighborhood around the same age. He can make me laugh so hard, I can't stop."

"Would you also see him on your school bus?"

"That's kind of a funny thing. It's like we had our own private world. We might say hi, but we didn't sit together or talk on the bus, or at school. Some of Jerome's boyfriends would tease him because he still liked to play in the dirt. They didn't know about our secret play and me. And as we got older, we had to hide the play even more, until finally things changed. Now and then we would talk about play, but he is busy playing in the band, and I was staying after school for girls' sports. We still keep our friendship quiet, and almost a secret. Our families know, I guess. What do you think?"

"It's very interesting. Play is such a very important part of development. I think you're lucky to find a friend to play with. It's a coping mechanism, meaning it takes your mind off things that are bothering you." They continued to talk about the importance of play in children's lives, and about Jerome, until the end of the session.

Finally, Dr. Thomas said, "I'm glad you told me about this, Mila."

As Mila headed back to her room, she felt lighter than she had in weeks. She couldn't help wondering about Jerome, where he was and what he was doing.

* * *

Mila's relationship with Rosalin grew stronger each day. She soon learned that Rose had been diagnosed with a learning disability that she compensated for with innate intelligence. She was especially talented with numbers, and she excelled in math and science. Mila's abilities were the flip side of Rose's, and they were constantly helping each other in their strengths. One late night after lights-out, they lay in bed exchanging stories. Mila had just finished talking about one of her play sessions with Jerome, when Rose decided to divulge a secret.

"There is something I have never told anyone, but I've wanted to, so here it is. Last summer, I was hanging out with friends one evening. It was getting late, and the sky was pitch-black. We were sitting on my friend Karen's porch, and we suddenly saw a massive object in the sky. It was lit up and moved slowly, low to the horizon, and then it slowed down and hovered. I guess it was what they call a UFO. It was a strange experience. We walked over to her back fence and looked up at an oval-shaped object. There was this tone—we all heard it. Then, without notice, it moved away toward the horizon and out of sight."

Mila sat up in bed, staring through the dark at Rose. "Whoa, that's completely bizarre."

"I know. We kept double-checking with each other to make sure we hadn't lost our marbles, you know? Did that really happen?"

"Did any of you tell your parents or contact the police?"

"My friend did, and get this…there were other police reports."

"And you think it affected your thinking?"

Rose paused, then said, "Maybe it had something to do with the tone."

Mila threw off her covers and sat on the edge of the bed. "Tone? What did it sound like?"

"It sounded like a low-pitched sewing machine that started and stopped. It only lasted about thirty seconds. That was it."

"Did it scare you?"

"That was the weirdest part of all. It didn't really scare us. We all just accepted it and only talked about it occasionally with each other. Now we just try to forget about it."

"That would be pretty hard to do. I mean, that's a big deal."

"You have no idea. Because something more than just seeing this thing had an effect on us that night. It was then I started to have a talent with numbers, because before the event, I was average at math. Now I'm working with advanced calculus problems." Rose hesitated, chewing on her lower lip.

"What?" Mila asked.

"Mila, you can't tell anyone!"

"Not even my little green friends?"

Rose chucked a pillow at Mila. "Seriously," she said. "Not anyone."

Mila wiped the smile from her face. "Don't worry, I won't say a thing, but Rose, I hope you're all right. Having an encounter is one thing, but leaving its effect on you? That's creepy. You might want to make an appointment to see Dr. Thomas. She's extremely cool."

* * *

Mila's schedule was jam-packed with her classes and a meeting with Sister Maria. Fortunately her meetings with Dr. Thomas had been recently reduced to weekly sessions instead of biweekly as they had been before. She stopped by the student center to check her mail and found a message in her mailbox that indicated her mother was visiting after Mass this coming Sunday. She had decided she would ask her mom for Jerome's address. She made her way to Dr. Thomas's waiting room and sat down, thinking about what she would say in her letter to Jerome. Dr. Thomas walked in minutes later.

"Hello, Mila." Dr. Thomas pulled Mila's chart and leafed through her file, then pulled out some notes. "Let's see, where did we leave off?"

"I think I told you about Jerome. Do you find it odd that I have a friend who is a boy?"

"Usually, during these years, our friendships are with our peers. Girls play with girls, and boys play with boys. They find familiarity and security with each other, but the most important issue is that children need to play. The more play, the better."

"Why?"

"There was a child psychologist, Jean Piaget, who explored how children think and reason. He described two kinds of play: fantasy and imitative. Both forms help develop imagination and intelligence. See? It's a good thing."

"Jerome always came to play with ideas. It was like he was already thinking about it before we started. I loved his ideas. It caused me to think about it as well. We did variations on a theme, and there was always a goal. Sometimes it was to grow and deliver the crops to needed families that were hit by a tornado. When he brought a bag of military toys, I knew it was going to be a battle. I think we had the most fun when we made up things from simple objects, like sticks and stones. Jerome had a collection of sticks, all different sizes, lengths, colors, and shapes. I collected stones and objects, like marbles, matchboxes, and pieces of string. It just went on and on and on. Jerome promised me we would always play and be friends."

Dr. Thomas stopped taking notes and looked at Mila. "You're really fortunate you had that experience. How long did it last?"

"It started to slow down and become less frequent when we got into middle school. Jerome had a special bell that he would ring from time to time. We called it the play bell. When I heard the bell sound, I could expect Jerome at the back door. Sometimes we just talked, but we always ended up playing in some way. As we got older, the play changed. We moved out of the yard and into our kitchens. We started playing with paper and pencil. Jerome taught me chess. We learned word games, number games, and occasionally board games, but they weren't quite as much fun as our own made-up games."

Since it was her assistant's day off, Dr. Thomas picked up a call that rang through, then placed her hand over the phone. "Listen, Mila, I have to take this. We'll have to cut this a little short today. Thanks for all the discussion. It's been really interesting. I'll see you next week."

* * *

The spring day was unusually warm, and all the trees and plants on campus were sprouting new buds. The water fountain had been turned on, and hundreds of crocuses surrounded the monument to Mother Mary. Mila walked quickly after Mass to the welcome center and saw her mother sitting comfortably in the lounge, as she had done several times before.

"Hi, Mom, how are you? Sorry I'm a little late. Mass ran over."

"That's OK, I haven't been here long. How are you?"

"Good. How are Anton and Dad?"

"Your father left to visit his mother. You remember, she lives in the Ukraine. He may be gone for a quite a while. He told me before he left that he did something wrong, but he didn't say what it was. I assume he was talking about you. I am not sure he will return. I am really sorry, Mila, for not recognizing what was happening you. It's my fault. I am so sorry."

Mila sat on the oak bench, and there was an uncomfortable silence. She searched for words that might help her mother. Finally she spoke.

"Look, you didn't cause this. If there is any blame, it's on him. We need to support each other, stay strong, and plot out a future. There will be a lot to think about, like our livelihood. What will we do without his support?"

Her mother used a tissue to wipe her eyes, then said, "I have started working at the post office. It's just part-time, but it could develop into a full-time job, and your grandparents are helping us. Your brother has a part-time job. I think we will be fine. Is there anything you need?"

"Yes. Could you send me Jerome's address?"

"Mila, I think they moved. I saw a For Rent sign in front of their house, and there hasn't been anyone around for a couple of weeks. I can check."

Mila tried hard to disguise her feelings. Her mother had no idea what this would mean to her. She tried to stay focused on their conversation.

"Well, send me the address anyway. Maybe they will have their mail forwarded. OK? I have a lot of homework, and I have to go. Thanks for coming by."

"Would you like to come home for a weekend sometime? I think it would be fine now."

"I think I will, maybe after my midterms. I'll ask Mother Angelica." Mila gave her mother a hug and a kiss. "Love you, Mom."

As she made her way back to the dorm, anxiety swept over her. *Jerome, where did you go?*

* * *

Mila picked up her pace to nearly a jog until she reached the dorm entrance. *Rose must be back by now*, she thought. She pulled hard on the banister, took two steps with one jump, and proceeded up the stairway in a rush to find her roommate. She needed to talk with Rose. She was the only one who would understand.

She opened the door and started to speak, but the room was empty, and Rose's bed was stripped of its linens. Mila sat on her bed, disappointed. Her mind was preoccupied with thoughts of Jerome neatly packing his clothes in his suitcase and organizing his toys into a special box, wrapping his sticks with small labels identifying their meaning.

Something crinkled under her leg. It was a small piece of yellow folded paper: *I am doing laundry. Rose. Of course*, Mila thought, and sprinted out the door, heading for the laundry facility in the basement.

She found Rose reading a recent gossip magazine from the collection that adorned the folding table.

"There you are. Thanks for the note!"

"Hey. Did you see your mom?"

"She told me Jerome and his family have moved. I have no idea where he is. I can't believe it." Mila's chin quivered as she wiped tears from the corners of her eyes and looked at Rose with an expression that said, *Can you help me?*

Rose gave Mila a gentle hug. Mila dropped her head on Rose's shoulder and cried softly, releasing the tension and frustration that had built up inside her.

"I'm so sorry, Mila. But don't worry. You'll find him."

"Yeah…well, we'll see. My mother invited me to come home. She told me my father left to visit his mother in Ukraine and I got the impression he's not coming back. So I think I will go home for a visit next weekend after midterms."

Mila helped Rose fold her laundry. The busywork distracted her and helped her relax. As they gathered up the clothing and placed everything back into the plastic bin, Mila said, "I had a disturbing dream last night. I was in the backyard, playing with Jerome, and my father came out of the house yelling at me. He grabbed me by the hair and started pulling me towards the back door. Jerome picked up a large stone and threw it at my father, knocking him unconscious. We just ignored him, and as he lay there, we returned to our play as if nothing had happened."

"Dream interpretation is beyond my skill level. You might want to run that past Dr. Thomas."

* * *

With midterms and the routine of the school week behind her, Mila stood at the welcome center door waiting for her mother to pick her up. This would be the first time she had gone home since her suicide attempt. Dr. Thomas had given her some advice as to how to proceed once she reached the house. She had told her to take her time getting reacquainted with the house, to focus on people, not things, and to avoid anything that might bring back thoughts of her father's behavior.

Her older brother, Anton, was out with friends when she arrived, and she found the house much the same. Her mother had rearranged the furniture in her bedroom and put a vase of fresh flowers on her dresser. She had mentioned perhaps going into town, doing some shopping, and catching a movie. Mila agreed, but asked for some time alone. She walked out the back door, wandered over to where she used to play, and knelt down in Green Acres. Several hard rainstorms had erased the roads and towns that once thrived there.

She sifted through the dirt, looking for remnants of past adventures. She glanced over the back fence into the familiar backyard, and she could barely make out Prairie Hills.

Within seconds, she was up and over the fence. Making her way to Prairie Hills, she saw an old stone fence and the remains of a bridge made of sticks. She sat down and touched the ground, moving both palms across the gravel. For more than ten minutes she just sat in the dirt, trying to imagine Jerome was there once again. *Jerome, where are you?* she wondered for the hundredth time.

She spotted a small tire half exposed in the dirt. It was something. She gently nudged the tire from the soil and brushed it clean. It had come off one of Jerome's trucks. It was symbolic. She remained at the center of Prairie Hills, grasping the small toy tire in her palm, imagining Jerome and her playing. In her mind, the scene played over and over, until she heard the familiar call from her mother.

"Mila…"

* * *

Sunday afternoon came quickly, and Mila found herself being dropped off after a nostalgic visit home. Rose had now become her best friend and confidant, and she couldn't wait to see her and tell her everything. Mila pushed the dorm room door open with her small suitcase. Rose looked up from the homework she was poring over, and her eyes brightened at the sight of her friend.

"How was your weekend?" Rose asked.

"Other than the flying saucers in my backyard, it was the usual."

"Very funny!" Rose closed the door behind her and whispered, "This morning I was working on my calculus homework, and I had no idea what I was doing. I didn't even understand the problem. Blank, blank, and more blank. I think the force left and took his calculator with him."

"Now you don't have to worry about being possessed by a little green alien force, right?"

Rose shrugged. "Easy come, easy go."

Mila laughed. Then, Rose came close, noticing a new necklace around Mila's neck. It was a silver chain attached to a small black circular object.

"Wow, what is that?"

"I found it in Jerome's yard. I already had this chain, so I glued a very small loop into the little tire, and presto. I love it. It's helping me a little."

* * *

The spring days grew warmer, and there were lectures, tests, performances, and an occasional mixer. Sessions with Dr. Thomas grew farther and farther apart. After Rose's transfer into basic math, they both found themselves on the honor roll, which made their families happy. Mila and Rose were asked to help at the senior graduation ceremony, and within days, they were packing to go home for the summer. Mila made sure she had one last meeting with Dr. Thomas.

"Well, Mila, you have come a long way since you first walked in my door. Don't you think? I mean, look at you. Your face glows, and you seem so happy. Are you looking forward to going home for the summer?"

"In some ways, I am. I really like a lot of people here, and if it weren't for you, I don't know what would have happened. Thank you so much. I feel like you saved my life."

"Mila, you've helped yourself. Did you ever get a chance to see Jerome?

Mila's expression immediately changed. "No, I haven't seen him. He moved away, but when I get home, I am going to try to find him." Mila paused and looked down at her lap, feeling suddenly awkward. "Dr. Thomas, I hope I'll see you next year. My grandparents have arranged for my return, and Rose and I want to room together again. I hope you have a good summer."

After a long hug, Dr. Thomas watched Mila leave the office. *I am sure she will be all right*, she thought.

During those last few days, and after intimate discussions that lasted long into the night, Rose and Mila exchanged phone numbers and made promises to see each other over the summer. Rose even said she would help with Mila's mission to find Jerome. There were station wagons, trucks, and cars pulling trailers that last day, and it seemed many students were crying and laughing at the same time. Eventually the parking lot emptied, and everyone went their separate ways. The halls were quiet, and everyone started what they hoped to be a good and restful summer vacation.

It wasn't long before Mila was home and had enlisted her brother to help her canvass the neighborhood. After asking every neighbor on the block, they determined that Jerome's father had been reassigned to a different workplace, but no one knew where. Mila's letters all came back Return to Sender. She looked in multiple telephone directories, and even stopped the postman one day. He knew nothing. The house behind her was eventually rented to a young married couple who quickly planted yards of thick grass in the backyard. Prairie Hills was transformed into a huge vegetable garden, and each time Mila approached the back fence, there was a large and angry dog barking in her face. Everything had changed, and Mila was left with her memories and a small necklace.

The summer was nearly over, and Mila had taken every class and activity that was offered by the department of recreation. She played summer soccer, worked on getting her Red Cross lifesaving certification, and read the complete collection of Ian Fleming's James Bond novels. Her mother kept her busy with household chores. Her favorite was the weekly laundry; it reminded her of doing laundry with Rose in the dorm basement.

She pushed open the back door with a large load of linens, which she hung carefully on the line. Without a cloud in the sky, the warm breeze made the sheets billow like sails. Mila thought she heard the sound of the play bell. It was very faint, but she was certain she heard it. Or was it just wishful thinking? Had all the searching come to an end? The sound faded, and her heart sank. She bent to pick up the laundry basket and saw the blue ball roll gently to a stop against the toe of her shoe. She remembered his promise. *Could it be?*

Mind over Maelstrom

Clarissa Martin lit a small wooden match. The flame was yellow with blue and red borders. She immediately dropped the match on the gray stone counter, while the flame continued to consume the thin square wooden shaft. Clare then placed her finger about a foot above the flame and moved it in a small circular motion, as if she was massaging the warm air flowing upward. Very slowly, the burning match lifted off the counter until it was about four inches above the stone surface. The flame consumed the match, while the remains lay suspended until she released the force and the black charred bits dropped back to the counter.

No one would see this. It was something Clare did when she was certain she was alone. It was a gift that she first experienced when she was two years old. Her Hispanic mother would dump a spoonful of loose red rice on the wooden surface of her highchair. This was a way to occupy her time as well as assist in the development of her fine motor skills. Clare, like most children at that age, would pick up the small pieces of rice using two fingers and place them in their mouth. She did this until it came to the rice beyond her reach. She then rotated her index finger in a circular motion ever so slightly, and the piece of rice would slide closer, within her reach. Even at that age, she sensed it was something she needed to hide, though she didn't know why. It was a mystery.

* * *

The halls of Jefferson High School were overcrowded during the five minutes between classes. Students scurried from their lockers to their classrooms, walking quickly to avoid being tardy since running in the halls was prohibited. Clare nervously stopped at the drinking fountain and quickly sucked up sips of cold water.

"Come on, Clare. We're going to be late for class. Dr. Lambert closes the door immediately at the bell," said Anu, her best friend.

"Thanks," said Clare, wiping the water from her chin. "My body needs water lately. Does that ever happen to you? At the weirdest times, I need water."

The two girls resembled speed walkers as they reached the physics lab doorway just as the bell rang. The science classroom was overly filled with an eclectic collection of science junk. Dr. Lambert was short, nearly bald, hard to understand, forgetful, and not very organized. But he loved his subject and collected specimens from each and every one of his field trips and travel excursions. He always had a student take attendance while he fiddled with the equipment for that day's lab experiment. He cleared this throat.

"As we have been experimenting with the various forces of physics—gravity, electricity, and motion—today we are going to take a look at magnetism. Who knows what magnetism is? Anyone?"

Collectively, the class avoided eye contact with their teacher. Many of the brighter students in the class had an elementary understanding of magnetism, but were afraid to answer for fear of being wrong. The athletes all sat together wearing their letter sweaters and never spoke unless it was absolutely necessary. There was some suspicion that they had prior knowledge of what was on the quizzes and tests, but no one could be sure. Finally, after the silence caused anxiety throughout the classroom, Clare raised her hand. It was unusual for her, as she and her friend Anu rarely said a word. She chose her words carefully, deciding to respond with a question as a kind of insurance.

"Isn't it the movement of electrons creating a field of opposite forces?" said Clare.

"Thank you, Clare. You at least have the courage and intelligence to take a shot at the answer. You're on the right track."

Dr. Lambert slowly walked across the front of the classroom with a blackboard full of equations behind him.

"All magnetism is due to circulating electric currents. In magnetic materials, electrons orbiting within the atoms produce the magnetism. In most substances, the magnetic effects of different electrons cancel each other out, but in some, such as iron, aligning the atoms can induce a magnetic field. So, in general, we can say magnetism is a phenomenon by which materials attract or repulse forces on materials, such as iron or nickel, to create a magnetic field. Your assignment is to measure the force of each magnet at your station using the equipment provided, then turn in your results at the end of the period. You can work in pairs."

The class started to disperse into their predictable pairs. Richard Bayliss was a senior and part of the athletic clique that had an arrogance that the really bright students could see right through. He made fun of people to elevate himself and make others think he was superior. He had secretly brought in a container of vegetable oil and poured it behind Clare's chair, in the path where she would walk. He and his friends watched as she got out of her chair and proceeded to the lab station. On her second step, both feet slid out from underneath her, and she went down, fanny first. Everyone stared. Richard and his friends laughed louder than most.

"Clare!" Anu reached out her hand to help her up.

"I'm all right. I slipped on this...*stuff*." She held her hands, which were slick and dripping oil. Anu helped her up and handed her a paper towel. Dr. Lambert had just happened to step out of class responding to a note from the office, missing the whole event.

"Those guys are assholes," said Anu. "Not to mention morons."

Clarissa and Anupabha were both attractive young high school girls who dressed modestly to conceal their well-developed bodies. Clarissa Martin's father was an American-born anthropologist, and her mother was Hispanic and worked as a speech and language pathologist at the local university. Clare's skin was the color of a sandy beach, and her hair was long and light brown. Socially, she was a very outgoing, extroverted teenage girl who usually dressed in a plain skirt and blouse.

Anupabha Vishnu was the daughter of a second-generation family who had emigrated from India. Anu was quiet and very introverted. Her father was an electrical engineer for General Electric, and her mother was a local pediatrician. The two girls were best of friends; both were in their junior year of high school and taking all the advance placement classes the school had to offer. The girls had placed in the upper 1 percent of their class on all the standardized tests and recently qualified for a National Merit Scholarship. Only the teaching staff had this knowledge, and they were betting on the two of them to score the highest in the school on the upcoming SATs.

Their neighborhood was in the older part of town, mostly two- and three-bedroom homes with large oak and elm trees that canopied the streets, filtering the sunlight, making the lush green lawns and red geraniums feel like a Hopper painting. Clare often read her literature assignments on the screened porch. There she could watch robins hop around the front yard, eating insects and earthworms.

The air today was cool from a recent rain. She recalled her grandfather telling her that robins didn't eat the seeds from his bird feeders. She dropped her school bag beside her chair and pulled out a pad of lined paper along with her reading glasses.

It was late afternoon, and neither of her parents was home from work yet. A breeze passed through the aluminum screens. It had been a long time since Clare had exercised her gift, although she always thought about it to herself. She sometimes would wonder if it was still there. Without hesitation, she looked around and then pointed at her glasses and began to move her index finger in a small circular motion. Then, almost as if it were a surprise, the glasses moved slowly toward her.

* * *

68

Clare's grandfather Ralph was her father's father, and a retired meteorologist who spent most of his time with his many hobbies: plants, pets, an organic garden, tropical fish, two cats, classical music, and a large reflector telescope. He had taught science at the community college for most of his life and occasionally would substitute for a few of the local TV weathermen. The family had bought him a new telescope for his birthday, and he had set it up on the second-floor bedroom balcony.

"What's the weather look like tomorrow?" Clare asked her grandfather.

"Whether it's cold or whether it's hot, we shall have weather, whether or not."

That was always Ralph's response, and it always made Clare laugh.

Ralph now lived alone after losing his wife to cancer six months ago. His bungalow on Pine Street was just a few blocks away, so Clare visited whenever she could to spend time with him. Her grandmother had been an artist and left behind a wonderful collection of watercolors that were on display throughout the house. The paintings were a combination of still life, landscapes, and portraits of the grandchildren. Ralph always talked about the work as if each one had its own story.

"Your grandmother painted this one when you were just five years old," he would say, "and she did it from a sketch she made when you were getting your first haircut. She said it was the only time you were still enough to get a likeness. Do you remember that haircut?"

Clare was used to the stories, and many of them were repeated with a different beginning or end. Her grandfather's memory was failing, and it was a concern for her parents, but she always listened intently.

"I do remember, Grandpa, probably because those were my first bangs."

Ralph's house was cluttered with weather maps, thermometers, barometers, and a special satellite feed from the local TV station. He had a small device on a pole that was attached to the exterior of the house and extended up above the roofline by ten feet. It would give him a variety of weather readings, including wind speed and moisture collection. His study was a maze of satellite images, beakers of various chemicals, and an ancient poster of a Mexican pyramid where the Mayans worshipped the sun god.

Clare loved science, and her grandfather's house was more like a science museum than a home. Growing up there was to experience a constant flow of experiments. The deck off the back of the house was surrounded by bird feeders, each a different type. The small garden was elevated and home to a strange collection of exotic vegetables. Ralph had attached a strip of copper around the edge of each box to keep out the slugs. He said it caused a small electrical charge when reacting to their translucent body and sent them running. He raised earthworms in a special container he kept in the garage. The worms came in handy on their fishing trips. There was a collection basin for rainwater, grapes that grew along the back fence, a large sundial in the middle of the backyard, and an old copper windmill that had belonged to his father perched over the door gable.

"That windmill came from my father's chicken coop," he said to Clare.

"Why is it so green?" she asked.

"It's made of copper. Because it has been left outside, the rain and air have caused it to oxidize. My dad worked in a tool and die shop and made it from scrap metal that he would bring home from work. When I was a child, about your age, he raised chickens on our property, and he made the windmill to let him know which way the wind was blowing, mostly so he could avoid the smell. When he sold the house, I asked him if I could have it. It reminds me of my youth, feeding the chickens, picking grapes off the fence, playing in the coop where I watched the chicks hatch. We always had fresh eggs."

The bond between Clare and Ralph was stronger than usual. Their mutual love of science was consuming, and often Clare's father would have to call the house to remind her it was getting late and time to come home. They grew special cacti, tested household foods, dissected small animals, and they always watched *Watch Mr. Wizard*, the children's science show, on Saturday mornings. As she grew up, Clare took every science class she could, joined the 4-H club, Girl Scouts, and attended a science camp every summer. She had to force herself to take other classes and needed to set aside time for learning social studies, drama, and art.

"Hey Clare, did I ever mention that I knew Mr. Wizard?" said Ralph one day while filling his bird feeders.

"Yeah right, and there's a Santa Claus. You're pulling my leg, right?" said Clare with a laugh.

"I went to LaCrosse State Teachers College—let's see, this would be around nineteen forty—and he was a year behind me. He was certified to teach science, but he had a real interest in drama," said Ralph, filling up the last bird feeder with thistle seed.

"I lost track of him during World War Two. I think he joined the air force, and then in nineteen fifty-one, I saw him on TV during a show from Chicago. It was called *Watch Mr. Wizard*. One of my favorite shows was when he used a can of sardines to lure a bear, and then they shot the bear with a tranquilizer. He shaved off a patch of hair, tattooed the skin, and extracted a tooth to determine his age."

"They wouldn't do that. I never saw that episode," Clare said with determination.

"It was an early episode, before they moved the show to New York City on NBC. They placed a small radio collar on the bear and tracked his movements for a year. It was part of a study to better understand their habits and how far they would travel."

Clare was mesmerized. She first got hooked on *Watch Mr. Wizard* when she was in fourth grade and often would go over to her grandfather's with questions. He never mentioned that he actually had met Don Herbert.

"Why haven't you told me this before?" she asked.

"I don't know. I only met him a few times, and I really didn't know him well. He was just an acquaintance. I remember he was born in Minnesota, and then his family moved to Wisconsin. He was a very nice person."

* * *

Anu studied more than most students. She'd inherited some math genes from father, but she had an unusual way with numbers, equations, algorithms, square roots, Brahmi numerals, differentiation, and Leibniz notation. Anu was the *only* girl in her calculus class. She often gave the teacher a moment of pause with her questions because it wasn't just her memory or her knowledge; Anu had a gift. Her tall, thin frame couldn't have weighed more than 110 pounds, and her black braided hair fell to the middle of her back. She would never be seen without her black-rimmed glasses and drab conservative clothes. Plus, she rarely said a word in class.

Her best friend, Clare, was much her opposite. They complemented each other in their classes and socially. Their recent project was to start preparing for the SAT testing to be held at the community college. They planned and plotted to maximize their performance by exercising, eating high-protein food like nuts, yogurt, and whole grains. For the first time in many months, they were getting nine hours of sleep and practicing yoga along with the normal routines of drills, memory cards, and intensive reading. While sitting in a lotus position, Clare asked Anu a question.

"Where do you think math and science meet?"

"Is this a trick question?" asked Anu. "They overlap, but..."

"If they're the same, when are they the same?" asked Clare.

Anu took a minute. "Minus forty centigrade is the same as minus forty degrees Fahrenheit on their respective scales. How's that?"

Clare sighed. "You're sooo smarter than me."

* * *

This was Darren Cross's third year of teaching math at Jefferson High. Calculus was the most advanced class the school offered to math students heading for the university. Being the only girl, Anu was a little uncomfortable in his class, but Darren went out of his way to engage her in activity and often would ask her to help pass out material. The boys in the class were all geeks and more interested in their slide rules, mechanical pencils, and the latest TI calculator.

The bell rang, and Anu took her seat and unpacked her materials. Darren erased the blackboard, sat at his desk, and, without speaking, visually took attendance. The chatter among the young boys in the class was all about taking the SATs, and many felt confident they would do well. Darren got up from his desk and addressed the class.

"OK. Take out a piece of paper and a pencil. This is a pop quiz."

Cries and moans of dismay came in unison from the class, except Anu, of course. The students loved to prepare for tests, especially when they were given extended time to solve problems, but quizzes were always just one question with little time to answer.

"Let's put some application to what we've been learning in the past weeks. Here is the problem. If you were climbing a mountain in a certain amount of time and then came down the next day in the exact same amount of time, there is at least one location, one point on the mountain, that you were at on both days at exactly the same time. What theorem explains this fact? I'll give you five minutes."

Many of the boys exchanged looks with lost expressions on their face. One student laughed and said, "The location was the overnight campsite? Right?"

"Very funny!" said Darren.

Anu said nothing, but immediately wrote something down on her paper and covered the answer with her hands.

Darren pulled up the chart that was covering the center part of the blackboard, revealing four names on the board: Minkowski, Chebyshev, Brouwer, Lebesgue.

"Hey guys, I'm helping you out. Multiple choice."

Darren watched the clock and gave them an extra minute.

"OK, pencils down. Show of hands. How many had Minkowski?"

Four hands went up.

"Show of hands. How many had Chebyshev?"

Eight hands went up.

"Show of hands. How many had Lebesgue?"

Three hands went up, and there was another group groan from the class as they realized that by skipping over Brouwer, that was the correct answer.

"And Brouwer?"

One hand went up.

"Anu. Why?"

Anu paused, gave it some thought, then said, "Brouwer's theorem says that any plane automorphism has a fixed point, Chebyshev deals with numbers, Minkowski with optimization, and the Lebesgue theorem refines the notion of an integral. It seems clear, it has to be Brouwer's fixed-point theorem."

The class was dumbfounded, and at the same time starstruck, and even Darren Cross had an expression of awe on his face. Not only did she know the correct answer, but was able to articulate why the other theorems would not work. In such a modest manner, Anu had made an impression that just might stay with all the people in that room for a long time to come. The bell rang and broke the silence. It was a relief, and the end to a form of mathematical humiliation. As they exited the classroom, faster than usual, many were thinking the same thing. *She is much smarter than I thought.*

* * *

If one paid attention to the weather fronts, the dark, clear nights were predictable. Providing Clare had all her homework done, she would walk over to her grandfather's house and join him on the deck to look through the telescope. The first thing Ralph showed her was the Big Dipper in the north, which could be high in the sky and upside down, or lower toward the horizon, depending on the time of year.

Ralph explained, "It's a bit longer than your hand at arm's length with the fingers spread. The two outer stars in the 'bowl' point toward the North Star. Polaris is part of a constellation called Ursa Minor, the Little Bear. The Dipper's stars likewise form part of Ursa Major, or the Great Bear. If you don't see any bears, don't worry. Constellations are invented patterns that began as pictures in the sky to help early people remember important myths and legends. Some constellations, such as spring's Leo the Lion, summer's Scorpios the Scorpion, and winter's Taurus the Bull, are prehistoric. They first appear in ancient Mesopotamian records at the dawn of history."

"How long have we had telescopes?" asked the ever-curious Clare.

"As for the invention, I'm not sure. It's hard to say. They came from the making of ground glass during the mid fifteen hundreds in the

Netherlands, I think. But it was Galileo who really used the telescope
to prove what Copernicus theorized earlier, that the planets in our solar
system were in an orbit around our sun."

"Was that a big deal?" Clare asked.

"Yes, it was. In fact, it was rejected by the church. They held to the
belief then that the earth was the center of our solar system, and everything revolved around it. It sounds funny now, but back then, it wasn't
so funny for Galileo. They almost executed him. They made him make
a public apology, excommunicated him from the church, and placed him
under house arrest," said Ralph, adjusting the telescope.

"That's crazy!" Clare said

"Seems so to us now, but back then, science and religion were not
always on the same page. Did you know Galileo invented the thermometer? I think he made his first thermometer in fifteen ninety-three. He
constructed a glass tube, about eighteen inches long, that stood upright
in a bowl of water. As the temperature varied, the water level went up
and down the tube. It was kind of crude, but it worked. Hey, it is getting
late. You probably need to get home. I'll get my sweater and walk you
back."

* * *

The spring season was more than half over, and it was normal for
Clare to be on the lookout for a big storm. The large cold fronts from
the north would collide with warm air coming up from the Gulf of
Mexico. If the timing was right, she would always make her way over
to her grandfather's house, where they would monitor all the weather
equipment that he had installed, including a small Doppler radar feed
from the local TV station. Every storm was an adventure, and they all
had different characteristics.

The rule was: the bigger, the better. These small pellets of ice dropped
downward, only to be caught in an updraft within the storm where more
moisture would freeze around them. Ralph explained to Clare that this
process repeated itself until the pellets would reach a certain weight,

and then they would drop to the ground. They once collected hailstones the size of golf balls. Clare's fridge had a plastic ziplock bag with specimens, and one time her father used them as ice cubes for his lemonade. On a late Friday afternoon while walking to their last class, Clare told Anu about the hailstones she had found.

"Hailstones are drops of frozen rain. My grandfather showed me a cross section under a microscope where he used polarized light to see the internal structure that the crystal forms. They had these little rings that resembled the cross section of a tree, except there were all these colors. You could measure how many times the hailstone was coated."

* * *

It was the end of a long week, and Clare gazed out the large windows facing west in her second-story classroom at Jefferson High School. It was the only class that she and Anu did not have together. Clare was in an advance placement literature class, while Anu attended her advanced calculus class. The lecture that day was on the work of Flannery O'Connor, the American female writer who lived and grew up in the South. Clare had turned in her assignment, students were shuffling papers, the teacher was erasing the blackboard, and there was only a minute left before the final bell.

Although it was only 3:30 p.m., it was dark outside. Clare could see large thunderclouds billowing upward like none she had seen before. Large amounts of electricity could be seen as sheets of lightning jumping between the bottom and tops of clouds. And then she saw a bolt of lightning hit the top of an old elm tree not more than a hundred yards away, followed by a huge clap of thunder. Everyone in the classroom flinched. Several yelped out loud as the sound reverberated in the high-ceilinged classroom.

The teacher was noticeably shook up and said, "It's just a thunderstorm. Don't worry, the bell is about to ring, and you will be on your buses soon. Could everyone please put their chairs up on their desks?"

The students were quiet, but their fear was palpable. There had been some severe storm damage to the school in the past, and the wind was tossing debris into the air. Some loose branches hit the large windows. Clare stood firmly, gazing into the storm, while students quickly shuffled out at the sound of the piercing bell. She could see the branch that had fallen from the elm tree next to the football field. *No rain...yet*, she thought.

Outside, wind whipped the trees, and small pieces of loose-leaf paper whirled like dervishes. A small, inverted umbrella tumbled across the high school lawn. From her time with her grandfather, Clare knew that this was an occluded front, that cold air had overtaken warmer air. It was the kind of weather that created tornadoes.

The teacher had finished packing up her things and was anxious to leave.

"Clare! We need to go!" she said sternly.

That snapped Clare from her trance as she grabbed her book bag and rushed to the door. She decided not to stop at her locker. Carrying her book bag with one hand and holding down her skirt with the other hand, she headed directly to her bus. The buses left promptly on time, as she well knew from the many times she had to walk home when she missed her bus.

The wind had picked up speed now to about thirty miles per hour, blowing dust and debris everywhere. All she could think about was getting to Ralph's house. *I wonder if he's home?* Clare got on the bus and spotted Anu.

"Wow, seems like a pretty big storm. I didn't even stop at my locker. Did you?"

"Yeah. I had to grab some books and my umbrella. There are a lot of branches down. Did you notice those flying projectiles?" Anu asked.

"Yeah. Do you want to come over to my grandfather's house with me? It's just a couple of more stops on the bus. If he's there, he'll be monitoring the storm activity, and we can watch it on his radar system."

By now, large pellets of rain were hitting the top of the school bus like a drumroll. The girls gazed through the bus windows. The entire sky was black, and the wind pushed sheets of rain across the large front lawn, which was peppered with small hailstones. A police car sped by, its bubble light swirling, the sound of the siren distorted by the wind.

The students on the bus were unusually quiet, and stop by stop, students opened their umbrellas just as they stepped off the bus.

Less than a quarter of a mile away, Ralph's instruments were in full gear. The wind speed monitor cups spun crazily, clocking the wind at sixty-three miles per hour. It was the highest speed he had ever recorded from his house. The barometric pressure was unusually low at 28.69 inches of mercury.

Ralph was adjusting his Doppler feed when he heard the community alert siren go off, a creepy drone that sounded when the conditions for a tornado existed, and warned the community to take cover.

Three blocks away, a funnel cloud touched down in an elementary school playground, sucking up everything in its path and taking out telephone poles and electrical lines. Fencing, a six-foot-long bike rack, and two large Dumpsters tossed in the air like paper kites. Shingles, sticks, papers, and dust thickened the air to soup. The narrow column spread across the neighborhood like a giant vacuum sweeper, ripping up trees, taking off garage roofs, and tipping over cars, before it retracted into the cloud from which it had come.

The surrounding airspeed now clocked at eighty miles per hour from the nearby tornado and ripped a very large tree limb from the old oak tree in Ralph's front yard. As he passed through the dining room, Ralph heard something crashing through the roof. The limb came through the drywall and hit the massive china cabinet, which toppled over, knocking him unconscious.

Clare stepped off the bus behind Anu, who had stopped to struggle with her small, frail umbrella. She held the aluminum frame together with one hand, but it did little to shelter them from the rain. Clare grabbed her arm as they both pushed forward against the wind and rain. She had heard the siren, and it made her stomach churn. She knew what it meant, that there was a possibility of danger. Her grandfather's house was only a block away. The street was cluttered with broken tree limbs and debris.

As they drew closer to Ralph's, Clare saw the giant limb poking out of the roof. The telephone line that connected the house to the street grid dangled from the exposed, jagged end of the branch. Clare stifled a yell and ran ahead. She wasn't even sure her grandfather was home, and as she leaped up the front porch stairs two at a time, she fervently hoped he wasn't. But her heart sank when she turned the knob and it gave. If the door was unlocked, that meant he was home.

Once inside, she could see the toppled-over china cabinet. The skylight in the dining room had shattered, and rain poured in, where she saw Ralph, unconscious, blood streaming from a cut on his forehead. He was trapped by the weight of the huge cabinet. Moments later, Anu was behind her.

"Is he all right?" asked Anu.

"I don't know yet," said Clare. She grabbed the phone on the business desk and dialed 911, only to realize there was no dial tone. She recalled the image of the line dangling from the branch.

She kneeled by her grandfather and took his wrist gently in her hand, feeling for a pulse. His eyes fluttered.

"What happened?" he asked. Before she could answer, he was out again.

The tree branch creaked and slipped downward an inch. Anu shouted and jumped backward. Clare looked up and could see the wind was still blowing hard. It could easily move the branch even further into the house. She needed to move Ralph to safety quickly.

Clare focused her thoughts and removed her emotions as best as she could, a skill that she would use in high-pressure situations throughout her life.

"Anu, grab his arms, like this." Claire pointed. "When I say pull, you pull him free."

The wind howled, causing the branch to creak ominously. Clare knew what she had to do, though she had never dreamed it would be in a situation like this. The biggest thing she had ever moved was a small wagon, and it had only been a couple of inches.

She held out her hands, channeling her entire being through her fingertips toward the cabinet where it lay on Ralph's hip. Slowly she arced her wrists back and forth in small semicircles. Anu watched in shock without knowing what to say. After what seemed like many minutes, the edge of the cabinet lifted an inch, then another inch, and another.

"Pull!" shouted Clare.

The cabinet continued to rise upward, now more than a foot, as Anu pulled Ralph onto the plush living room carpet. Clare gradually lowered the cabinet and the weight of the branch down to the floor without a crash.

She instructed Anu to run next door for help before rushing to her grandfather.

"Grandpa, can you hear me? Are you all right?"

His eyes opened gradually. "What happened?" His voice was weak.

"Lightning hit the oak tree just outside the house. A large branch came through the roof. It knocked the china cabinet on top of you. Where are you hurt?"

"My wrist hurts, but my legs are OK. Are you OK?" he asked.

"I'm fine. My friend Anu went to the neighbors to call for an ambulance. We need to get you to the hospital."

"Good idea," said Ralph.

Clare wiped his forehead with a warm, wet paper towel and could hear the ambulance siren getting closer. Time was a blur. The paramedics were in the house before Clare could speak to her grandfather again, and started all the proper procedures. Once they had him on a stretcher, they started giving him oxygen and moved him into the vehicle.

The lead paramedic had just finished with a few questions for the two girls, when he said, "His vitals look good. We're taking him to the county hospital for observation, but at this point, his wrist may be fractured or sprained, and he may need a couple of stitches on his forehead. Otherwise, I think he'll be fine. Do you have any questions?"

"I don't think so," Clare said.

"Did that branch hit him?" asked the paramedic.

Clare froze. She hadn't anticipated questions like that. *I mean, isn't it obvious?* she thought.

"Yes, exactly," said Anu, having just walked up from the porch. "I think it hit him in the forehead."

"Well, you're lucky that cabinet didn't fall on him. OK, will you contact his family?" asked the paramedic on his way out the door.

"He's my grandfather. I'll call my dad," said Clare, calmer now.

Anu sat down next to Clare on the couch, and they did not speak for some time. They were both exhausted. Several minutes passed in silence, and then Clare spoke.

"You're wondering what happened, right?"

"Well, it *was* a magic show," said Anu.

"No one knows about this, about what you saw. I don't use it at all. It's something I've been able to do since I was real little. I can't explain it, you know? It's beyond me."

Anu said, "In calculus, we would call it a phenomenon, an infinite series of derivatives, a calculated manipulation of space and time, creating an action that usually results in a change."

Claire laughed. "Right. Exactly!"

Ralph stayed only one night in the hospital before he was able to come home. Although he had some bruises and a few aches and pains, he was cleaning up his yard and tending to his garden within days. He decided to have a new skylight installed in his dining room. Clare and Anu got right back to prepping for the SATs, and their friendship would continue for years to come.

The Callanish Stones

Galen was up early as usual, got dressed, and made his way downstairs. The fire in the family fireplace had gone out, so before putting on his fleece jacket, he laid a couple of slabs of peat on the coals and left for the beach.

It was a long walk, about a kilometer, to the east coast of Lewis Island, Scotland, most of it traversing an expansive, peat-covered plateau of low rolling hills. Dunes along the ocean backed the white sandy beach. The coastline was severely indented with a number of coves, and the cool, moist climate chilled the morning air.

When Galen finally crested the dunes and dropped down to the beach, he knew the tide would be out. At low tide, it was easy to walk on the hard, wet sand and scavenge for fresh seafood left behind in tide pools. He'd brought a nylon string bag in which to carry home butter clams, sea scallops, and an occasional Atlantic char.

He had been on the beach only minutes before he saw a body crumpled at the edge of the high-tide mark. Galen broke into a run. As he got closer, he could tell it was a young boy, facedown in the sand. A faint pulse thrummed against his fingers when he placed them gently on the boy's neck. At least he was alive. A long gash had welted up at the boy's temple, but it was no longer bleeding, probably because of the cold water, Galen thought. Galen tried gently to bring the boy around, with no luck. He took off his fleece-lined jacket to wrap around the boy's torso, then sat back on his heels to assess the situation.

Galen had just turned seventeen and was nearly six feet tall. He was a strong young man, mainly from loading crates of salmon into trucks headed for Stornoway. With driftwood everywhere and tough strands of dried seaweed abundant, he could construct a sled that he could pick up at one end and drag back to the farm.

As he worked, the sound of noisy guillemots scouring the beach for their breakfast kept him company. Their squabbling over bits of dead crayfish was as familiar as the waves breaking gently on the sand. Once he'd finished the sled, he carefully rolled the boy's body onto it and covered him as much as possible. He picked up the end of the sled closest to the boy's head, making sure he was properly elevated, and headed home.

Galen MacLeod lived with his family on their farm ten miles north of Carloway, on Lewis Island, along the Outer Hebrides. The nearest village was Garenin. The MacLeods raised sheep and barley mostly, and they always planted a small vegetable garden. Galen's father worked in Carloway, at the Harris Tweed mill, where he managed the machine-spinning and vat-dyeing process that produced distinctive twilled cloth. Galen, his mother, and his sister managed the farm, but Galen was always looking for extra work. He helped cut peat for a neighbor and loaded seafood into trucks headed to markets around the island. He was trying to save enough money to travel to the mainland and see the likes of Edinburgh and Inverness.

The MacLeod family had deep roots in Lewis Island. The first MacLeods had settled there in the mid–seventeen hundreds, all members of the Free Church of Scotland. Galen's father, Adair, was born on the island and had inherited his father's land, as well as a hundred more acres from his uncle, whose land joined theirs to the north, and now raised his family in the same house where he had been born and raised. More than six hundred Blackface sheep roamed the farm. Their meat was free of superfluous fat, and their wool brought the best price at market.

Galen pulled his makeshift sled across the beach and into the marshy landscape while trying to find a path that would make the pull a bit easier. The vegetation that pushed back as far as he could see was a mixture of grasses, peat, and rosy heather. Although it was midsummer, the temperature rarely got above seventeen degrees Celsius. Galen could still hear the large guillemots, though more birds had gathered in search of food exposed by low tide.

As Galen pulled, he looked back occasionally to see if the boy had regained consciousness, but his eyes remained shut. Galen tried to imagine how the boy had ended up on a remote, deserted beach. He could only figure that he somehow fell off the ferry that brought tourists up the coast of Lewis en route from Harris to the Port of Ness. The ferry usually stopped midway up the island's coast so that passengers could debark and tour the famous Callanish Stones.

Constructed around 4000 BC, the thirteen huge monolithic stones formed a circle fifteen meters in diameter. From an aerial view, the formation of the stones resembled a somewhat distorted Celtic cross. The site had undergone limited archaeological study in 1980, and although a burial cairn of human remains had been discovered, there was evidence that the configuration formed a calendar system based on the alignment of the moon.

Because Galen's farm was so close to the site, there were times when tourists in search of the stones would show up at the farm, seeking directions. Galen's younger sister, Rhona, would sometimes tell people that giants who lived on the island refused to be converted to Christianity by Saint Kieran and were turned into stone as a punishment.

Just then, Galen saw Rhona in the garden and shouted, "Rhona, get Mom. Hurry!"

In jeans, a white blouse, and a dark blue sweater, Rhona's blonde hair hung well past her shoulders. She had just turned fourteen and was in many ways as independent as her brother. Her mother had taught her piano from an early age, she raised her own sheep, and she had learned advanced analytic mathematics all on her own. No one in the family knew that Rhona spent much of her time amongst the stones, and had recently had an experience she shared with no one.

"What's wrong?" Rhona shouted back.

"Never mind! Just get Mom!"

Rhona heard the urgency now in his voice, dropped the garden spade she'd been working with, and ran to the house.

At the front gate, Galen put down the sled and unlatched the iron catch. He could see his mother and his sister approaching as he picked up the sled and continued toward the house.

"What happened?" his mother asked.

"I found him on the beach. He must have washed up in the high tide. I tried to bring him around, but there's a gash on his head. He must have hit his head and fallen…maybe off a boat, like the ferry."

Rhona picked up the other end of the sled, and they continued to the house. Galen's mother lightly touched the gash on the boy's pale skin.

"Let's get him into the extra bedroom. There are some pajamas in the linen closet, and some extra blankets. I'll call your father."

The MacLeods' fieldstone-built farmhouse was two stories high with white window casings and three fireplaces. It was larger than most residential houses in the area. It had been added onto each time the house was handed down to the next generation. By now, there was more room than the family needed.

Ishbel MacLeod was a well-built woman with strong features, light-brown hair, and an intellect that surpassed her husband's. As feminine as she could be, she found herself cleaning out the sheep pens or slogging around in a muddy field more often than not. Most of the time she wore worn-out jeans, an oversized sweater, and old boots. She worked hard to maintain the farm, oversee the hired help, and raise two teenagers. Ishbel had met Adair in college, where she was studying mathematics and hoping for a career in teaching. She never got into the classroom, but she knew how many hectares there were in an acre. But that knowledge was no good to her now. She picked up the phone and called Adair at the mill.

When he answered, she told the story in a rush and finished with, "What do you think we should do?"

"I'll call the police, but you should call your friend Jillian. Isn't she a physician's assistant? I'll try to get home early, but the police will be there soon enough, too, OK?"

"Thanks, honey. I'll give Jillian a call." Ishbel went back to the bedroom and told her children that help was on the way.

* * *

Dr. Rebecca Collins had her own room, while her colleagues, James and John, shared a room at the Doune Braes Hotel, a small bed-and-breakfast snuggled in an alcove of the main street of Carloway. As she lit a candle and lay back in the hot bathwater, she tried to let her mind relax. Her work schedule had been grueling, and there was a lot of data to cross analyze and interpret.

Dr. Rebecca Collins headed up the archaeological team that focused closely on the stone formations in Britain. It was part of a two-year study that had started in England, and they were now examining the stone formations of the Outer Hebrides. The team of three academics was hoping to shed new light on the long-standing debate about whether the earliest stone formations around 4000 BC were due to colonists moving into Britain or if the indigenous population gradually adopted the new agricultural lifestyle themselves.

In Carloway for only a few weeks, her team was excavating the Callanish Stones site. The preliminary findings showed that the first colonists were likely to have traveled across the western seaways, a hypothesis backed by findings such as French pottery fragments found just ten inches under the buildup of soil.

Dr. Collins had handpicked her team: Dr. John Healy from England's University of Liverpool and Dr. James Maxwell from Stanford University in the United States. John was an expert in radiocarbon dating, and Jim handled all the logistics of reclaiming artifacts and accessing the layers of human activity. Thus far, they had constructed a database of all known fourth millennium sites and used a program of radiocarbon dating to understand the chronology of activity on Lewis Island.

Recently divorced, Rebecca was a driven researcher who traveled constantly, worked very long hours, and published extensively in prestigious scientific journals. It was her writing and credentials that had won them the funding and contracts with the media. The Arts and Humanities Research Council of Great Britain had funded the project, so two camera crews had been with them for more than a year. The BBC crew was a two-person crew that worked out of Stornoway, and the Smithsonian / National Geographic team was a four-person crew based in Glasgow that provided them with helicopter support for transport to various locations.

Water sloshed from the bath as she reached for the memoir *Just Kids,* sent to her by her niece in the United States. It was an emotional and touching love story that provided some relief from her academic and scholarly work. She reminded herself they would only be in Carloway one more week before she'd be able to get back to the University of Edinburgh in time for the holiday. Meanwhile, she tried to relish the hot bath, since she'd only had time for quick showers in the past month. She had an early morning the next day to meet the media crew at the site, but she was determined to soak and read for a while. Still, her eyes grew heavy quickly, and, with a sigh, she placed a piece of torn paper in her book, wrapped herself in an oversized towel, and headed off to bed.

* * *

The Carloway Constabulary arrived at the farm within a half hour of Ishbel's call. She met them at the door and led them upstairs to the spare bedroom where the boy lay, still unconscious. They took a few photographs, then asked Galen and his mother to help them complete a report that included all the details thus far. They asked to be notified as soon as the young boy became conscious. At that time, if there were a reason, they would return to question him. In the meantime, they would cross-check his description against any missing-person reports and let them know if any information came of it. As they left the farmhouse, Jillian pulled up in her old Range Rover and approached the door.

Ishbel waved her inside and up the stairs.

Jillian sat on the edge of the bed and opened her medical case. She took the boy's vitals and drew a blood sample to test. She looked in his ears and eyes and listened to his lungs with a stethoscope. The electronic thermometer beeped.

"His temperature is a hundred and one, which is above normal, but other than that, he seems OK. He could be fighting off a virus. His blood pressure and his breathing are normal. I don't think he's in a coma so much as an extended state of unconsciousness. The blow to his head is probably the reason for that," she said, again touching her fingers to the gash. "This isn't deep and probably won't require stitches. I'll discuss the situation with the doctor tomorrow when he comes in. If the boy hasn't regained consciousness by then, you may have to bring him in. I am afraid that's all I can do for now. What did Adair say?"

"He called the police, and he's probably on his way home now. Thanks for coming, Jillian. I'm so glad you live nearby. It makes us all feel a bit safer. Call me if you think of something, won't you?"

It was less than a half hour before Adair came through the front door, his face creased with worry. He had talked with the police on the drive home, trying to extract information. Most of all, he wondered what the boy's family was thinking.

Ishbel took him to the guest room where the young boy lay under the covers in an old pair of Galen's pajamas. His light-colored hair was short, and his features were pleasant, like many young boys that age. She pointed at the contusion on the boy's temple and said that was probably the reason for the unconsciousness. Later, they all convened at the dinner table.

"How are you feeling, Galen?" asked his father.

"It's been a weird day," Galen said, shaking his head. "I never expected anything like this."

"Who would?" his father said. "You saved his life, son. I'm proud of you. It was a courageous effort."

Rhona spoke up. "Galen thinks he may have fallen from a ferry heading up the coast. You know how they come close to shore to let the tourists stop to see the Callanish Stones? What do you think, Dad?"

Adair took a moment and then said, "It makes sense. Let's see what the police turn up. If someone were missing from the ferry, you'd think they would know by now. I will call them again in the morning."

After dinner, and when all the dishes were washed and put away, Galen went outside to sit on the front porch. Rhona eventually followed.

She knew her brother was upset. In the deepening darkness, Galen stared toward the distant hills that rose to a plateau and flattened out. As he and Rhona sat, it grew fully dark. The aurora borealis gradually lifted itself from the horizon and lit the night sky with a shifting panorama of colors.

Rhona watched until the colors flared up and dissipated. Then she yawned. "I'm going to bed. It's been a crazy day. Life is usually so quiet around here."

"I know," Galen said. "But don't worry, everything will be Okay."

* * *

As usual, Galen woke early. He dressed and went to check on the boy. As he gently pushed open the door to the extra bedroom, he saw the young boy sitting up in bed and rubbing his eyes.

"Morning," Galen said, keeping his voice low and calm. "How are you feeling?"

The boy looked at Galen in bewilderment. "Where am I?"

"You're at our farmhouse, a little more than a kilometer from the ocean. I found you on the beach yesterday morning. You're lucky to be alive. Do you know what happened to you?"

Ishbel tiptoed in and stood behind Galen. She was still in her bathrobe, but she had a steaming cup of coffee in her hand.

Rhona appeared and whispered to her mother, "Dad was up early and left for work."

The young boy looked at the three of them as though they were from outer space. "My head hurts. I think I was on a boat and I hit my head."

Ishbel walked over to the bed and put her hand on his forehead. "Your temperature feels normal. It must have spiked sometime during the night. That's a good sign."

The sound of the phone ringing downstairs startled them all. Ishbel hurried down to answer. It was Adair calling from his office in Carloway.

"I called Port Ness, and there are no reports of anyone missing from yesterday's ferry. Is the boy awake?"

"He's sitting up in bed, but he doesn't remember what happened. He thinks he was on a boat and hit his head. Did you talk with the police?"

"They're still checking, but nothing yet. We'll just have to wait a bit. Well, at least he's awake. Take care of him, Ish. I'll be home as soon as I can. Love you."

Ishbel found some of Galen's old clothes from when he was boy and brought them into the bedroom. "Would you like to get cleaned up a bit? Afterward, here are some of Galen's old clothes you can wear for now. Are you hungry?"

The boy nodded.

"Well, come down to the kitchen when you're finished. I'll have a nice hot breakfast ready in no time."

After breakfast, Galen and Rhona decided to tour their guest around the farm. They both knew there was something exciting that might be happening in the barn.

Before they left the house, Galen asked the boy if he remembered his name.

"I think my name is Ryan. It's the first thing that comes to my mind."

"Then Ryan it is," said Rhona. "Come on, Ryan, we want to show you the sheep."

All the buildings on the farm were made from fieldstone, and the oldest buildings still had thatched roofs. Although many farms in the area were crofters, the MacLeods were full-time agriculturalists with a sophisticated farming system that was part livestock and part crop generating. When harvest time came, they often hired as many as thirty workers to bring in wheat, barley, and oats. The sheep that were about to lamb were in barn number three. Galen unlatched the gate, and they walked into the lambing barn.

"How do you know when a sheep is ready to have its baby?" Ryan asked.

"Just prior to lambing, the ewe may separate from the flock and locate a quiet area for herself."

Rhona added, "She'll smell the ground, dig it up a bit, and paw at it. When she lies down, it's time."

The three of them watched the restless ewes milling about in the barn. There was much to see on the MacLeod farm. They spent the day showing Ryan around, which culminated in a drive to the highland, where the majority of the flock roamed and the dogs managed most of the work.

* * *

On a rainy, windy afternoon, the Collins's team suspended their work at the site and gathered at the Lachlan Pub in Carloway, where the BBC crew had set up their camera, some audio equipment, and a soft light. When asked what brought them to Lewis Island, Dr. Rebecca Collins responded as the video rolled.

"We're excavating the Callanish Stones site because we have decided to turn our attention away from the mainland and towards the seas that formed an important travel link between the islands and Britain. These Outer Hebrides sites, which are an important maritime zone, have surprisingly been given little scholarly attention in the past. Archaeological findings, such as the bones of farm cattle from the fourth millennium BC, and European pottery, along with advances in radiocarbon techniques, have given new life to the theory that European colonists settled in Britain and brought farming practices with them."

It was the last setup, and the final take, before the crew took a break. They were heading up to the site to gather some B-roll after lunch, when Adair walked into the pub and sat at the bar, where he ordered himself a corned beef sandwich. As a city councilman, he had met Rebecca a few times, and had recommended their accommodations. It was good public relations for Carloway and Lewis Island to have the study underway, as it helped with their efforts at increasing tourism. Rebecca took off her radio mic and walked over to Adair.

"Mr. MacLeod, how are you? I wanted to thank you for your recommendation that we stay at the Doune Braes Hotel. We needed a place that provides full service and Internet, not to mention the tender mutton and scallops. How are things at the mill?"

Adair was always polite and diplomatic with visitors to Carloway. As a councilman, he was responsible for efforts to boost the local economy, but at the moment, his mind was elsewhere. He had just left his office, where he'd spent a good part of the morning trying to figure out which ferries had traveled either up or down the coast in the past couple of days. There had been strong winds overnight that took out some of the phone lines along the coast, so he had only been able to leave voice messages.

He struggled to focus on Rebecca Collins and her polite questions now.

"The mill is busy, thanks for asking. I'm glad the hotel is working out for you. I grew up with Bennie Boyd. He's a good fellow and tries hard to please his guests. How is your project going?"

Rebecca was an attractive woman in her late thirties with a pleasant smile and long brown hair pulled back in a ponytail. Each time he had met her, she had been dressed the same: khaki slacks and a dark blue sport coat over a white shirt. Her vintage wire-rimmed glasses made her look like a professor. There was something immediately appealing about her manner, not pushy or brash, but gentle and genuinely concerned for others.

She was frowning now as she contemplated an answer to Adair's question about the project.

"Well, it's days like today that set us back. We drove up to the site this morning, and the wind was just too much. We had to pack it in."

Adair smiled. "When the wind comes off the ocean from the northwest, it picks up speed as it climbs up into the highland. It's a wonder those stones have stood up for so long. Are you finding what you came looking for?"

"The surveying and excavation are complete. We're using a new three-D computer graphic model gathered from satellite thermography, and John has detected some unusual electromagnetic readings from the inner circle of stones. We have found some amazing artifacts and some kernels of wheat that we can subject to carbon dating, but we're still working on a theory for the purpose of the stones themselves. Do you have any ideas?"

"There have been all kinds of stories, but nothing scientific. When I was growing up, I heard it was some kind of calendar system that helped ancient farmers with their crop planting, but others say it was used as a religious site for marriages, funerals…that kind of thing. Now it's mostly a tourist attraction. Maybe your work will provide a more scholarly explanation."

Rebecca's colleagues were up and ready to leave. The film crew had finished their lunches and left the pub, and there was much work to do. Adair was still waiting to hear from the ferry companies or the police.

"Well, we are finding a lot of new information that might shed light on what purpose the Callanish Stones provided, and I'll make sure we send you our preliminary findings when we have them. Good seeing you again."

* * *

By late afternoon, Rhona took Ryan back to the farmhouse so Galen could tend to some chores. Rhona and Ryan went straight to the kitchen, where Ishbel stood on a stool searching a high cupboard shelf for something to get dinner started.

"Mom, do you need help?"

Ish shook her head as she stepped off the stool. "How was the tour? Did you see some sheep, Ryan? Any luck with your memory?"

"Just the same as this morning. And even that's more like a feeling than a memory."

"My friend Jillian spoke with the doctor. He told her when there is head trauma, you can experience something called retrograde amnesia. Most of the time your memory will come back. You remember what you did today, right?"

"I remember waking up here. Then we went out all day. Before that, all I see is a boat."

Just then, Adair came in and greeted everyone. "Ryan, how are you feeling? Any improvement?"

"We were just talking about that," Ishbel said. "Jillian said he has a type of amnesia that comes with head trauma and that the memory usually returns gradually."

"That's good news. I wasn't so lucky. There are no reported missing people from the ferry system, and the police have had no missing-person reports. So that's a dead end. It looks like you're stuck with us,

Ryan, at least for a while. Maybe Rhona can work her magic on you. She believes in that kind of stuff."

Rhona's face indicated her displeasure at his remark.

Galen walked in and headed straight for the mudroom to wash up. "We have a new lamb, Dad. I took care of it, and everything went well."

Ishbel looked at Rhona. "Can you cut up an onion? And be careful. I just sharpened the knife."

Rhona pulled a white onion from a mesh bag and placed it on the large wood cutting board. It was only a minute before she cried out. She dropped the knife on the cutting board and grabbed her index finger.

Ishbel looked at her in exasperation. "I told you to be careful. Here, let me see." She pried the girl's fingers open. Blood ran down her arm. "It's not too bad. Here, hold the cut closed, stick it under the faucet, and apply pressure. I'll get some gauze and tape."

Ishbel kept a first aid kit in the small bathroom off the kitchen. After they washed off Rhona's hand and applied some more pressure, she laid down a piece of medical gauze and wrapped it so the tape pulled the separated skin together. "Keep applying some pressure. I don't think you'll be practicing piano for a while, which should make you happy," Ishbel said with a wry grin.

After dinner, Rhona took Ryan out to the porch, hoping for another show of the aurora borealis. Sure enough, the horizon started to light up and gradually become green. The rest of the family joined them on the porch to watch the lights.

"What is that light?" Ryan asked.

"Aurora borealis is the scientific name," Galen said. "Most people just call them northern lights."

The dark blue horizon began to emit a green swirl of color that blended to pink, then yellow, and back to green.

"What makes the colors, and why does the light move?"

"The color's caused by highly charged particles in the atmosphere colliding together. The charged particles move like a solar wind and are directed by Earth's magnetic field. Our science teacher told us the lights were named after the Roman goddess of dawn, Aurora, and the Greek name for wind, Boreas. They occur near the time of the equinox, which was a week ago. They aren't harmful or anything."

"I remember this," Ryan said suddenly. "I saw this from the boat. Does this happen everywhere?"

Adair knew that, because of their latitude, the lights were especially active in the month of July.

"If the night is clear, and the temperature is just right, there is a lot of activity off Lewis Island. But if you saw this recently, then you must have been on a boat nearby. This could be another piece of the puzzle."

* * *

After dinner and a short meeting at the hotel that night, Jim Maxwell asked Rebecca if she would like to share a nightcap. They had been friends for more than ten years, and this would be the third project they had worked on together. Jim had known Rebecca's ex-husband, an engineer for British Petroleum stationed in Belfast. This was the first time they'd been on a project since the divorce that left her son in the custody of her ex.

"I was sorry to hear about the divorce," Jim said. "Was it a shock for you?"

"Not really. We were both working a lot and going in different directions. Tom was home more than I was. My work took me all over the place. We were in marriage counseling for a while, but it was hard for me to keep a schedule. That's why he got custody. And I could hardly argue that. I was away so much. I missed Christmas one year. Do you believe that? Our son needed to be in a school in one place where he could have friends and play soccer, and he and Tom loved to sail out of Belfast Harbour."

Jim poured them both another glass of sherry and looked at Rebecca, who now seemed sad.

"Do you talk with them much?"

"Yes, usually, but it's been two weeks. They were planning to sail the coast of Ireland. I probably won't hear from them until they get back sometime next week. When Ryan was younger, he almost drowned in a pool. I had a premonition that something had happened. It was frightening. And when I was ten, I was involved in a boating accident that made me afraid of the water. That's why I didn't sail with them. Last night I had a nightmare that involved a sailboat and water, and it has me on edge. Tom said he would call as soon as they returned."

"Maybe you should give them a call."

"I have, but I just get voice mail." Rebecca looked at her watch. "Thanks for talking to me, Jim. I needed that. But it's getting late. Think I'll turn in."

* * *

The following day dawned bright and clear. Galen was loading bails of barley and supervising the men working the farm. Adair had left for Carloway, hoping to find out something about the missing boy. Rhona had asked her mother if she could take Ryan to see the Callanish Stones, and as soon as they finished cleaning up after breakfast, she and Ryan headed north on foot.

Rhona knew the most direct way to the stones was to keep to the single-lane path until they reached the valley, and then pass over the outcrops of granite. As they walked, Ryan recounted a dream he'd had the night before.

"There was a large, jagged mountain suddenly coming up out of the ocean. It was green and surrounded by clouds. I must have been in a boat, because there was a sound of a rock ripping a hole in the bow, and the boat turned over. I hit my head and grabbed a life vest. Then I was in the water. And that was it. Do you think that's me remembering what happened, or was it just a dream?"

"Could be." Rhona was distracted now because she could see the stones. She pointed. "Look, Ryan, there are the stones. I don't see any visitors, which is good. Come on, let's go."

* * *

The research team was scheduled to be at the Callanish Stones site early that morning, but they were stranded in Carloway waiting for repairs to their vehicle. The local mechanic was replacing a tie-rod to the front wheel that had to be brought over from Stornoway. They decided to use the time for planning, as the garage promised they would be on their way by early afternoon. Rebecca was nervous after her talk with Jim and tried to reach Tom on her cell phone for a second time, only to hear the same message. She called Tom's sister, Gina, and found out that no one had heard from Tom yet, but they were expecting a call anytime.

"Thanks, Gina," Rebecca said. "Please call if you hear something."

Jim had overheard the conversation. "Is everything OK?"

"I just talked to Tom's sister. She hasn't heard from them either, but expects to anytime. Apparently they changed their plans and headed northwest to visit Saint Kilda. Do you know where that is?"

Jim shrugged. "I haven't heard of it, but that doesn't mean anything. There are so many small islands in the area. They could be anywhere."

"Any news about the car?"

"They have the part, and they're working on it. Shouldn't take long."

"Let's pack up so we're ready to go when it's finished. I wonder what the cell phone availability is around the smaller islands?"

* * *

When Rhona and Ryan reached the stones, the sky was clear blue, and there was no one in sight. At the center of the circle, the largest stone stood at least ten feet high and about a foot thick. In the center was a pit bordered by smaller stones. From the center of the circle, stones of varying sizes and shapes spread north and south at ten-foot intervals, forming the shape of a Celtic cross.

The foot traffic of many visitors had worn paths in the thick grass around the site, especially around the base of the stones. Rhona and Ryan walked amongst the stones as if they were in a church. There was something about the place that was very humbling and spiritual, as most visitors described it. It felt as if the stones were placed there to pay reverence to life.

Rhona spoke up suddenly. "Ryan, come here. This is what I want to show you."

Ryan moved to her side and bent down to peer at where she pointed at something growing at the base of one of the stones.

"See this plant behind the wild grass? It's called yarrow, and it has healing power. I've used it before. Technically, it's called *Achillea millefolium*. If you break the stem and extract some of the liquid from the plant and apply it to your skin…Watch."

Rhona removed the bandage from her finger and applied a small drop of liquid to her cut. "It takes about twelve hours, but it is amazing. It's my secret, and now you know."

"Does it only grow here?" asked Ryan.

Rhona pondered, and then said, "I don't think so, but it is very rare. I think people may have planted it here because this was a special place. That's what all these stakes are for that you see around here. There's a team doing research right now. My father told me they are professors who are trying to find out more about the meaning of the Callanish Stones. Isn't this place cool?"

Ryan looked up at the sky. "I feel like I should have known that."

"About the plant?"

"About the people working on the site. I feel like I know about that stuff."

Rhona laughed. "Don't be silly. You're just a kid. You couldn't possibly…Hey look!"

Some birds landed at the edge of the site.

Ryan asked, "What kind of birds are those?"

"Avocets and sandpipers. They come inland from the ocean." In the distance, they could hear the sound of a car. "Probably tourists," Rhona said, and sighed. "I was hoping we could have the place to ourselves for a little while."

* * *

Rebecca sat in the backseat of the car, looking over her notes, when her cell phone rang. She glanced at the screen and saw her sister-in-law's name. She answered immediately.

"Gina, have you heard anything?"

"We got a call late last night from the Royal Navy out of Harris Island. Apparently there was a distress signal from a boat off Saint Kilda Island. When they went out there with a helicopter, they saw a sailboat partially submerged just off the island coast. The description matched Tom's boat. They didn't see any people. They said they couldn't land the helicopter because it's just one big, steep piece of rock. The island is not populated. They are going to go back today by boat and do a search."

Rebecca closed her eyes tightly. This could not be happening. After a long pause, her sister-in-law continued.

"It doesn't mean there aren't survivors. Let's just pray and hope they got to shore. I'll call you as soon as I know more."

"Thank you, Gina. Yes, please call me." Rebecca ended the call and started to cry.

Jim turned to her from the front seat. "What happened?"

Through her tears, she explained what Gina had told her.

"Should we go back to Carloway?"

"No. There's nothing I can do until I hear from Gina. I'd rather go crazy here than in a hotel room. Let's go on to the site. I might just stay in the car, though."

John pulled up about a hundred yards from the Callanish Stones and parked the car. They could see a couple of young people from where they were, but it wasn't unusual to see visitors around. Jim and John got out of the car as Rebecca leaned her head against the window and closed her eyes.

Jim looked at the kids, then back to John. "I hope they read the signs. I just want to make sure they haven't messed with our installations. You know kids. We'd better check it out."

Rhona and Ryan were sitting in the grass talking when the two men approached them.

"Good morning," said Jim. "How are you young people doing?"

"Good morning," said Rhona. "We're fine. Are you part of the research team?"

John wandered off to check the archaeological areas under way, leaving Jim to handle community relations.

"So you know about that?" Jim asked.

"Of course I do. I am Rhona MacLeod. You know my father, Adair MacLeod."

"Of course. Fine man." Jim continued to talk with the two young people while John checked the installations "Do you live nearby?"

Rhona and Ryan had stood up by then, and could see a woman getting out of the car.

"Yes, about a kilometer away, over that ridge. Our sheep wander this way sometimes, but the loch keeps them from getting close to the stones."

John had finished checking the work sites and had returned to tell Jim that all was well. Rebecca was walking slowly toward them as if mesmerized.

Suddenly, Ryan took off at a run toward Rebecca.

"What the...?" Jim started to go after him, but he saw Rebecca drop to her knees, her arms outstretched, then wrapped tightly around the boy as he reached her.

They sat like that for a long time, Rebecca sobbing the boy's name repeatedly. Beyond them, fieldstone walls trimmed low rolling hills that flattened as they reached the ocean.

Rhona asked softly, "Is that Ryan's mother? How can that be? My brother found him on the beach yesterday morning, barely alive. He couldn't remember anything."

They stood quietly a while longer, watching the reunion.

Then Jim said, "She just found out that her ex-husband's sailboat was wrecked off Saint Kilda Island. Ryan was supposed to be on that boat with his dad. Nobody was found with the wreckage. She was afraid that..." Jim trailed off, then continued. "The place they found the boat is forty kilometers northwest. The kid must have made it through the night and the tide brought him here."

Still holding her son, Rebecca talked quietly. "Ryan, what happened?"

"We hit something, the boat went over, and I hit my head." The boy's face paled, and he started to cry. "Mom, I don't know what happened to Dad and Uncle William."

Rebecca soothed him. "I talked to your aunt Gina. The navy has a search team out there right now." She put a bright smile on her face. "What do you say we go thank the nice people who took you in? I'm sure your aunt Gina will be calling very soon."

In the living room of the farmhouse, the smell of peat burning in the stove gave a comforting and ancient aroma to the place. Sitting together in the living room, Rebecca explained the morning's events.

Rebecca's cell phone rang, and she could see it was from Gina. She looked over at Ryan and said soothingly, "It's your aunt Gina, sweetie. Let's see what she has to tell us."

Rebecca listened intently, then covered the phone with her hand and said to Ryan, "They found your dad and uncle William. They're fine." Then she spoke back into the phone. "Don't worry, Gina. Ryan is here with me. I'll explain later, but could you patch us through to them on the other line? Ryan really needs to talk to his dad right now."

Ryan took the phone. "Hello?"

"Hey buddy. It's your dad."

Everyone in the room looked at the expression on Ryan's face and smiled. A reunion was in order. Galen drove mother and son to Leverburgh Naval Base. Rhona's finger healed in record time, and Rebecca's team completed their work, spending an extra day packing up the equipment before shipping out to Edinburgh. The Callanish Stones, dark regal spires of metamorphic gneiss rock, remained intact, awaiting an explanation of their past.

Yellowknife

After the harshest winter in twenty years, spring came early to Minneapolis-Saint Paul. By mid-June, the weather was hot and humid. William packed his suitcase for a trip that would take his family to one of the most remote places in North America. His father, Jason Danforth, was a thin man who everyone said resembled James Dean. He was a senior engineer with the Occidental Petroleum Company and project manager for a new exploratory assignment. The company wanted to survey the upper part of Great Slave Lake, located in Canada's remote Northwest Territories.

"How cold does it get?" Will asked his mother, Julia.

"Not that cold in summer," she said. "I don't think you'll need your long underwear."

"Can I bring my bike?" Will asked, still packing.

"No," his father said. "There's no room for anything that large. Just bring the essentials, like your clothing, and maybe something to keep your mind occupied, like your science book."

Will looked at his father in disbelief. "It's summer, Dad. Give me a break!"

The first leg of the flight was on an Air Canada 747 stopping over in Edmonton on its way to Anchorage, Alaska. The flight, which took nearly two hours, lifted off the Saint Paul runway on time and within minutes broke through low-level clouds on its way west. Will gradually fell asleep, while his parents discussed their travel plans over coffee. Julia had planned the trip carefully and took this time to bring Jason up to speed, making him feel confident that all their reservations were in place.

The jumbo jet was making its first stop, and was on its approach to the Edmonton Airport, when Amanda, Will's fourteen-year-old sister, complained privately in a whisper to her mother. "I can't believe we're using Dad's business trip for our family vacation. I thought we were supposed to visit Grandma in Florida?"

"We were, but your dad is scheduled to be here for two weeks, and he really didn't want to be here alone. Besides, seeing this part of Canada could be very interesting."

"Did you sign us up for that camp?" Amanda asked.

"Will doesn't want to go to camp. He thinks it's just for girls."

"Is it?" asked Amanda, concerned.

"No, it's a camp for kids interested in the arts. I'm sure there will be plenty of boys."

"Then why does Will think it's just girls?"

"Because Will thinks anyone who isn't interested in math and science must be a girl."

"Mom, that's totally sexist," Amanda said.

"Maybe you should explain that to Will," Julia said calmly.

The wheels finally touched down, and the large jet landed smoothly. The layover in Edmonton was only an hour, but they had to transfer to a Canadian Airlines DC-3 prop plane for the last leg to Yellowknife. The flight would take only an hour and would put them into the local airport just around 11:00 a.m., with enough time to get their car, find their cottage, and get unpacked. The plane carried only forty passengers, and it was the first time the kids had been in a plane with propellers. The ride was rough with air turbulence, which made everyone a little uneasy. Soon the captain came over the PA.

"This is the captain. We are starting our descent to the Yellowknife municipal airport. Please make sure your seat belts are buckled and your seats are in an upright position. We should be on the ground in about ten minutes."

Only moments later, the captain came on again.

"This is the captain. We have a change in our landing location. All passengers please fasten seat belts and put your seat backs in the upright position."

Jason looked at his wife. "I wonder why they have to change the landing location?"

Without further notice, the DC-3 suddenly banked heavily to the left and began its descent to what looked like a highway running along the edge of the large lake below. Amanda clutched her mother, frightened by the plane's abrupt movement.

"Are we going to be all right?" Amanda whispered to her mom.

Again, the captain came on the PA. "Standby, all flight attendants. Take your seats and prepare for emergency landing procedures. We will be landing momentarily."

Julia looked at her husband with fear in her eyes. Jason said, "I'm sure we'll be fine. Just make sure your seat belts are fastened, and hold on."

It felt as if they were in a scene in a movie. They could hear snatches of dialogue from the other passengers as the flight attendants tried to keep everybody calm.

The DC-3 touched down on a long, straight stretch of highway as if it were a daily procedure. This part of the highway ran along a bluff high above the lake. Just above the trees and looking out over the great lake, one could see the skyline of Yellowknife to the east.

As soon as the plane wheels rolled smoothly to a stop, the captain switched on the PA. "Ladies and gentlemen, I'm happy to report a successful landing. We're sorry for any discomfort this may have caused. Airport personnel are on their way with a shuttle bus to take everyone to the airport, but we ask that you remain seated until the emergency ladder can be move up to the exit door at the front of the plane."

Will was peering out his window at Great Slave Lake. From his vantage point, it looked as big as an ocean. Suddenly, on the distant horizon, he saw what looked like a green tessellation of light hovering above the lake. *What could that be?* he thought.

Canadian officials met the passengers at the exit door to ask the usual international customs questions and then some. They were concerned that someone on the plane could have caused the technical problem. After a quick debriefing of each adult, nothing seemed out of the ordinary. All passengers boarded the shuttle bus and departed for the airport. Jason stood close to the pilot discussing the event with his copilot and overheard their conversation.

"What do you think happened up there?" asked the copilot.

"We just lost instrumentation. Everything electrical went dead, including the radar. It would have taken a strong magnetic force to cause the interruption. Pretty mysterious. I'm just glad it was a clear day so we could see the highway."

* * *

The Danforths picked up a rental car at the airport and headed to Yellowknife. As they drove along the lake toward the Sitting Bear Bridge, which spanned the bay, Julia noticed that the trees and flowers were about two weeks behind the plants in Saint Paul. She assumed the role of teacher and tour guide, skimming information from the classic Frommer's travel guide, *Canada*.

"Yellowknife is the capital of the Northwest Territories. Great Slave Lake is one of the largest in North America. It covers eleven thousand square miles, and is over two thousand feet deep in places."

"That's almost a mile," Will said in amazement "Why'd they name it Great Slave Lake?"

Julia thumbed the pages of the book until she found what she was looking for. "It says the lake was named for the Slavey Indian tribe. Europeans developed Yellowknife soon after the discovery of gold in the mid eighteen hundreds. The region is still important for gold, zinc,

and diamonds, but also supports a major commercial lumbering industry. The lakes and rivers in the province are ice-free for only four months
of the year."

"Maybe I'll find a diamond," said Amanda.

"Look at the power plant," said Will, pointing. "Dad, do you think
it uses water from the lake to operate?" Its vent stacks billowed large
plumes of white smoke into the bright blue sky.

"It looks like a major diesel-electric plant. It probably provides most
of the electrical power for the region," replied Jason.

They passed a building called the Wild Cat Café that marked the
edge of Old Town, Yellowknife's designated historic district. With a
gazebo at the center of its well-groomed circular park, it was home to
members of the arts community looking for an unusual place to live.
Most of the buildings were built prior to 1920 and had undergone major
renovation over the years. The Danforths' three-bedroom cottage was
near the end of Latham Street, just north of Kinoda Pier. Settled early by
a large mining company, the housing had been converted into comfortable cottages with full conveniences.

Jason Danforth had a good position as a research project engineer
with the Occidental Petroleum Company. He specialized in petrochemi-
cal exploration and had been assigned to explore the northern shoreline
of the lake as part of the Millennium Project. If successful, the company
expected revenues of $2.8 billion over the next five years.

Jason had worked his way up in the company after graduating
from the School of Engineering at the University of Michigan. Jason
met Julia there, who was then studying to be an elementary school
teacher. Since graduation and Jason's position with Occidental, Julia
had been working as a third-grade teacher at Ellwood Elementary
School in a suburb of Saint Paul, Minnesota. Jason and Julia married right out of college, and Amanda was born two years after their
graduation, followed by the birth of William two years later. The
family had enjoyed the comforts of Saint Paul's Glen Lake suburb
for the last ten years. The cottage was more than Julia had expected,
thinking the housing would be somewhat primitive given the remote
location. She took her time methodically unpacking the suitcases,
and Jason called the office to ask his manager, David, about the
equipment.

"Most of the equipment is due to arrive tomorrow," Jason said once he got off the phone. "I told David about the emergency landing, and he was really surprised. He said the return arrangements could be made direct because it would be a later flight."

Jason walked over to Julia and gave her a hug. "And what are you going to do to keep busy for the next two weeks?"

"I brought plenty of schoolwork," she said, smiling. "I just hope the kids are happy here. You know Amanda. She wants everything to be perfect."

"Don't worry about her. She'll adapt and make friends. And Will loves an adventure. He'll fill us in on the pH makeup of the lake water. Just rent a bike and make him a lunch. He'll find his own way."

The moon settled over Great Slave Lake to the southwest and reflected off the glass tabletop as Jason and Julia enjoyed a glass of wine on their first night in Yellowknife. A late spring brought on the sounds of frogs from the nearby wetland, and the night was cool, making for good sleeping weather. The Danforth family had arrived and settled into their accommodations in Yellowknife. In spite of an early start and a shaky landing, they all looked forward to the next couple of weeks in the Northwest Territories.

* * *

Everyone was up early, and Jason was the first out the door as a horn sounded out front. Will went with his mother to drop off Amanda at Camp Willow, located on the east bay of the lake, not a mile from the town. An old lumbering camp, the twenty-acre facility had been completely renovated with a grant from the National Arts Council of Canada. Offering dance, drawing, ceramics, and Native American crafts, the camp ranked at the top among Canadian arts camps. The summer schedule was to run two consecutive two-week sessions, from nine to four each day.

When they pulled up out front, Amanda grabbed her backpack, nervously spilling the contents.

"Shit!" she hissed, then smacked her hand over her mouth. "Sorry, Mom!"

"How come she can swear and I can't?" complained Will.

Students lined up at the student center to pick up schedules and supplies. Will waited in the car as Julia went along with Amanda to help her register.

Amanda looked nervous and insecure for a change. Julia tried to reassure her.

"Just try the first day, and see how things go, OK? It could be really great, you know? You can call me if there's a problem."

Amanda grabbed her bag and headed off for her first class. Suddenly it was Julia's turn to be nervous. She didn't know anyone running the camp. Would her daughter be safe with strangers? She took a deep breath and lectured herself as she had Amanda. *Just give it a try.*

Will fidgeted impatiently in the car, wondering what was taking his mother so long. "Where have you been? It's been, like, two hours," he complained.

She laughed. "Try twenty minutes. I just needed to get Amanda settled. She was a little nervous. Do you remember last summer when I dropped you off at Blue Lake Camp? You didn't want me to leave either."

"No way. I loved Blue Lake," he said strapping into his safety belt.

"Yeah, in the end, but do you remember the first day?" Julia asked, looking into his eyes and expecting an honest answer.

"I guess so," Will conceded, "but can we get going, Mom? I need some time to pick out the right bike."

The Klondike Trail bike store was better than Will had expected. Apparently, the locals loved bikes, and there were many to choose from. Will picked out a top-of-the-line bike and added some extras that could help out in a pinch. The silver titanium Cannondale BX was brand new and had never been ridden. He carefully watched his mother's face as they rang up the rental price for two weeks, wondering if it was too much, then thought what the heck, they didn't have to pay camp tuition for him.

Once they got back to the cottage, Will scurried around looking for his old track sneakers.

"How long will it take you to get to the park, Will?" asked Julia as she packed a sandwich for his lunch.

"It's less than five miles," he said, "and I might stop along the way if I see something I like. So maybe a couple of hours." He was ready finally and grabbed his lunch from Julia. "See you later, Mom."

"Be careful," Julia called after him.

Will took one more quick look at the map and took off north.

The trails were different than what Will was used to, narrower, and not always clearly marked. He sped through a towering white pine forest that must have been over a hundred years old, using every exposed tree root as an opportunity to jump his bike.

The trails were a mixture of dirt road and off-road through state woodlands. A lake breeze filtered through the woods not more than a hundred yards from the trail. Will could see the end of the trees ahead and what looked like dunes rising from the lakeshore. The sand slowed the bike down, and Will had to peddle hard to get over a ridge. Once he topped that, he could see the entire expanse of Great Slave Lake. It was huge, he thought. Powerful.

Ahead he could see a small finger of sand reaching into the water. It was a perfect place to stop and take a break. Will walked out on the spit and gently set his bike down next to a large log that had drifted ashore. He took off his sneakers and socks. *Freezing*, he thought as he walked in the shallow water. The size of the lake was immense, stretching north about fifty miles and nearly thirty miles across. As he remembered, it was the second-largest freshwater lake in Canada. *And it's so deep... That's why it's so cold.*

As Will walked across the small, narrow peninsula, he noticed how pristine and fine the sand was, different from the sand in Minnesota and the shore of Lake Michigan. *What makes the sand different?* he wondered. It was something he could ask his dad tonight at dinner. With the exception of small outcroppings of stone, the peninsula was nothing but pure sand, untouched and without evidence of any recent visits by people. As he perused the beach, he noticed something reflecting in the sunlight. He approached the reflection and brushed aside the sand, exposing a smooth green disk. He dug deeper. The disk was the top of a three-foot-diameter cylinder that seemed to go straight down into the sand without end.

What could this possibly be? A property marker? Maybe the Canadian government has a special way of marking the border of the lake?

It was always exciting for Will to discover something he couldn't explain, and this was beyond his understanding. But it was getting late, and he was supposed to be home in time to help with dinner. He could always come back and explore further, he reasoned. Maybe his father would know something about it.

* * *

Julia spread a red-checkered tablecloth on the table. The cottage was outfitted nicely to provide most of the comforts of home, including some pretty antique drinking glasses.

"I loved the camp," Amanda told her mom when Julia had picked her up. "The dance class is a little advanced, but I think I'll get by. I made some friends, too."

Julia smiled. Amanda seemed to be her old self again.

The dinner table was more than a meal; it was a ritual for the Danforth family, where everyone discussed the happenings of the day. Everyone seemed to be in a pleasant mood except their father, who was frustrated with the late arrival of the equipment from Saint Paul.

"They said it would be here ahead of us, but it didn't arrive until late this afternoon. This could put us behind schedule."

"I did some grocery shopping for the week. There's a shopping plaza in Old Town. It's hard, without having a lot of my own staples, and the selection of food here is a bit different. There is a lot of fresh fish, so I hope we all like fish."

Julia passed the pasta to Amanda, who added, "I was really afraid I wouldn't like the camp, but it's fun. Will, I think you would have really liked it. We're going to make ceramic pots, and I like my dance teacher. Dad, do you know Laura Dorini? Her father is Dominic?"

"I didn't know they were bringing their daughter," Jason said. "We should have them over, if it's all right with everybody else." He looked over at Will, noticing that he was unusually quiet.

As the others rambled on about shopping and Amanda's new friends from camp, Will thought he'd explode before he got a chance to talk about what he'd found. Finally his father asked, "Will, how's the bike? Did you see anything out there in the wild?"

Will paused before answering. "I took the trail up along the lake towards the national park, but I never got that far. I found a small peninsula of sand jetting out into the lake and just hung out there for a while. The sand is totally different from back home. What makes the differences in sand, Dad?"

Just then the phone rang, and Julia answered. She covered the mouthpiece as she said it was for Amanda.

"Just like at home. Constant calls from her friends during dinner," said Jason irritably. "You can call her back after dinner."

Amanda frowned at her father. Julia told the girl Amanda would call her back shortly and hung up the phone.

Will interrupted impatiently. "Dad, what about the sand?"

"The composition of sand is based on the geology of the region. Sand is essentially small grains of rock from the earth made up mostly of quartz. It's usually washed over millions of times by water that constantly reduces its size. The makeup of the sand depends on the rock and mineral compounds in the area."

Julia sensed something much bigger behind Will's questions, and said casually, "So, just a sandbar, Will?"

Will looked out the window before speaking. "There was this green disk that went down into the sand as if it was the top of something. It had a shiny metallic surface."

"Maybe something washed up from the lake and was covered by the sandbar," said his father. "I doubt it was placed there."

"I know, Dad, but it was kind of weird. It seemed like something official, like some kind of marker put there by the government. I've never seen anything like it."

"They may do things differently in Canada that we know nothing about. I want you to have fun, not to get in trouble, so please be careful." Julia got up from the table, hoping this was the end of the conversation.

Will's father was silent for a few moments, and then said, "If I get a chance, we'll take a spin up the shore road, and you can show me the spot, see if we can figure it out."

Will spent most of the next few days exploring downtown Yellowknife, visiting the historic buildings that were established during the early mining days. There were handball courts just off Main Street where he picked up a few games with some of the local kids. Their talent for handball was better than he would have thought. He didn't win a single game.

Amanda invited him to camp as a visitor, and he took her up on it. He sat in on a day-long wood carving class. The students in the class were carving totem poles and painting them with poster paint in multiple colors. The class was being taught by an older woman whose hands were scarred from carving mishaps over her forty years of work. Dressed in blue jeans and a tan shirt, her long gray hair braid was always coiled and pinned at the back of her head.

She carved with one of the most unique knives Will had ever seen. The handle was made from white bone that was embossed with ancient-looking symbols. Will followed the teacher's directions and carved a small totem with four faces, trying to depict four different emotions. It was difficult, and often it was the use of paint that finally created clear expressions.

Will walked down the hall to the watercooler not really happy with his carving. On his way back to his seat, he noticed a native Indian boy had made a painting of a green bar.

"What's your name?" asked Will.

"Remer," said the boy.

"Hey Remer, nice painting. Can I take a look?"

Remer handed Will the painting, and he observed a figure on a bed with a green bar above. When Will looked down at the image, he was reminded of the shape he had seen from the plane. As he bent down for a closer look, his digital watch went dead and stopped. *Strange*, he thought, handing the painting back to the boy.

"What is the meaning of the image?" Will asked the boy.

"It comes from a story my grandfather told me."

"What was the story about?" asked Will.

"He said the green bar is around when we need help. It fed my family for a winter when the snow was too deep to leave the house, and it fixed my sister's broken arm. It's beyond us, and it's been here for hundreds of years."

Will had been able to resist going back to the sandbar partly because there was so much to do in the town, but also because the incident on the sandbar had not been fully explained. He had asked people in the town if they had ever seen the green bar, but folks looked at him with blank stares. And now the Remer story. *There must be some connection*, he thought.

"So what is this, and where does it come from? Do people know about this?" Will asked Remer questions as fast as his thoughts could generate them.

The bell rang, and Remer looked at Will with a blank stare, unwilling to share any more information. The teacher made an announcement that it was time to clean up and put the materials and tools away.

* * *

Jason and Julia had made plans for a weekend trip to nearby Wajja Town, which was inhabited entirely by native people. They would leave early the following morning. When they got back, Will thought, he would make a return trip to the peninsula and further investigate the marker. It was the only thing to do.

The trip to Wajja would take three hours. They planned to camp at a national campsite near the small village, just on outskirts of a larger town called Snowdrift. They arrived by 1:00 p.m., set up camp, and had lunch.

The campground was on Lake Wajja, a small lake used by local people and set up by the Territories mostly for visitors from Yellowknife. The campsites were primitive, but there was plenty of firewood and a central well for water. As experienced campers, the Danforths picked a site on high ground overlooking the lake and part of the village where there was a general store with enough supplies to make even Amanda comfortable for a night.

Julia had done some reading about the local Blackfoot, Kootenay, and Slavey bands and how they lived. Physically, they resembled the coastal natives known to white people as Eskimos, and relied on caribou, fish, and waterfowl for much of their food. Some sold their arts and crafts in Yellowknife for extra income, but it wasn't much. From their campsite, the Danforths could see the local women walking barefoot along a dirt road, carrying clothes and groceries. Half-dressed children followed behind them. It was a harsh existence for people who lived most of the year in a subarctic climate.

When Julia and Amanda went into the village to shop, Will and his dad went about gathering wood for the evening fire. Once that was done, Will sharpened sticks for marshmallow roasting while his dad started the fire.

"Dad, did you ever find out what happened with the plane landing?"

"After the landing, I heard the pilot commenting that the instruments were working fine and there was no logical reason for the malfunction, except that it would have taken a strong magnetic force to cause the behavior. That was about it. Last week, I heard from a supplier who works in this area, and he said it had happened before, right around the same time of day. I asked him if it happened often, but he didn't know. He said it was something no one really wanted to talk about. Anyway, we are taking a direct flight out on the only airline that has a jet service from Yellowknife, so we'll be fine when we leave. Is that what you were worried about?"

"I wasn't worried, just curious." While Will sharpened the last stick for marshmallows, he asked, "Dad, could your project mess up the lake?"

Jason turned his attention away from the fire and looked at his son. "No…not at all."

"Is there any danger to the environment?" Will asked.

"There used to be, but now we use insertion pumps, so there aren't any oil rigs or drilling stations on the water. The devices attach themselves to the lake bottom and are controlled by fixed microwave signals. The seals are monitored by submersible microcameras, all of which is viewed on monitors at the offshore facility. Plus, if the project is successful, it will help build housing and schools for the local people."

"Hey, nice fire, guys," Julia said as she and Amanda walked hand in hand into the campsite.

Behind them, the full moon was larger than usual as it set over the lake like a giant glowing ball. Although it was summer, the evenings were cool, and cricket song filled the night air. The family settled around the campfire to roast marshmallows.

Will piped up. "Dad says that not far from here is where they found the largest dinosaur remains in North America. They used to fall off those tall cliffs during the glacial age—"

Amanda cut him off. "Gee, that's fascinating, Will," she said sarcastically.

"Fine. What do you want to talk about? Shopping?"

Amanda sat up straight, her eyes glinting mischievously. "Mom went to a psychic! He looked like a real medicine man, with long gray hair, bracelets, and tattoos."

Julia tried to sound casual. "I liked the sign in the window. It was a circle with a word in the center that I thought was native. Later he told me it meant 'ask.'"

"Did he read your palm?" asked Jason, grinning.

"He didn't read palms or have any cards. He had a pouch he called his medicine bundle that contained stones, herbs, and amulets. He just asked for a strand of my hair."

"What did he tell you, Mom?" asked Will.

"He said I had an older sister who lives on the East Coast, and that she was married with three children. He said I'm a teacher and have an interest in dance," Julia said softly. "And he mentioned my interest in healthy foods and that I was going to live a long life."

"That's all true!" said Amanda enthusiastically.

"Did you give him your social security number?" asked Jason, again in fun. "He might have had an Internet connection under his robe."

"Stop teasing, Dad," said Amanda, defending her mother. "She takes these things seriously, and so do I."

"You tell him, Amanda," said Julia, not at all bothered by the comment. "I didn't get the last thing he said. Something about a green bar."

A chill went down Will's back. Should he tell them what he'd seen from the plane window that day? Or tell them the story Remer's grandfather told him?

"Maybe the green bar is a symbol for money," said Jason. "You're going to hit the lottery, and we'll be rich." This got everyone laughing. "Come on, what do you say we turn in?"

It was getting late, the fire had died down, and they had pretty much consumed all the marshmallows. Tomorrow they would break camp, drive back through the mountains along the eastern side of Great Slave Lake, and be back in Yellowknife in time for dinner.

* * *

The next morning, the warm sun glowed over the foothills, a striking reminder of the glaciers that, over millions of years, had formed, moved, and receded in the area, creating prairie landscapes, heavily forested areas, and grasslands. After coffee and breaking camp, the family drove west along the lake, spotting a herd of moose and caribou heading for the marshland along the Slave River. The southwest wind, called Chinook, was mild. It funneled itself east through the mountains from the Pacific Ocean. Julia told stories of the native people from Asia thousands of years ago who were the sole human inhabitants of what was then a vast wilderness territory. Amanda and Will both wondered if everything she said was true, but then again, it didn't really matter.

"Did you ever hear of the Secret of Spring?" asked Julia. "It's an ancient Slavey Indian tale that says long ago, winter seemed to last forever and blankets of clouds covered the earth. The snow never stopped that winter, and the sky was as black as coal, while the ground was silvery ice.

"The animals were all freezing, waiting for the season to end. According to the legend, the bears had stolen spring and taken it up into the sky through a hole in the clouds. A group of animals, including wolves, fox, caribou, and a mouse, went on an expedition to find the bears in the upper world. Soon they came to a large blue lake where they saw a tiny hut. When they peeked inside, they saw two bear cubs huddled together. When discovering the mother was out hunting, they took the bag hanging in the hut that was holding the "warmth" the bears had stolen.

The animals headed straight for the hole and leaped through, carrying the bag with them. As they hit the ground, the bag opened, and the spring rushed out, melting the snow and opening the clouds to the sun. The trees' leaves opened, the flowers bloomed, and the whole valley leaped to life, and the animals rejoiced. The bears summoned their courage to return and were forgiven, as plenty of sunlight and warmth spread joy everywhere. The Secret of Spring was revealed, and there came a time, in the late months of winter, where the animals all knew where they had to go to find the beginning of spring."

"Dad, where does she get these stories?" asked. "Does she make them up?"

"It's a legend," said Julia, "and legends are usually based on some truth."

* * *

The next morning, Will made ready for a second trip to the peninsula. He shoveled in his breakfast and rinsed it down with some orange juice, and waved to his mother. He stepped off the back porch and onto his bike in one fluid movement.

He had been thinking about the sandy peninsula and the green disk all weekend, planning his return trip. He had thought about what he would take with him, including his camera, a Swiss Army knife, a Walkman, and a bottle of water. The ride up the lake trail went faster than before, as Will now knew a more direct way. Getting to his destination was more important than the jumps he would normally perform.

The pines swayed in the wind as he downshifted through the sand. He pedaled hard up the ridge, and stopped just short of the peninsula in amazement. He had left the cottage around 9:30 a.m., and as he glanced at his watch, it was now roughly 11:00 a.m. To the right of the landmass, about a hundred feet away, was a translucent green bar of light, hovering over the spot where he'd discovered the disc. He sat down in the sand and gazed at the light from a distance. He got out his camera and took several pictures.

What could it be, he thought, *and where did the tessellation come from?*

Will sat in the sand and looked at the object for several minutes without moving closer. Finally, he got up and moved slowly onto the peninsula, pushing his bicycle through the deep sand. He was reluctant to get too close to the object. Fleetingly, he thought of going back home and contacting authorities. But then he heard a low bass sound that seemed to come from the vibrating green bar of light. He stopped, now about three hundred feet from the object, and stood perfectly still, afraid. He didn't understand what he was experiencing.

As the low bass sound continued, the green bar became a thick rectangle of translucent green light that hovered over the top of the disk in the sand and slowly lowered itself down, making contact with the top part of the object. Multiple beams of thin white light connected to the disk. The intensely concentrated light sparked and crackled up and down their lengths as if electrical signals were being transmitted back and forth.

Then, in a split second, the vibrating light, and the green rectangle, dissolved into thin air. The low bass sound was gone. After a few minutes, he decided to approach the spot where the bar had hovered to take a closer look. There was no sign of anything, just fine, pristine white sand. Will cautiously dug down, expecting to find the top of the disk, but nothing was there. He looked east, over the white-capped surface of the lake. Completely normal.

Will scanned the huge rock cliffs along the shoreline, as if they might provide an explanation to his recent experience. The lake water was choppy, and the small whitecaps were like an endless pattern of soapsuds making their way toward shore. He got on his hands and knees and put his ear to the sand, listening for the deep bass tone, and heard nothing but the low rush of blood in his ears as if he'd clamped a seashell over his ear.

He took off his backpack, reached for the bottle of water, and drank slowly. Then he remembered the photographs. He had taken three photos from a distance of the event. He grabbed the camera from his backpack and checked to see how many photos were left. Just one. Holding the camera as far away as possible, he snapped a shot of himself, then listened as the camera began to automatically rewind. Now the only thing in his mind was getting the film developed. Once he had that, he could tell the story with proof of what he'd seen.

Once back on his bike, and in his rush to leave, a driftwood branch from a log buried in the sand, caught the spoke of his bike wheel, and hurled him off the bike and high into the air. As he landed, his head hit an outcropping of stone, and he was knocked unconscious. He lay there in the sun alone, motionless. Ants crawled over his hand. A seagull flew over, searching the water's edge for dead fish.

Suddenly the low bass sound returned, and from the horizon, the tessellation of light slowly approached the boy's body. The bar hovered over Will, transmitting several beams of bitstream light to and from his body, and then disappeared as suddenly as it had appeared.

It was almost an hour before Will regained consciousness. He looked over at his bike, upside down in the sand, and he could see the spoke in the front wheel was badly bent. His head hurt. He looked at his watch. It read 10:35 a.m.

He didn't remember falling. He touched the side of his head, and there was dried blood that extended down his neck. He was slightly disoriented. He decided to check his bike, make some repairs, and be on his way back to the cottage, where he would tell his mother everything. The trip back was slow and took twice as long. Will stopped several times to rest along the way. He felt slightly nauseous, and as he approached the cottage, he stepped off and walked his bike the last fifty feet.

"How was your ride? You're back early," said his mom as he walked through the back door.

Opening his backpack, he said, "It was good, but I think I took a fall and hit my head. I might have been knocked out, 'cause I don't really remember the fall."

Looking him over, Julia noticed a scrape and swelling on the side of his head. "I'll say you did. Where did this happen?"

"It was up near the peninsula. My watch says eleven fifteen, and the one on the stove says one fifteen p.m. Which one is right?" he asked his mother.

Julia looked at the stove clock. "This one is right. Maybe your watch got wet and stopped, but I need to put something on this cut. The blood has run down to your neck. Let me clean this up."

"Ouch! That hurts, Mom."

"Sorry, you took a hard hit. This could even use a stitch. You know, Will, you might have been unconscious."

"That's odd. I don't remember drinking this bottle of water, and look, my camera pictures have been shot."

Will continued to listen to his mother while he unpacked his backpack. "I need to lie down and rest," he said.

"Rest, but don't sleep, Will. You may have a concussion."

That night at dinner, everyone was fully aware that Jason was upset with the lack of progress at work. This was a very important assignment, and if he could not find the necessary coordinates, it could possibly jeopardize his job.

"We've found nothing so far, and things are not looking good. The heat-sensitive satellite pictures tell us there is an abundance of oil and gas reserves about a mile out over the lake, but we have not been able to locate the exact coordinates. Without a point to start, the survey can't move forward. There has been success in the Yukon and the Mackenzie Valley at rates of thirty thousand barrels per day in their initial finds. If we don't find a location soon, we may be leaving early, and I may have to dust off my résumé."

Will looked to his mom and said, "Hey Dad, maybe you should consult with Mom's psychic. You know…maybe a strand of your hair?"

"This isn't funny, Will," said his father. "We're budgeted for a certain amount of days here, and tomorrow may be our last attempt at finding a location."

"Jason, he fell and hit his head while riding today on his bike," said Julia with some concern. "In fact, maybe I should have taken him into emergency for an X-ray."

"I feel fine, Mom," said Will.

"But is the bike OK?" asked Jason, still concerned about his work project.

Will looked out the window at the bent spokes on the front wheel of the bike. *Not a good time*, he thought.

"Are you going out tonight?" Amanda asked her father. "I need to drop off my film." Then she turned to her mother. "Mom, can we take it in after dinner? I really want to see some of the pictures I took at camp."

This got Will's attention. "Me too. I have a roll of film."

As always, the family shared in cleaning up after dinner, rotating who did dishes. Jason gassed up the rental car after he dropped off the kids' film. The gas pump refused to operate, and he looked around for an attendant, but the small office was deserted, and no other customers pulled into the bay. He sighed, frustrated.

The corner of his eye filled suddenly with a green glow, and he turned toward the bay. The light moved over the bay, toward the filling station. A low bass hum grew louder in his ears. Suddenly the gas pump engaged and a car pulled in and came to a stop in the adjacent lane. Jason blinked and shook his head. The previous few minutes of ordinary time were blank.

He thought, *Maybe I should call in another satellite guidance system and see what happens when I cross-reference the two.*

* * *

At his office the next morning, Jason worked hard with Dominic to get a location. Finally they were able to get the second satellite feed to cross-reference with the first stream of information, and that was all they needed. The dual readings gave them a pinpoint location for their primary drill location. The longitude was 60.653, and the latitude was 40.833. After taking a locally rented helicopter to the site, they found the depth at exactly 1.67 kilometers. When they inserted the laser gauge to test the pressures, all the readings sounded familiar to Jason, but the success of finding the location flooded his thinking.

His crew was ecstatic. Everyone on Jason's team worked extra hours to finalize and complete the project by the end of the week. Will and his mom quietly returned the damaged bike, and he promised to work off the extra cost for the damages by finding a summer job. There were postcards to mail and souvenirs to buy. Amanda fired her pottery on the very last day of camp, and the raku glazes were amazing.

* * *

It was time for the family to get back to Saint Paul. They had packed everything the night before, and Jason had picked up the film on his way home from work. He walked into the kitchen and tossed the film packages on the table, where both Will and Amanda were sitting eating the last bag of chips and finishing up the Diet Cokes.

"Here are your pictures, kids. I hope you're packed, because I'd like to get an early start to the airport. We've got an early flight, direct, no layover."

Will hadn't even heard his dad. He looked through his photos, and all the shots were of the lake and a plain sandy beach. There was no evidence of the green light bar he recalled so vividly.

The last shot was a close-up of Will that he would have had to have taken himself.

"These pictures don't seem right. Hey Dad, can we stay another day or two?"

Jason had finished packing his work materials and sat looking over their travel reservations. He gave Will a look that said it all.

Will laughed. "OK, OK. Just kidding."

* * *

The following morning, they reached the car rental around 11:00 a.m., and Will noticed the digital clock on the dashboard had stopped. By the time he got his father's attention, it had resumed. *Foiled again,* thought Will.

The jet lifted off the runway into a clear and sunny morning. As the plane banked right, Jason looked out his window and pulled Julia over for a look. Great Slave Lake looked majestically reverent and untouched.

"Do you see something on the lake horizon, like a green light?" Jason asked, trying to keep the location in sight.

"No, I don't see anything," she said, paying more attention to her journal writing than the plane's small window.

"You know, when I filled up the car the other night, the solution to our problem just came to me. I mean, the idea of getting a second satellite position just popped into my head."

"And I'm glad it did. The project was successful. As to the why… there are certain things that are beyond our understanding," said Julia as she returned to her journal.

Jason released his seat backward and rested his forehead against the window glass. He listened to Will and Amanda bicker over a game of Boggle that Amanda was clearly winning.

Within moments, Jason was looking down on a bed of clouds, very happy about the success of his work. Julia was reading over her schoolwork, and Amanda was now thinking about the cost of the phone bill her parents had not yet received.

As for Will, he sulked over the Boggle loss, and kept looking intensely at his pictures, especially the empty beach shots and the picture of himself. He found the expression on his face and the look in his eyes unfamiliar. In his mind, there was confusion. There were missing pieces to that second bike trip to the sandy peninsula. No matter how hard he tried to remember the sequence of events that late morning, there was a void. *It must have been the fall*, he thought.

Philomen

For Kes, the ocean was as much a part of daily life as getting up in the morning, eating breakfast, and going to class. The beach was just a short walk from where he lived. Although the ocean had claimed his father's life, visiting the shore and walking along the beach was a ritual that Kes had practiced for as long as he could remember. When he was younger, his favorite spot was an old wooden water tower, built over an abandoned railroad track, where he could sit and look out toward the bay. Then, as now, Kes loved to watch approaching storms or the rising surf, and even today, he looked toward the ocean for answers to his questions.

Kes lived with his mother in a two-bedroom apartment near the downtown center of Omena, a small historic oceanfront town deep within the national seashore park. After school, Kes often walked along the beach, lost in thought as he searched for collectibles. His bedroom was a museum of unusual objects that he had discovered on his shore sweeps. Whereas most kids collected shells, large crab parts, stones, or the feathers of birds, Kes favored man-made objects. His lifelong collection included forty fishing bobbers and a lifeboat buoy with the markings of a US Navy destroyer. In fact, he collected *only* objects that represented man's creations—lost details of ships, pieces of flags, driftwood from sailboats, and bits of cloth. He had come to see the objects in his collection as symbols of a search not yet finished. There seemed to be no limit to his collection, just as there seemed to be no limit to how many mornings he gazed out at the tide.

Sometimes Kes walked so far along the shore that he was late coming home. This scared his mother, an elementary school teacher, though she knew how strongly the ocean pulled at her son. She feared he might fall in, be swept away, lost in some horrible accident like that which took her husband only months before Kes was born. They had learned when Kes was young that he had airborne allergies, requiring him to carry an inhaler. Often when he left the house, he would forget it. She had sent the Omena Police Department to look for Kes more than once, concerned about an allergic reaction, but each time he was found happily searching some new area he had discovered in the remote parts of Cat's Head Bay. Now that he was fifteen, Jill's frantic calls to the police dispatcher were less frequent, and even she had to admit that her son's extraordinary swimming abilities gave her less to worry about.

When Kes was only two years old, Jill had insisted that he learn to swim, and he had eagerly agreed. He mastered the lessons learned in his swimming classes, and when older, he took all the Red Cross lifesaving courses.

Now that he was in high school, Kes was on the varsity swim team. He certainly had the right kind of build for a swimmer—a long, stretched-out frame supporting a smooth, muscular body. A pleasant-looking boy, he was easy to pick out in a crowd with his short blond hair, small ears, and metal-rimmed glasses. The feature noticed by those close to him was his blue-green eyes, which seemed to recede into a space without end. Only two freshmen had qualified for the varsity swimming team, and of the two, only Kes competed regularly, actually leading the team in three events. He had set a school record with his sidestroke in the two-hundred-meter individual relays.

No mom was louder or more animated at the swim meets than Jill, who nearly fell out of the bleachers when her son set the school record. Jill and Kes took joy in each other's lives—except in one area: the ocean. Since the death of her husband, Jill had stayed away from the ocean, rarely visiting it and never fully trusting it.

Because Jill was a teacher, it was natural that school was an ever-present fact of life for Kes. The importance of school had been drilled into his head, and all the other teachers knew him. Because many of his teachers were colleagues and friends of his mother's, they were like extended family. This could be troublesome, too, because they expected him to be on his best behavior and do well in his studies.

Kes did not find schoolwork very hard. He was quiet, kept to himself, loved to read, and always did his homework. He even made the honor roll twice, which, as far as he was concerned, was enough. What he didn't like was the regimentation and structure of school. Kes needed to learn more than time in school permitted. Just when a subject was starting to get interesting, it was time to stop and clean up.

Recognizing his frustration, Jill helped him continue to study at home. If he were studying the transformation of a monarch caterpillar into a pupa, and eventually into a full-blown butterfly, she would coach him through the project.

Like his classmates, and his teachers, Kes looked forward to breaks in the educational calendar, and now spring break had arrived at last, along with warmer weather. He looked forward to this time to himself.

After school let out that Friday afternoon, Kes was home by three o'clock, already peeling off his school clothes as he walked in the front door. The kitchen window was open, and a warm breeze blew in. Sun flooded the rooms, unobstructed by a single cloud.

A message on the refrigerator informed him that his uncle Carl was coming to dinner. He also read through a list of chores that his mom wanted him to do before she got home. He looked at the note much longer than it took to actually read, thinking, *Maybe I didn't see the note*, but quickly dismissing the idea. Starting the spring break like that could prove disastrous, and he would not risk such a setback.

With a sigh, Kes began his chores, resigned to the reality that any explorations along the ocean shore would have to wait until tomorrow morning. Besides, he was really looking forward to Uncle Carl's visit.

Carl was his father's only brother, and Kes practically considered him his dad. A commercial photographer, Carl traveled much of the time, but he always included time for Kes when he was home. Last summer, they went camping together in the Olympic Peninsula for two weeks. While Carl snapped photos, Kes explored and collected. They hiked Hurricane Ridge and feasted for three days on fish they caught fresh from Crescent Lake.

One of the things he liked best about Carl was the way he made plans at the beginning of each day, but always allowed room for spontaneous changes. Lunch was whenever, dinner came late, and there were no alarm clocks. These trips gave Kes an anchor to the world. In the darkness of a small pup tent, there were stories every night, often about how his father and Carl grew up on a rural farm in Iowa. It was on these chilly nights that Kes had the chance to reveal his fears and talk about his dreams.

Tonight they would have a chance to catch up with one another.

When Jill came home, her arms filled with grocery bags, she found a home in perfect condition. Kes had tidied the entire apartment and washed the dishes, leaving them to dry in the warm afternoon sunlight. She was pleased with the maturity he had shown. She hadn't been certain that he would come straight home, much less see the note.

Jill was still putting the groceries away when Kes came in with a bag of ice, the last chore on his list.

"Does the place look OK?" he asked, knowing already that he was in good shape with her after two hours of work.

"It's perfect, Kes. Thank you."

Kes stored the bags of ice in the freezer as Jill returned to unload the bags of groceries.

"What time will Carl get here?" Kes asked.

"He said around five thirty, which probably means seven thirty," Jill said, turning her attention from the groceries to the fresh flowers she had bought. She cut the stems and pulled out her favorite large plain glass vase. "How did you do on your biology paper?"

"I don't know. I'm not sure Jenkins will like the subject."

"Why?"

"Because I did my paper on chewing gum."

Astonished, Jill turned to him, the vase with the flowers half arranged held in her newly manicured hands, a luxury she allowed herself at the end of each week.

"Chewing gum was introduced in the United States in the eighteen sixties," Kes told her. "It's an extract from the sap of a Mexican jungle tree called the sapodilla. The Aztecs called it *chicti*, and it was a favorite of Santa Ana. Did you know that early gum had no taste?"

"No, I didn't, but that sounds more like social studies than biology. Do you think that was such a good choice? You know how he is—probably the most conservative teacher in the whole school."

"Whatever," Kes replied with a shrug. "He may not buy it, but I did a lot of research. I think it's good."

Jill said nothing more while she finished arranging the flowers and started to cut up tomatoes.

It was Kes who broke the silence. "I'm really glad it's spring break. I need some time off."

"Me too," replied Jill. Self-confident and well educated, her most notable accomplishment was a children's book that had been published recently. It would bring in extra money for Kes's college fund, but Jill knew that the favorable literary reviews meant at least as much to her as the money.

"Is there anything else, Mom?" Kes asked. "I need to take a quick shower."

"I think we're all set," replied Jill, glancing quickly at the kitchen, with its natural wood and Mexican tiles. "Thanks for the help."

An attractive woman in her late thirties, Jill had never remarried despite several proposals, although there were times when she wondered if it was the right decision. Carl's willingness to help raise Kes was a blessing. Dinner with him and Kes was a weekly event that happened without much formal planning, a sort of glue that held them together.

An hour and a half later, earlier than she had predicted, Carl came up the stairs carrying so many things he couldn't even ring the doorbell. Kes heard him thumping and answered the door. He had two bottles of Mendocino Valley wines, a six-pack of Diet Pepsi, three French baguettes, a large box of photos, and two bags of pistachios hanging from a small canvas backpack. His golden retriever, Jasper, slipped between his legs and seemed to be trying to dig his way through the door into the apartment.

"You have so much stuff!"

"I always have too much stuff," Carl said. "Where's your mom?"

"Kitchen," Kes said.

Such an entrance was a weekly ritual. Carl was always late for dinner, but once there, he might stay for several days, since he always carried a sleeping bag with him in his pickup truck. Eating dinner was another ritual, which they might string out until ten o'clock, when Carl would reach for the photos he had brought. Most people take their vacation film to the closest pharmacy and come back a week later to pick up their snapshots. Not Carl. He spent hours printing and dry mounting the color pictures on a large format paper.

One of the earliest products of Carl's love for photography, hung nearby on the dining room wall, was a picture of his parents just before they were married. They were at Sunset Beach, Jill in a small two-piece bikini, her youthful hair a radiant blonde. Phil, tall, handsome, and well tanned, had his arm around his future bride. Both were squinting, their hands blocking the sun, as if they were saluting the photographer.

Whenever the word "father" came up in casual conversation, the image of this photo flashed in his mind. Kes had heard many stories about his father—from Jill, from Carl, from his grandfather—and the composite memory of them washed over him whenever he wondered what *his* father was like. Still, all those stories were imagined, while this photograph was real, a document of an actual moment, with a real physical record of his father.

Tonight, Carl gave Jill his most recent favorite shot—a photo of Kes pulling in a large trout from a stream not far from the base of Mount Rainier. Carl's photos had documented Kes's voyage through childhood to his teens, and this one, too, would eventually be framed and added to her collection.

Jill brought out a dinner of baked chicken, rice, beans, avocado, and a French baguette, while Kes filled all the water glasses. They held hands and gave thanks for their company and food.

"What's been your favorite class this year?" asked Carl.

"That's easy. Psychology. My teacher is so cool. He makes it really interesting. He comes up with cool projects."

"Like what?"

"I did a paper on comparing Sigmund Freud with Carl Jung, and their theories on dreams. It was really interesting. Mom helped."

Jill listened as she recalled the project and the amount of research required. She and Kes had spent hours in the library. Carl slipped Jasper a piece of chicken under the table without notice.

"So, what did you learn?" asked Carl.

"Jung believed in three levels of awareness. The first level is when you're awake and going about your everyday life. The second level is when you're asleep and you're dreaming. But the third level is the weird one. Jung called it the 'collective unconscious.' It's like a collection of experience that exists outside of each individual. Everything that's ever happened to people throughout history collects in this pool, and we all have access to it through our unconscious minds. When we do certain things or are drawn to certain images, it might be because we are aware of it from that unconscious pool of experience. Jung felt that we tap into all that collective experience especially when we are asleep, which is why he was so interested in dream interpretation."

"That sounds like *The Twilight Zone*." Carl hummed the theme from the popular TV show.

"More like *The Outer Limits*, really. Jung believed that the collective unconscious consisted of forms and images he called 'archctypes.' The forms and images are universally recognizable, so they more easily influence you and the way you think or dream. Right, Mom?"

"You're explaining it better than I can. Go ahead."

"OK. In my paper, I used the example of the mother archetype. The Earth Mother of mythology symbolizes the mother archetype, like Eve or Mary in Western Christian traditions. So, the mother archetype is our built-in ability to recognize a certain relationship, that of mothering. And, 'thank you, Mom,' that is in place for me, but in my case, it's the inner child archetype that often embodies a playful, creative side of the self that shows up in dreams. What I learned in this assignment is that when someone's father has failed to satisfy the demands of the archetype, he could spend his life seeking a replacement. Jung says we draw on our collective unconscious usually through the dream process. So dreams are good things."

Jill laughed.

Carl said, "I usually forget my dreams. Maybe I need to take a psychology class. I guess, when I think about it, there are similar images that exist in all cultures. Things repeat themselves. Sorta like our dinners together."

Jill sensed it was time for new conversation. "I think clearing the table and loading the dishwasher is a universal theme. Kes, would you?"

It was after midnight before Jasper got his chance to lick the ice cream dishes clean. By then, all three were exhausted and ready for sleep. Jill opened the sofa bed while Carl retrieved his sleeping bag.

Kes paused as he locked the back door and stood looking west, between the hardware store and the marina building, toward the only view of the bay from their apartment. Late at night, the reflections on the water shimmered and formed abstract shapes that changed as they moved toward the horizon. He would be up and on his way early the next morning.

Saturday morning he woke to sunlight slicing through his open bedroom window, a cool breeze from the ocean, and the sounds of gulls. Kes looked at the thermometer attached to the glass pane of his window: seventy-four degrees. He already had his destination planned, Victoria Beach, named for a girl who had nearly drowned there before Kes was born. Victoria, it was said, was a young girl caught by a riptide as her friends and family watched helplessly. After that, people stayed away for a long time. Eventually people returned to the beach, mainly locals, many of them kids who biked the two miles to reach the remote location.

Since today was Saturday, the first day of vacation, Kes was sure he would find kids hanging out at Victoria Beach. It would take him an hour to get there by surfboard, more than if he walked, but paddling up the coast was part of the adventure—and that was the whole purpose of his being.

Kes had heard the story of Victoria Beach in a variety of forms and had biked there before, exploring the rocky ridges, as well as the pristine sand. He had visited the beach a month earlier and found part of a wooden mask that had washed up on shore. Although most of the color had faded, the mask seemed to be a bird's face carved from a coconut shell. *Where could this have come from?* Kes had wondered.

The wind was blowing hard enough that Kes heard some loose shingles flap on the roof of the apartment building as he washed his face, dressed, and headed for the kitchen. He packed a sandwich in his water-proof pack, grabbed his net bag, picked up his surfboard, and closed the door quietly so he wouldn't wake his mother or Carl. He left a note on the refrigerator: *Gone out for a while—Kes.* He and his mother had joked that he might as well make a master of this note and run off a hundred copies at the library, since this was essentially the same note he always left. Within moments, he was looking over the landscape, with the town on the edge of the bay, with the barrier dune beyond, and then the ocean, stretching out to the very end of the horizon.

The town beach had access points where the Park Service had built cedar boardwalks extending over the barrier dune to the open beach. In national parks, beaches were open to everyone, and swimming was largely unsupervised. Kes made his way into the water far enough so that he was behind the surf, then started paddling north. Past Cambria, Kes made his way straight for Piedras Point, remembering to watch closely for the cliff edge with the large, looming redwoods. As he rounded the first cliff, Victoria Beach came into sight, already inhabited with a few kids.

The inlet was about a half mile wide, cut off at both ends by severe cliffs. Redwoods and cedars protected the cove along the steep rock cliffs in every direction. The beach itself was flat, the sand nearly pure white, reaching into the bay several hundred yards before dropping off quickly into a hundred feet of deep blue water. The drop-off and swirling undercurrents made swimming dangerous.

The closer he got, the louder the kids on the beach got. They had a boom box blasting while they played Frisbee. From a distance, he could make out a white structure centered midway along the sandy beach. *What could that be?* he wondered as he picked up his stroke and made his way to shore.

He could now see that the white structure was a lifeguard stand. The wood was new and the paint fresh, although the design of the lifeguard stand was old. The new stands were all made of aluminum pipe. There was no way someone could have towed the stand to the beach from nearby. Even though everyone else on the beach seemed oblivious to the lifeguard stand, Kes was curious, and when he got close enough, he could see that the materials used in its construction were unusual. The two-by-fours were a full two inches thick and four inches wide, not the modern, planed-down approximations. The hardware, the umbrella, and the chair itself were also odd, as if they were made in an earlier time.

Kes climbed up and sat in the stand's chair, looking out over the entire beach and shoreline. He had fantasized many times about becoming a lifeguard, as if something was calling him to the job. He sat in the chair for more than an hour, still dressed in his traveling gear, watching kids swim on both sides of the stand. No one said a word to him—or even acknowledged him. Only a few white clouds peppered the horizon under the bright sun at two o'clock. *This must be what it feels like to be a lifeguard*, Kes thought as he looked out toward the wide blue expanse.

Eventually he made his way down from the stand, picked up his board, and headed back out into the water that was flowing south. Looking back, the lifeguard stand was casting long shadows down the beach while the red-and-white candy-striped umbrella moved slightly in the light offshore breeze.

How did the lifeguard stand get built so quickly? It usually takes the Park Service weeks to put in a few steps or make a simple repair, yet this stand appeared almost instantly! Why build a stand on such a desolate area, especially one that's not even identified as a public beach?

These questions—and more—swirled in Kes's head as he paddled toward Omena Bay, and he promised himself to ask Carl and his mother if they knew anything about the lifeguard stand when he got back to the house. Or maybe his friend Jim, who worked at the sheriff's office, might know something.

The offshore breeze had picked up, and as the tide was now coming in. Kes looked toward the southwest and saw some dark clouds on the horizon, though still at a distance. *Probably a rainsquall*, he thought as he paddled to shore and picked up his board, deciding to walk the rest of the way home on foot.

By the time he reached the apartment, it was 6:30 p.m. He found a note from his mother that she and Carl had gone to see a movie. Kes was disappointed because he wanted to tell them about the discovery he had made at Victoria Beach. Instead, he put on some music and heated leftovers from last night's dinner while Jasper followed him around begging for food.

The memory of the empty lifeguard stand at Victoria Beach lingered in his mind. *If no one was watching the beach, why the stand?*

He checked the weather on the radio and confirmed his findings on the television that good weather was in store through most of the next week. The squall had passed over with light rain, and the sky was clearing to the west. Kes decided that he would return to the beach the next day, and if no one were there in the chair, he would assume the responsibility of the lifeguard on duty, at least for the day. He would get up early the next morning and dress in his swimsuit, grab his megaphone, and apply some official white sunscreen to his nose.

By now, he was tired from a long day of travel and experience along the coast and at the beach. He finished his dinner and waited for his mom and Carl to come home. He knew they often stopped afterward for coffee and hours of talk.

Why is the lifeguard stand there? Who would put it there? he kept thinking.

After finding and organizing all his stuff, Kes decided at ten o'clock to call it an evening and get some sleep. He took Jasper out for a short walk, then made ready for bed. The sky had cleared, leaving the stars and planets illuminating the town. The moon had just completed its lunar cycle and was now full, casting shadows throughout the small streets. Kes set his alarm clock and made his bed before going to sleep. (His ritual was to make his bed at the end of the day, not always a custom that he and his mother were in agreement about.) With the events of the day swirling around in his head, Kes fell into a deep sleep.

Long before daybreak, Kes awoke from a dream and sat up briefly, remembering it in detail: He was wandering an unknown beach surrounded by Greek temples, wearing white boxer shorts, leather sandals, and a gold wristband. His hair was wet from being in the water, and in the distance, a mandolin was playing. Suddenly a girl cried out for help. The water was light emerald and perfectly still. Animated and moving in slow motion, Kes plunged in and swam toward her. When he reached her, she seemed only eleven or twelve years old, but once he got her to shore, she appeared to be much older. She wore a tie-dyed shirt and acted as if nothing unusual had happened—as did the others on the beach, whom he didn't know.

Kes sat on the beach completely exhausted, having saved a young girl from drowning, only to find that when he stood up, he was now on a mountain, looking down into a fertile valley. A winding country road led down the mountain to an old stone bridge, which crossed over to the rich green meadow where flocks of sheep were grazing. He noticed Greek ruins on the horizon, with a man seated in them, and in the distance, he heard a name, *Philomen*.

Kes glanced at his clock—4:30 a.m., not yet time to get up. He thought for a moment that he was ready to start the day, but his thoughts shifted back to the dream, and gradually he drifted back into sleep.

Kes hit the snooze button twice before finally waking from a deep sleep. The clock next to his bed told him the time was nine thirty, though everyone in the house—even Jasper—was still sleeping. Kes noticed Carl in the living room, on the sofa, sleeping next to an empty bottle of Napa Merlot. He could vaguely remember his dream from the early morning hours, but he now focused more on getting his things together for his return to Piedras Point. After dressing, he grabbed an orange juice box from the refrigerator and left his mother the usual short note: *Gone out for a while—Kes.*

With his surfboard under his arm, he set off along the bay. Once he was outside town, he used his board to shortcut the trip across the shallow water and up the coast. The weather that day was identical to the day before. Small white clouds gathered near the horizon, but it was predominately blue sky and bright sun.

As he approached Victoria Beach, he rounded the inlet's edge and saw the beach not two hundred yards ahead. A few young surfers were catching the morning tide, learning to surf the smaller waves, but Kes immediately focused on the lifeguard stand. A young man in his early twenties was sitting there today. He was tan, except for the white sunscreen on his nose, and he was peering intently through his sunglasses at the swimmers in the water.

Kes was disappointed. *Why wasn't he here yesterday?* Young bathers were swimming in front of the bright white lifeguard stand with its new lifeguard. The imagery startled Kes as he paddled up to shore about fifty feet south of the stand. Walking closer, the lifeguard looked very familiar. He glanced down at Kes and greeted him by name.

"Hi, Kes! How was the trip?"

He seems to have been expecting me, Kes thought.

"It was fine," Kes heard himself mumble. "I caught some current off Piedras Point and made good time. How did you know my name? Who are you?"

"I'm assigned to this beach," the young man answered. "It looks like it's going to be a busy day. Would you like to work here with me? I could sure use some help."

"But you don't even know me," Kes said.

"I know a lot about you," replied the lifeguard. "How's your mother?"

"You know my mother?"

"I knew her when she was young. She is a very special person."

"She's a lot older than you, you know."

"I suppose you're right," said the lifeguard, laughing. "How are you doing in school?"

"School's OK," replied Kes. "Do you know my uncle Carl?"

"I just happen to know your uncle Carl. He must be around your mother's age. Are they friends?"

"Yes," said Kes. "Did you know my father? He died just before I was born."

The lifeguard paused a moment. "Yes, I knew him…He would have been proud of you. He loved you, even before you were born. He lives on in you now, Kes."

Kes was genuinely startled, and the lifeguard tried to explain.

"That's why your mother worries so much about you—you're the only part of him that's left for her," said the lifeguard. "Do you understand?"

"I guess I do. Do you live nearby? I haven't seen you here before."

The lifeguard looked out to the wide expanse before answering. "I've come a long way, mostly to see you and tell you how precious life is."

Suddenly, a small cloud covered the sun, and both Kes and the lifeguard turned quickly as they heard a young girl cry for help a hundred feet out from shore. The beach had a reputation for crosscurrents and undertows produced by riptides in the Gulf Stream not far from shore. The hot summer months brought the stream closer to shore, causing a strong crosscurrent in the bay as they converged with cool water from the north. Both Kes and the lifeguard could see the girl was struggling to stay above water, and they both ran through the shallow water before diving into the surf.

The drowning girl was a strong swimmer, but as the two approached, they saw her disappear beneath the surface. Kes and the lifeguard did a dive to find her thrashing body. Kes immediately saw the girl not five feet below the surface. He grabbed her long blonde ponytail and pulled her to the surface. She struggled and resisted, but Kes was stronger, and overpowered her by placing his muscular arm around her chest. Then, with a sidestroke, he brought her to shore.

Only minutes had elapsed by the time they reached the beach, and Kes immediately cleared her throat and began mouth-to-mouth resuscitation. With several depressions to her chest, the young girl coughed, then again—a good sign. By now, everyone had gathered around, watching Kes as he continued working over the girl. The girl's mother held down her legs while Kes, using all of his lifesaving skills, gradually brought her back to life.

The mother and daughter held each other, both crying, but so happy and grateful that she was alive with no apparent harm done. Kes lay back on the sand, exhausted. His legs and knees were weak. The people on the beach were talking about his skill and heroism. Few had ever witnessed such an event.

The girl and her mother gathered their composure and thanked Kes, who was still lying flat on the sand, looking straight up into the sky, not fully comprehending what had just taken place. Suddenly he remembered the lifeguard. Kes sat up and looked around, but he was nowhere in sight. He stood up and looked out over the shoreline, but saw no one. When he glanced over to where the lifeguard stand had stood earlier, it was gone. He asked some of those still gathered around him about the lifeguard and the stand, but no one seemed to know what he was talking about. No one on the beach recognized his description of the person or the structure.

What happened? I couldn't have imagined the lifeguard stand, not two days in a row! And the lifeguard—he was so real, our conversation so vivid!

Kes found his surfboard and grabbed his net bag. He opened the bag and used his inhaler to help clear his breathing. Without delay, he paddled toward Omena Bay as fast as he could, and home, where he could tell his mother and Carl what had happened and about the lifeguard who said he knew them.

As soon as Kes opened the door to his house, Jill saw from the look on his face that something had happened. She had seen this look before, the time when he told her their dog of ten years had been killed by a car.

Kes sat down in the living room—something he never did. He began the story from the early morning of the following day to the moment he came home. By evening, Kes had told his mother the story four times, each time describing the events with greater intensity and more detail.

Jill didn't know what to think. Carl had left earlier, but promised she would call and get his opinion. That was important to Kes, because Carl was part of the conversation he remembered having with the lifeguard. Maybe he could shed some light or give an explanation as to the mysterious disappearance of the person and the lifeguard stand.

Now Kes wanted to know more about his father's death. Jill had told him a few things over the years, but she never saw the need to go into many of the details. Now there was a need.

"We were at the beach. Your father saw the girl flailing in the water and then saw her go down. He grabbed a fishing buoy and went in after her. He got the buoy to her, but the current was so strong, he was pulled down once he let go of the buoy. Your dad's quick thinking and courage saved the girl's life, but after a huge search, we never found Phil. I didn't tell you this when you were younger because..." Jill paused, then went on. "Because I was afraid you would blame him for saving the girl. I was afraid you would think he chose her over you."

"Why would I have thought that?" Kes asked. "It doesn't make sense."

"Children are very literal-minded, Kes. When something happens to them or around them, they think it's connected to them. Like when parents divorce and the children feel it was because of them. I didn't want you carrying that kind of burden around when it wasn't necessary. Your father wasn't making a choice. He was just doing the right thing."

Kes asked his mother about the girl and her whereabouts.

"I recall her name was Victoria, and she lived in the neighboring town of Genesee...She must be about twenty-five now."

"We have to find her."

Jill could not refuse such a serious request. Besides, it might help resolve the issue, even though she feared that it would cause her to revisit the long-ago pain of losing her husband.

The next day, Kes called a classmate who lived in Genesee, asking if she knew of anyone named Victoria or Vicky. She told him that the only person she knew named Vicky was a young woman, in her midtwenties, who worked at the art supply store off Larson Street.

Kes asked his mother if she would take him there so they could find out if the young woman was the same Victoria who had so narrowly missed drowning fifteen years ago. Jill agreed, hoping this might bring some closure to the recent events.

Genesee was a ten-minute drive from Omena. Jill parked the car, and the two of them proceeded across the street to the art store. By now, they were both in search of answers to questions they had not yet completely formed.

Kes and Jill found Victoria cutting mats and framing pictures. She was a striking young woman, with long blonde hair and chiseled features that called out to be photographed. Jill began to introduce herself and Kes by describing where they lived and who they were, but Kes interrupted.

"Were you involved in a swimming accident, not far from Piedras Point, when you were a young girl?"

Victoria said nothing, as if she was thinking and considering carefully her answer about something so obviously important. Finally, she spoke.

"When I was about eleven years old, I almost drowned at a place they now call Victoria Beach. I got caught in a riptide from a crosscurrent in the bay that pulled me under the water. I tried to fight it, but it was too powerful. A young man saw what was happening and swam out to save me. He brought a large buoy and extended it to me. I grabbed on and held my breath until I was released from the undertow, but the same riptide swept him away."

Jill placed her arm around Kes.

The young woman described the incident as if it were a part of her past that she tried to forget. Ever since then, Victoria explained, she had a reoccurring dream of the accident.

"But last Saturday night it was different. I had a different dream. The beach was surrounded by Greek temples, and the water was emerald green. I could hear mandolin music. A young boy wearing white shorts, sandals, and a gold wristband walked toward a mountain on a winding road. In the distance I heard someone saying, 'Philomen.'"

Kes had already told his mother about his own dream, and they were transfixed as Victoria told them of hers, virtually the same as his. *How can this be?* he thought.

Now Kes related his dream. He told her about the other recent events of his life, and they talked for a long time, exhausting first one, and then another, theory that might explain the strange occurrences. At last, all three fell silent.

"We need to stay in touch," Victoria said to both Jill and Kes. "I hope I can call you if I need to."

Outside, Jill opened the car door and slid into her seat, pausing before she started the engine. The sunlight was much lower than when they had arrived, and the post office near where they parked looked like an Edward Hopper painting. She chose to drive home along Route 6, the rural road that ran along the coast, past large vineyards and a Texaco gas station that looked as it had in the 1950s.

"What do you think, Mom?" Kes asked softly.

"I don't know what to think," Jill replied after a few moments.

Jill turned onto a gravel road Kes could barely remember. She had brought him here often in the past, though not much in recent years. The winding road led to what had been a livestock farm at the turn of the century. Eventually, the eighty-acre farm became a community cemetery, named for the farmer, Cannon. High up on the ridge, beyond the wind-shaped row of cedars, was a lovely site overlooking the ocean, where the view of the setting sun was especially dramatic.

Neither had spoken a word, but Kes knew where he was and what this was about. Kes and Jill walked together up a path that meandered through large stone monuments from the 1920s, to a more recent and modest headstone at the top of a grassy knoll. The sky was a patchwork of clouds with thin streams of sunlight highlighting areas throughout the meadow-like cemetery. Jill and Kes knelt in front of the headstone. In the distance, they could see a thin slice of ocean with white breakers headed for shore.

As they looked at the headstone, they saw afresh the striking, bold letters scrolled across the top of the gray marble: Philomen. As Kes had grown older, there were only certain times and events that he would kiss or hug his mother.

But on this day, as the new spring wildflowers swayed at a distance in the ocean breeze, he closed his eyes, turned on his knees, and hugged his mother as never before.

Saving Grace

"Should I believe in God?" Nicho asked his mother as he helped her fold laundry.

Nicho's mother continued to fold the white towels while she fashioned the right answer to her son's question before responding.

"Our faith teaches us that there is the Father, the Son, and the Holy Spirit," said his mother.

"You mean there are three Gods?" Nicho asked, half joking.

"They are all one," she said.

"So even though I haven't seen him yet, I should believe?"

"You were baptized when you were six months old, and you had your first communion just a couple of years ago, remember? Now you're twelve, so trust me, the Lord is with you, and yes, you should believe," she said, looking him right in the eye.

"I'm thirteen, by the way," Nicho said.

"Almost," his mother said.

The twelve-year-old boy told everyone that he was thirteen because his birthday was only three weeks away. As far as he was concerned, that was thirteen.

Nicho Rodriguez lived in a two-bedroom flat with his parents and his older brother, Jasper. He walked six blocks to St. Vincent School, which housed students grades K–8. The school was the educational arm of St. Vincent de Paul next door. Nicho's parents sent both of their children to St. Vincent's because it was safe and close to home.

His family was Roman Catholic, but his parents were not actively involved in the church. They were busy working, raising their boys, and supporting their families back in Puerto Rico. Nicho's father worked as a city bus driver, and his mother was a nurse's aide at New York Hospital downtown.

Nicho was a normal seventh grader, new to the upper school and in the throes of puberty. He had spent two years as a Cub Scout, and had just begun his first year as a Boy Scout in Troop 101. He played soccer with his friends on the school playground, collected comic books, and served as an altar boy at St. Vincent.

The altar boy position was a result of his close relationship with the parish priest, Father Gomez, who also coached the school baseball team. Nicho's own father was a big baseball fan, and he had been taking Nicho and his brother to baseball games since a very early age. Their father played one year with the Ponce Lions, a semiprofessional baseball team. There was a family divide over which team they supported. Nicho's father was a Yankee fan, and his sons were big Mets fans. Nicho started playing T-ball when he was five years old, and his love of the sport carried through to Little League, then school teams. Nicho was the first-string shortstop for St. Vincent and led the team in hits. His family attended his home baseball games and cheered him on from the small, battered bleachers.

* * *

144

Grace Rivera's twin brother played second base for St. Vincent's team, and she and her mother often attended the games. Nicho knew Grace from elementary school, and they were now in the same social studies and English classes. Grace had long black hair that she always wore back in a ponytail. An excellent student, she helped tutor students in the lower school. She had started paying attention to Nicho when his hits put runs on the scoreboard and resulted in a big win against their rival, St. Luke's Academy.

Grace dressed in the traditional school uniform each school day: white blouse, blue-and-green plaid pleated skirt, and white kneesocks. For after-school games, she would run home to change into her casual street clothes. If her mother knew there was a game, she anticipated her daughter's whirlwind entrance, followed by the mad rush to get back to the baseball field, such as what was occurring now.

"Mom, are you ready? The game starts in fifteen minutes," said Grace as she pounded up the stairs to her bedroom, peeling off her uniform before she reached the dresser.

Her mother, Rosalita, yelled from the downstairs kitchen, "What's the big rush? We always get a seat. It's not Yankee Stadium."

Grace quickly slipped into some jeans and pulled a dark red school sweatshirt over her head, then traded her loafers for some sneakers.

Their apartment was an older three-bedroom walk-up above a small hardware store where Grace sometimes worked part-time on weekends and in the summer. Her parents were first-generation from Ponce, Puerto Rico. Grace's father worked in the post office, and her mother did some babysitting for the neighbors and family members.

Only rent control made it possible for these families to live in this neighborhood. There was constant fear that the landlords would decide to remodel and redevelop the entire building. But for now, things on Hester Street were normal, and at this time of the year, the most exciting event in late afternoons was the baseball field that St. Vincent shared with PS 10.

"Mom, we'll be late again. Michael is waiting for us to show up! Don't forget your purse and your keys. Come on, I want a good seat," said Grace, standing by the door.

"OK, OK, I'm coming. How can you be late for a game that lasts two hours?" said Rosalita, closing the door and making sure it was locked.

The spring weather was slightly cool, but it didn't stop the baseball season from getting in full swing. The St. Vincent baseball team was three and one, losing only once to St. Lawrence in extra innings. The team they faced today was Brother Rice, a wealthy prep school from Queens that had won the league title the previous year. This would be St. Vincent's toughest team yet.

The game was scoreless through three innings, with really good performances by both pitchers. It was the bottom of the fourth inning when their best hitter smashed a ground ball right at Nicho. Normally it would be an easy throw to first base, but the ball hit a stone in the dirt infield and took an unusual hop over Nicho's glove and hit him in the forehead. Nicho stopped the ball, picked it up, and threw the ball to the second baseman and got the force out at second. It was the end of the inning. The umpire called time, and he went out to where Nicho was holding his hand over his forehead. Father Gomez left the bench and ran out to help Nicho, while his teammates gathered around. He had taken a hard hit to the center of his forehead, but held back any expression of pain.

"Nicho, are you all right?" asked Father Gomez.

Nicho's family was standing up in the bleachers, looking across the field fearfully.

Nicho's brother put his arm around their mother. "Don't worry, Mom. Nicho's a tough kid. He'll be all right."

At the other end of the bleachers, Grace grabbed her mother's arm. "Mom, that's Michael's friend, Nicho. He got hit by the ball. Look, Mom!" she said, shaking her mother's arm now.

"I see," said Rosalita. "He'll be all right. Look, see? He's getting up and going back to the bench."

Father Gomez assisted Nicho to the bench as the crowd stood up and applauded. He wiped the boy's forehead clean and placed a Band-Aid over the cut. He scooped a handful of ice from the cooler into a towel and made Nicho hold it against the bruised area. Nicho was able to stay in the game as the next few innings went scoreless.

Finally, it was the last inning, with the scored tied at 2–2. Grace's brother, Michael, was on second base after hitting a single and stealing to second. With two outs, Father Gomez motioned to Nicho to come over and sit next to him.

"How are you feeling?"

By now, Nicho had taken two aspirin, and the Band-Aid had stopped the bleeding. Any residual pain he may have felt was taken care of by adrenaline.

"Are you kidding, Father? I feel great. I can't wait to bat!"

The air was still, and families in the stands were once again on their feet. His team knew he was the best hitter they had, and cheers erupted from the bench when he stepped into the batter's box.

Nicho was tall for his age, with broad shoulders and a muscular frame. He kicked the dirt and did a practice swing with his bat. The pitcher from Brother Rice knew this batter would be a challenge. Nicho pulled the hard batting helmet down. The large white bandage glowed distinctly on his forehead like a medal of honor.

"Batter up!" the umpire yelled.

Nicho stepped up to the plate. The count worked its way to 2–3 as Michael got the hit-and-run signal from Father Gomez.

"Come on, Nicho! You can do it!" yelled Grace from the stands.

The pitch was a fastball down the center, likely to be a strike, which would send the game into extra innings, but Nicho remembered what his father had told him: *Keep your eye on the ball until it meets the bat.*

Nicho's bat came around with all the velocity he could muster and connected with the ball, sending it over the pitcher's head and straight into center field. By the time the ball hit the outfield, Michael had rounded third base and headed home. The game was over. St. Vincent 3, Brother Rice 2.

The crowd and the bench went wild. Nicho's family jumped up and down, hugging each other as the players ran to congratulate Nicho for the victory. Michael grabbed him by the waist and lifted him upward, while the coaches exchanged handshakes.

* * *

Saturday morning was a quiet time in the church. Father Gomez met with the altar boys around 10:30 a.m. to go over the Mass schedule and help orientate any new boys to the procedures. He relied on Nicho to help make the younger boys feel comfortable. Nicho had started working in the ministry in fifth grade, and now he was the senior boy. The church could not afford to give the boys money, but there was a seniority system. Nicho now assisted Father with baptisms, funerals, and marriages, for which he got tips that provided him with spending money.

Nicho entered the church through the rectory back door left open by Father. The large, thick wooden door creaked as he lifted the latch and pushed forward. Although the original church had been built in 1896, it was in good condition, having undergone major restoration in 1926 and 1952. When the neighborhoods were bustling with commerce, the collections provided the needed support for improvements and regular maintenance. The new slate roof was a major capital campaign that lasted for three years. With the roof now complete, the interior ceiling was about to be replastered and painted.

The church design was based on the equilateral form. When the main arch was drafted, the radius was exactly the width of the opening, and the center of each arch coincided with the point from which the opposite arch sprang. The long nave had two aisles on each side, and a larger center aisle. The walls were constructed of heavy limestone blocks, with a brick exterior and a plaster interior. The transept was decorated in dark oak, with engravings along the top sill.

There was a simple but majestic quality to the interior of St. Vincent. The original stained glass gave the east and west light avenues of illumination as distinct columns of colored light poured across the pews and onto the hand-carved Stations of the Cross. When New York City tour buses stopped at St. Vincent, it was because of its crucifix, which was suspended in the center of the transept, directly over the altar.

The crucifix had come from a church in Italy that was destroyed in an earthquake around 1892. The fifteen-foot cross was hand hewed from virgin oak, and the figure was painted in a traditional and realistic manner. The frail body hung limp and stretched downward from the extended weight produced by gravity. The Christ figure was oil painted in flesh tones that resembled the Aramaic people who lived and occupied Palestine during the time of his life. The particular attraction was the expression on his face as his eyes fixed upward on the heavens, as if he was speaking directly to the Father. The parched loincloth was tied to his body with rope, and blood ran from the nail piercings that attached him to the massive wooden cross.

Nicho was early and entered the solemn space quietly from the back door near the sanctuary. He stopped and genuflected as usual, then glanced at his reflection in the mirrored surface of the window casings. *I forgot my bandage*, he thought. Although it hadn't required stitches, the cut on his forehead was two inches long and had been previously covered with an oversize bandage.

If there was ever a time when the church was quiet and still, it was Saturday morning. The morning light entered from the east through the long, slender stained glass windows above the sanctuary. These original windows depicted the episodes of Christ's life and cast dusty sunlight down the main aisle.

Nicho walked quietly toward the lectern, then turned to face the crucifix. He was young and respectful. The church, Father Gomez, and the school were the centers of his life. It was the only spiritual environment he had ever known. He looked around and saw no one, but the smell of incense lingered from yesterday's Mass. Nicho looked up at the crucifix and knelt down, crossed himself, and prayed.

"In the name of the Father, the Son, and the Holy Spirit," he whispered, "forgive me for my sins and bless my family, my mother, my father, my brother, and my grandparents, and any help you can give our team would be much appreciated. We want to win the division title this year."

Stillness filled the room. The massive walls of the church extinguished the sounds from the streets outside. The sunlight had shifted and reached Nicho's face as he peered forward and stared into the eyes of the crucifix. Then from *inside* his head came a voice.

"Bless you, my son," said the voice. *"May the Lord be with you."*

Nicho's eyes opened wide. *Where did that voice come from?* he thought. In the distance, he could hear Father Gomez opening the door and welcoming the other boys. Nicho stood up and proceeded to the rectory to join the other altar boys.

"Hey Nicho," said Father. "I didn't know you were here. How are you feeling this morning?" Father Gomez peered at the spot on Nicho's forehead where the bandage had been. He frowned. "Well, I've heard of fast healers, but this takes the cake. There's not a scratch on you."

Nicho put tentative fingertips where the bandage had been, feeling only smooth, unbroken skin. *How could that be?* he thought.

"Excuse me, Father, may I use the bathroom?"

"Of course," said Father Gomez. "We'll wait for you in the conference room."

Nicho opened the door to the small corner restroom and gazed into the tiny mirror. He rubbed his hand back and forth over his forehead. The cut was gone. His skin was smooth. *That's unbelievable*, he thought. *What the heck happened to me in there?* Nicho quickly washed his hands, unlatched the door, and made his way to join the others.

When the meeting was over, Nicho made his way to the playground, where kids of all ages were playing games, using the swings, and flying kites over the church. He jumped over the low fence, crossed the baseball field, and headed for home. On Hester Street, he saw Grace pulling a basket cart loaded with groceries, slowing her walk to a creep.

"Hey Grace. What's up?" said Nicho, running ahead to catch up with her.

"Hi, Nicho. How are you feeling?"

"I'm all right. Can I pull that cart for you?"

Grace breathed a loud sigh of relief. "Would you? That would be great. I just picked up some groceries for my mom." She stared at Nicho for a moment. "I thought I saw some blood yesterday."

"Just a little scratch. It's fine now." Nicho was anxious to change the subject. "What did you think of the win? Michael had the hit-and-run sign," said Nicho bashfully.

"We loved it! You came through with that hit, Nicho. Michael wouldn't stop talking about it all the way home."

Grace was dressed plainly, her hair pulled back in the usual ponytail, her face unadorned. It was the first time she had ever spoken to Nicho alone. As they walked along the busy street, surrounded by a mass of different people, street kids, and a few motorcycle riders in leather, they spoke to each other at length, ignoring the world around them, and without much eye contact. Finally they approached the front of Grace's building, walking as slowly as possible.

"Thanks for the help," said Grace. She reached for the cart handle and touched Nicho's hand lightly. It was not a mistake.

"No problem. I should be going. I've got some homework to do."

"Yeah, me too," said Grace. "I'll see you in school."

Grace walked up to the front door and took out her keys, giving one last glance and wave to Nicho. He stood on the sidewalk until she was safely inside, and then he lingered for a moment. *She's so nice*, he thought. *No, that's not it.* His stomach felt like Jell-O, and his hands trembled slightly.

Grace sat in front of her mirror brushing her hair. Her eyes weren't on the task at hand. Instead, she was staring at the picture of her brother's baseball team. Michael had his arm around Nicho, and she found herself daydreaming about the recent events, especially the walk home from the grocery store. *Nicho is nice looking*, she thought.

That night, Grace went to bed early with a headache. She was not feeling well. When she woke the following morning, her head continued to pound. She and her mother had planned to go shopping right after church the following day. Rather than disappoint her mother, Grace took a couple of aspirin and got dressed for the day.

Walking from store to store along Orchard Street was a pleasure for her mother as she searched for bargains. They walked into the lingerie store looking for Grace's first bra. After making their purchase, Grace was grateful to her mother for making this event easy. She had selected the most inexpensive bra she could find, and in a fleeting moment, she caught her mother's expression of sadness, wiping away a small tear from the corner of her eye.

Grace had grown unusually close to her mother as they had cared for her grandmother together in her late years. When she was feeble, weak, and close to passing, Grace and her mother kept her looking beautiful. With touches of makeup, fresh sheets, and a collection of clean nightgowns, they had worked hard with the people from hospice to make her comfortable. Grace remembered some of her last words.

"What you do for me, Grace, someone will do for you."

When she passed, the family came together for a Puerto Rican–style funeral, including a full Mass at St. Vincent and a family gathering at their house afterward for a sharing of pictures and memories. Her *abuela* was the matriarch of the family. She had raised six children on her own while working full-time in a nearby textile factory and cleaning the local barbershop in the evenings for extra money. All of her children graduated from high school, and Grace's mother, Genoveve, had received an associate's degree from the local community college. Her diploma hung in the apartment living room on proud display.

By the time they finished shopping, Grace admitted to her mother that she wasn't feeling well. Her mother felt Grace's forehead. It was hot. Once they got home, she took her temperature, and it registered 104 degrees. Genoveve phoned her husband, Miguel, and because it was Sunday, they decided to take her to the emergency room at Bellevue Hospital. The emergency room was overcrowded, and they waited four hours before they admitted Grace with flu-like symptoms. She was isolated in a special part of the ward, and they immediately started to administer a battery of tests. By midnight, they told her parents that this was a serious virus, possibly life threatening. Grace could lapse into a coma while her body fought the dangerous virus.

Miguel adored his daughter. He could not imagine losing her. Holding back his tears, he spoke to his wife.

"Genoveve, this cannot be happening, not to our Grace."

She looked into his eyes, and as always, they provided him with the comfort he needed. For many years, since Miguel's bout with cancer, Genoveve had been the foundation of the family. Although Grace was her cherished daughter, she remained emotionally steady, providing the support for Michael and Miguel.

* * *

That next morning, the main office was jammed with students arriving late. For all seventh graders, religious education was required, and usually held the first period of the day. The nun who taught the class was near retirement. Nicho sat at the back of the room, next to the window, as Sister Rita lectured.

"The Catholic crucifix was not widely used before the fifth century AD," she said in her authoritative manner. "Prior to the fifth century, the Lamb of God was the most common symbol to represent Christ. Today, the crucifix is recognized as the universal symbol of Christianity, symbolizing the sacrifice of Christ and the consequent redemption of mankind."

Nicho gazed out the classroom window from the second-story building and watched the lawn crew work on the baseball field. *They should drag the infield...get rid of those stones.* But while his thoughts were on baseball, some of the nun's words reached his ears. *Maybe God can speak through the crucifix,* he thought.

At lunch, most of the baseball team sat together. Some had sack lunches, while others bought from the school's hot lunch line. The girls all sat together on the east side of the gymnasium, while the boys were on the west side. Father Gomez walked down the center aisle and made sure everyone finished before leaving for the recess area outside.

On the playground, the girls huddled in the corner, passing notes, looking into small mirrors, and talking about their favorite television shows. The boys played soccer using two parking cones as a makeshift goal. Nicho blocked a soccer ball headed straight for the goal with his body, then fell to the pavement, ripping a new hole in the side of his pants. The girls flinched, but still tried to act as if they ignored the game.

The bell rang, and everyone scurried inside, the girls to their lockers, and the boys made a line at the drinking fountain. The idea of paying attention to girls was new to Nicho. It wasn't long ago that he was playing with toys outside his building, watching cartoons, eating pork rinds, and drinking Kool-Aid. He paid little attention to his appearance, but had started paying more attention to the behaviors of the older eighth-grade boys. There was a style to their shoes, and there was this wave in their hair.

At practice, Nicho spoke to Michael. "Where's Grace? I didn't see her in school today."

"She's really sick," said Michael just as Father Gomez called his name. "I'll tell you about it later."

The day flew by with papers due, tests, and practice, and Michael never got around to mentioning his sister's condition. At Bellevue Hospital, doctors had begun administering the normal procedures to combat the flu, but until the cultures were complete, they did not know which virus to fight. After forty-eight hours, they determined that it was the Hong Kong flu, and started to give her the neuraminidase inhibitor Tamiflu. By then, Grace's condition had taken a turn for the worse.

Without the public knowing, there had been an outbreak of the type A H2H3 influenza virus, and four people had died. Each hospital in Manhattan had several patients who were in serious condition. Grace was one of them, now comatose, fighting for her life.

"What can be done?" her father, in tears, asked the doctor.

"We are monitoring all her vital signs, and we can just hope the medicine starts to take hold. We got off to a late start because, until recently, there were no reported cases of this virus in New York City. Right now she is stable, but weak. Maybe you could say a prayer," said the attending internist. Miguel held his wife and stood silently watching their unconscious daughter.

The end of the week came quickly at St. Vincent. The baseball game after school was away. The team loaded their gear into the secondhand bus and began their ride to Brooklyn Heights, home to the large regional high school, St. Andrews Academy. St. Vincent scored six runs in the first inning off a double by Nicho and a triple by Michael. The final score was 6–1, and everyone celebrated on the bus ride home.

Michael sat next to Nicho on the bus and finally mentioned to him that Grace was in the hospital with a serious case of the flu.

"What do you mean 'serious'?" asked Nicho.

"She's in a coma. My parents are really worried because her blood pressure is starting to drop. We're all going to the hospital tonight."

Nicho worked at holding in his feelings from Michael and his friends. When he got home, the house was quiet. His father was working, and his mother had left a note saying she was visiting her sister in the Bronx. Nicho sat down on the couch and stared at the blank television screen. On the shelf above the TV was a small plastic crucifix. It gave him an idea. He locked the door behind him before heading out toward the church. It was only 4:30 p.m., and he was pretty sure the church would be vacant. The old door creaked familiarly as he entered from the back door of the rectory.

"Hello?" he said.

There was no response. He slipped down the hall to the back of the church. He stood silently looking around to see if there was anyone in the church, but saw no one. The Stations of the Cross loomed large around the interior walls of the church, where fourteen carvings depicted Christ's sufferings and death.

Nicho walked forward to face the crucifix, crossed himself, and knelt down to pray. He whispered, "God bless my family, but I need some help for Grace."

A voice replied inside his head, *"Touch my feet. Go to her. Pray."*

"Excuse me?" said Nicho.

And that was it. The voice was gone. He stood up and pulled a nearby chair over to the place directly below the looming crucifix. He climbed up, and with the help of his toes, his hand grasped the foot of the ancient wooden crucifix. He prayed.

"Dear God, please help Grace, who is suffering from a serious virus. In the name of the Father, the Son, and the Holy Spirit. Amen." Nicho dropped his hand to his side and looked into the eyes of the Christ, waiting for the voice to respond. Instead, he heard a soft, familiar voice from the entrance of the church.

"Nicho! Is that you?" It was Sister Maria, Nicho's friend from his work as an altar boy. "What are you doing standing on that chair?" she asked.

Nicho stared down at the chair, then said haltingly, "I...I think I was in communion with God, Sister."

Sister Maria was one of the youngest, sweetest nuns at St. Vincent. She laughed softly and said, "It's all right, Nicho. Sometimes when we are young, we think the crucifix has a special power. But God is everywhere. Why don't you come down? Put the chair back before Father gets here. I have choir practice in ten minutes. Do you need any help?"

"No. Thank you, Sister." Nicho stepped down awkwardly, slid the chair back to its resting place. He retreated through the rectory and opened the back door with both hands. His body seemed to know where he was going before he did. He crossed Allen Street to the Bowery subway stop. Bellevue Hospital was only one stop away.

The hospital engulfed an entire city block, and Nicho was not sure where to enter. Traffic was heavy as he crossed the street and headed toward the large sign that read: Emergency. Once inside, he made his way to the waiting room and spoke to the receptionist.

"I'm here to see Grace Rivera," said Nicho.

"Visiting hours are seven to nine p.m. You're early," said the young Hispanic girl.

"I can't wait that long. Is there any way...?"

"Are you family?"

"Pretty much," said Nicho. "I really need to see her. Please?"

"Don't tell anyone that I let you in. She's in room six ten."

Nicho scurried into the elevator and pressed the Door Close button repeatedly.

The elevator bell rang at each floor. The door opened, and Nicho walked quickly, watching the numbers on the rooms until he got to 610. The small sign in the glass panel of the door read: Limited Access. Nicho ignored it and pushed the door open. There were two double beds in the room, but only one was occupied. Grace lay in her bed, connected to a variety of monitors.

A vase of yellow flowers decorated the table next to her bed. He could hear the PA calling a doctor's name in the distance. He walked up to the edge of her bed, stopped, and crossed himself. She appeared to be asleep. The heart monitor was making a regular beeping sound that was reassuring. Nicho took her hand in his and remembered his recent church experience.

"In the name of the Father, the Son, and the Holy Spirit, may the Lord be with you. I love you, Grace. Please get better."

Grace lay in her bed still and silent. Her breath came in soft rhythms. Nicho sensed it would be wise for him to leave before visiting hours began. Instead of taking the elevator, he opened the door to the exit stairway and made his way down the stairs to the first floor without being noticed.

* * *

The sun warmed the air outside, but the inside of the church was noticeably cooler. Grace's mother covered her head with a white mantilla veil as she entered St. Vincent Church for early Mass. The community of people who gathered for early Mass was usually older. Genoveve held her rosary, genuflected with one hand grasping the dark oak pew, then entered her usual row and knelt to pray. The large, lifelike crucifix loomed heavily over the altar, and the sound of light piano music filled the vaulted room. Mass had been a ritual for most of Genoveve's life, but today was different. Thoughts of Grace lying in a hospital bed, unconscious, had denied her sleep most of the previous nights. She prayed to God to help her daughter get better, and several friends touched her shoulder as they passed. That morning, as the east light filled the center aisle, Father Gomez mentioned Grace in his prayers.

"And for the Rivera family, their daughter Grace, hear our prayer."

As Mass ended and Genoveve got up to exit her pew, she saw Michael standing at the back of the church, under the flamboyant arch, with his hands folded. She couldn't help thinking the worst, and her knees wobbled as she approached her son. She didn't like the look on his face.

"The hospital called and said we needed to come right away. There's a change in Grace's condition," said Michael calmly.

"What exactly did the nurse say, Michael?" she asked, near tears. "Is she all right? Tell me."

"She said things on the floor were really busy and she would explain everything when we get there," Michael replied, feeling helpless.

Genoveve and her son left the church, flagged a cab, and stopped by the house to pick up Miguel before leaving for the hospital. The cab ride to Bellevue was quick on a Sunday morning. It was not regular visiting hours, but the head nurse had left a note at the reception desk to let them up. The hospital staff was cleaning, bedding was being changed, and nurses walked to and from rooms grasping medical charts. Michael and his mother held hands as they approached the room, preparing themselves for the worst. As they turned the corner on the open door, they saw Grace sitting up in bed, talking with a nurse.

Genoveve swayed and put her hand out to steady herself. Tears coursed down her face as she rushed to her daughter's side.

"I'm much better, Mom. Don't cry." Grace patted her mother's hand. "Hey Michael," she said before sucking some orange juice through a straw.

"Wow, you really do look better," he said, smiling.

"I'm sorry," said the nurse. "When I called, a patient in the hallway had fallen, and I didn't have much time to give you the details. I hope I didn't worry you too much. I just wanted you to get over here as soon as possible to see how improved she was. The fever broke in the middle of the night. It must have helped disable the virus. She woke up this morning around seven thirty feeling much better." The nurse pulled the breakfast tray away from the bed. "The doctor was in about a half an hour ago and said he wants to monitor her today, but she can go home first thing in the morning. How does that sound?"

"Thank God you're all right. I was so worried. How do you feel, Grace?" asked her mother.

"I'm a little weak, but I'm feeling much better. It's funny, but I remember feeling a hand on my arm, and something lifted. Maybe I was dreaming," said Grace.

Genoveve asked the nurse, "What did she have? What kind of virus?"

The nurse looked over the chart. "She had a severe case of the H2N3 influenza. The medication has limited effect on that strain. Mostly the white blood cells have to fight off the contagious cells, and the body helps by creating a high temperature. The doctor said her recovery was unusual. I'd say it's beyond our understanding. You can touch her. She isn't contagious anymore."

Genoveve crossed herself before hugging Grace, and Michael kissed her hand and held it to his cheek. His sister was well.

At St. Vincent the next morning, many kids gathered on the school playground before the dew was off the grass. Nicho noticed that Michael was absent. He asked Father about him.

"Good morning, Father. Have you seen Michael?"

"He called into the office this morning and said he was picking up his sister at the hospital today and that she was coming home. It's good news," said Father Gomez.

"Did you know his sister, Grace, was sick?" asked Nicho.

"Yes. Her mother had asked for a prayer at Mass. It sounded serious. I'm glad she's better."

Nicho just hoped she'd be in school the next day.

* * *

Nicho forgot to set his alarm and was running late. Normally he would walk to school, but his father agreed to drop him off on his way to work. Nicho got to his first class, Religious Studies, right at the bell.

"That's cutting it close, Nicho," said Sister Rita.

Taking his seat, Nicho replied, "Yes, Sister. I overslept. Sorry."

Sister Rita took attendance and started their morning with the Lord's Prayer.

Nicho's thoughts were elsewhere. He had not yet seen Grace that morning in school. Their classes were in different parts of the building. He deliberated what he might say to her. It made him nervous, or anxious, or both. Should he mention his visit to the hospital? He decided to write a note and give it to her at lunch.

> *Dear Grace,*
> *I heard about your illness. I'm glad you're feeling better. I said a special prayer for you while you were in the hospital.*
> *Love, Nicho*

Love, Nicho, he thought. *I can't say that...not yet.*

He erased the word "love" and wrote: *Fondly, Nicho*. Better. He folded the paper twice and placed it in his front pocket. It was the first note he had ever written to a girl.

The lunchroom was noisy and more crowded than usual. The eighth-grade class was eating with the seventh-grade class today because they were going on a field trip and the bus had to leave early. In addition, today was pizza day, and many students were getting hot lunch. It made the line go much slower. Nicho walked with his tray toward the same spot where he and his friends always sat, but he could see from a distance that it was already taken by a group of eighth-grade boys. Then he saw Michael waving to him from another table, and he felt relieved. His eyes traversed the gym for Grace, but she was not there.

Where is she? he thought.

* * *

Illiana grabbed Grace's arm and gave it a tug. "C'mon. We'll miss lunch."

Grace was in deep conversation with Sister Maria, explaining to her the details of the illness and her hospitalization. Finally she gave way to Illiana's tugging.

They stopped at their lockers and jammed their books into the narrow compartments while grabbing their sack lunches. The halls were quiet, as nearly everyone was in the gymnasium by now.

Walking hand in hand, Grace asked Illiana, "Do you know Nicho?"

"Rodriguez? Yeah, he's been in our class forever. Why?"

"What do you think of him?"

"OK, what's up with Nicho?"

"Just wondering. Forget it."

By now the gym was packed. There were groups of students, mostly seventh graders, sitting on the floor, eating lunch. There was an extra contingent of nuns patrolling the aisles. A small group of eighth-grade girls had just finished eating their lunch and were getting up when Grace and Illiana walked into the gym. They quickly slipped into the seats and sat down.

"Where's your sister?" asked Nicho, finishing his lunch.

"She's here, somewhere," said Michael. "There she is." He pointed. "She just came in with her friend Illiana...over there."

Nicho finished his pizza and contemplated his next move. He had never passed a note before. He decided to ask Michael for help.

"Hey, are you finished? Let's go outside," Michael said.

"Do me a favor, would you? I wrote down some assignments for Grace. Would you give this to her before we head outside?" said Nicho quickly, trying to sound as casual as possible.

"Sure," said Michael as he squashed his lunch bag into a small ball and took a jump shot into the wastebasket.

"Hey, here comes your brother," said Illiana. "And Nicho."

Nicho hung back as Michael approached the table and handed the folded piece of paper to his sister. "This is for you..."

Nicho felt weird. *Maybe this wasn't a good idea.* Gradually, he came forward.

"Hi, Nicho," said Grace. "How are you?"

"Fine. I heard you were really sick. I'm glad you're back," said Nicho, standing a couple of steps behind Michael.

"I'm feeling much better. Thanks."

Michael interrupted, impatient to get going. "We're heading outside. See you later." The two boys made a beeline for the exit and out onto the playground area.

Grace grasped the note in her hand and quickly slipped it into her pocket, but the exchange did not go unnoticed.

"What's up with that?" said Illiana.

"It's probably just a grocery list my mom forgot to give me," said Grace, forcing her voice to remain neutral. Intuition told her the note was from Nicho. Her brother would not pass a note to her.

A natural snoop, Illiana was not to be put off so easily. "Is that from Nicho?"

"You just saw *Michael* give it to me, didn't you? Come on, let's go," said Grace, getting up in an effort to distract her friend from the interrogation.

Grace decided to duck into the restroom, and told Illiana she'd meet her at the lockers. She went into one of the stalls and latched the door. *This requires complete privacy*, she thought. She read the note quickly, then again, and then again, slowly. She flushed the toilet unnecessarily, then slipped the note back into her pocket.

Beginning sometime in third grade, all of Grace's girlfriends engaged in the ritual of passing notes. It was silly stuff, and more about the process than the content, but this was her first note from a boy, and it did not feel silly. At all.

Nicho and Grace had English class together the last period of the day. Grace had decided she would say something to Nicho, but she didn't know when, perhaps just before class. She stopped at the drinking fountain, and as she finished and turned around, Nicho stood there waiting.

"Can I see you after school?" he asked.

"Sure, where?"

"Let's meet outside the rectory, at the back door," Nicho said.

Grace nodded. She was caught off guard. This was new territory. They both sat in their English class, several rows apart, preoccupied with the idea of the meeting.

The sun had passed over the rectory, and everything was in shadow. The roses had not yet fully bloomed. The birdbath of the Holy Mother in her traditional pose needed painting. Nicho rested his shoulders against the cool brick wall, waiting for Grace. The moments seemed like hours as he rehearsed his words. Finally the door opened.

"There you are," Grace said. "What's up?"

"There is something more I wanted to say, that I didn't get a chance to go into in the note," said Nicho.

"Like what?"

"While you were in the hospital…" Nicho trailed off and bit his lip. "Let's step into the church. I want to show you something," he said, moving toward the door at the rear of the church.

"Why the church?" asked Grace.

"Just follow me," he said.

Grace was intrigued, and followed Nicho inside.

The church was empty, but that could change at any moment, so Nicho headed quickly to the crucifix. He looked into Grace's eyes and said, "I prayed for you to get better."

"Thank you, Nicho. That was so sweet."

"No," he said, his voice urgent now. "I mean I really prayed, like I've never prayed before, and he answered. He made you well. Nothing like this has ever happened to me before."

Grace searched the boy's face. His dark eyes were lit with such intensity, she knew he meant every word he said. That was all that mattered.

"I believe you, Nicho. I'm better, and I'm here," she said.

"Do you think we can see each other?" he asked. "Are we old enough to do that?"

Grace couldn't help laughing, but said, "We can figure out something." Then, without any hesitation, she glanced around the church, and seeing no one, she kissed him softly on his lips. "Nicho, you're going to be late for baseball practice."

* * *

A week later, and many times after that, Nicho went back to the crucifix with sprains, cuts, scratches, and headaches, but never again was there a voice or a healing effect. After much thought, he decided to keep the details of what had happened to himself.

There came a spring dance where Nicho and Grace danced close together. There was a water balloon fight at a school picnic, and there were long walks on Hester Street. There was a sunny bus ride to Central Park, phone calls, friends' parties, and family celebrations. After winning the division title, and during the early days of summer, Nicho and Grace fell in love. It was a summer they would always remember.

Wavelength Duet

Camp Montague had been changing the lives of young people since it opened in the early 1920s. Every summer, beginning in mid-June, the camp was home to high school students studying music, art, theater, and dance. Forty cabins were nestled in the sprawling woods that smelled of pine. The roads and paths, made of the red clay that was a geological hallmark of the island, connected the cabins and cottages with the Panamure Center. Located on the eastern edge of Prince Edward Island, the camp was tucked into Cardigan Bay and consisted of nearly four hundred acres of rolling meadows, woodlands, and beaches that were surrounded in turn by potato farms. The local geography mixed eroded red stone cliffs, tall grasslands, and salt marshes along with professional artists from all parts of the world. The faculty came to conduct, direct, and inspire the elite art students who traveled from as far as Europe and Asia to attend what was considered to be the gem of East Coast summer camps for the arts.

Only the die-hard *Anne of Green Gables* fans made the trip to Prince Edward Island Provincial Park to visit the famous house at Mayfield. Other than tourism during the summer, the sleepy, historic island kept to itself, with the exception of its famous arts camp. The economic infusion provided by the camp's summer residents was a welcome one. With the exception of a few students on scholarship from the Canadian government, endowments, and private sources, most of the students came from upper-class families who could afford the camp's tuition and room and board.

The rustic cabins were constructed from local rough-cut lumber produced by sawmills where great blue herons walked along the beaches in early morning. The long red dirt road to the camp dropped below sea level before elevating itself once again near the camp's entrance. The road was lined with aging sugar maples whose branches formed a canopy that cast the road in lush, filtered green light. The large stone entrance, reminiscent of the turn of the century with tall iron gates, made students feel as if they were entering the home of royalty.

1938 was a harsh year in Canada. The Depression had taken its toll on the potato farmers and the industry on the island. The capital, Charlottetown, still had hundreds of people living on welfare. Some of the local farmers had sold their farms and taken jobs in the fisheries, where they harvested oysters, redfish, and herring. The once quaint and popular vacation spot for the wealthy had dropped to all-time low levels. In North Rustico, the new lobster market had brought some hope for a recovery in the economy, and there was a new Christie's Biscuits factory opening in Primrose. Although the war in Europe was stressful, the immediate challenge of keeping families fed was the biggest worry for the island's residents. Folks from all parts of the island had lost relatives to the horrible aggression of Germany in Europe, and many people arrived weekly from Great Britain to escape the bombing. Amidst the world's political differences, Camp Montague continued on, isolated, and often detached from world problems.

Students had begun arriving at camp as early as mid-June, when the cabin counselors were there to set up the cabins. Each cabin had four double bunk beds and a separate divided area for the counselor's bed. To the rear of each cabin was a changing room with a counter, sink, toilet, and a hand pump for well water. There was a small redwood shower stall that was gravity fed from a holding tank on the roof. The temperature of the water matched the temperature of the air, and on a hot day, it was possible to get a warm shower. Students took ten-minute shifts pumping the water up to the holding tank by hand. Only the Panamure Center and the auditoriums had electricity. Each cabin had one kcrosene lamp that was managed by the counselor for illumination at night. There were no candles allowed, as they were considered to be a fire hazard. Everyone shared in the cleaning of the cabin, and there were random checks by the dean each week. Cabins that were found to be unacceptable were put on probation, and privileges were restricted.

All the students wore blue trousers and white shirts while they were at Montague, a precaution with the security of the student body in mind. With the influx of tourism, school officials could easily identify one of their own. By the weekend of June 15, everything was running smoothly as the last few students arrived.

* * *

The bus ride to Boston's Logan Airport seemed like an eternity as the rain and wind gusted in from the harbor, past the naval shipyard, and across the Tobin Memorial Bridge. The city bus pulled up next to the sign that read: Departures.

"How long is the flight?" he asked the stewardess standing at the gate.

She looked at the young man dressed in olive-green cotton pants, a short-sleeve white shirt, brown leather boots, and a Boston Red Sox baseball cap that barely covered his light-brown hair. His parents stood nearby trying to read the one-page flight schedule.

"It normally takes two hours," she said. "We should be in Charlottetown by noon."

The Pratt and Whitney engines roared, and the propellers would blow your hat off if you didn't hold on to it tightly, which is exactly what Jamie McCloud had to do as he walked across the tarmac and grabbed on to the railing of the ladder leading up to the DC-3. With a small bag slung over his shoulder, he climbed up the steps and boarded the flight destined for Charlottetown, Prince Edward Island.

The rain and wind from the Boston Harbor made the event even more miserable for Jamie's parents as they stood watching through a large, wet window from the hangar office. The rain droplets running down the glass mirrored his mother's face. This was the first time Jamie had left home on his own, and they were worried. The DC-3 wheeled around and revved its engines, and the rain immediately disappeared from its wings in a trail of mist that sprayed the ground crew and all the bystanders.

Jamie's father was a high school art teacher at Logan High, one of Boston's largest high schools, and his mother worked part-time as a nurse at Mass General Hospital. The family was part of the Irish Catholic community in Boston's north side, and Jamie was the first generation born in the States. Jamie was attending Montague as a birthday gift from his grandparents, who, wealthy from an import business, often found themselves searching for ways to support their grandchildren.

The plane's engines accelerated, and the tail spun around once again, pointing the nose of the aircraft northwest at the end of the long runway, which was obscured by the rain. Within seconds, the wheels lifted, and the DC-3 pushed through the low ceiling of clouds. As the roar of the engines faded, Jamie's parents stood motionless. His mother's head lay against her husband's shoulder while he kept his arm wrapped around her small frame.

He's gone, thought Jamie's father. In those final moments, John McCloud sensed a transition, a passage that gave him an emotion he had never experienced. His young son had crossed a bridge and could not return. All the childlike experiences and emotions he loved so much were now gone as the plane door closed behind Jamie. *Bittersweet*, he thought as he held back his tears while his wife trembled and cried quietly in his arms.

The DC-3 was a relatively new plane that cruised at around 230 miles per hour. After about an hour in the air, its first stop was Portland, Maine. In preparation for landing, the plane reduced altitude to fifteen hundred feet and circled the Portland airport. The rain had stopped, and the clouds were beginning to break up and move off the coast eastward, out into the Atlantic Ocean. Jamie had survived his first takeoff and landing without an abundance of fear. However, there was that feeling of safety when the wheels first touched the runway.

* * *

Anne Marie Courtier stood flanked by her mother and father, who were in turn flanked by two large suitcases that bulged at the seams and held more clothes than she would ever need.

As it emerged from the clouds, the DC-3 had lowered itself from the sky and landed safely. Anne's mother glanced at her watch to see if the plane was on time. Anne watched the plane taxi to the hangar and the giant propellers come to a stop.

Raised in the small town of Blue Hill, Anne had studied dance for eight years and played the clarinet. She had convinced her parents that Camp Montague was the perfect camp for her artistic interests. Her father, David, was a local architect who had designed several buildings in downtown Portland.

The Courtier family had immigrated to the States around the turn of the century from Quebec City. Anne's grandfather was a leading politician in the Conservative Party of the Canadian government. The family moved to Blue Hill when her father was invited to join the architectural firm of Stewart, Strauss, and Young. Anne was musically gifted as well as analytical, organized, and studious. She studied French and had occasionally taken riding lessons at the Blue Hill Riding Club.

Anne kissed her parents and boarded the plane quickly, as if it was the local school bus and this was her first day of school. Her excitement had built over the spring as she imagined, over and over, scenarios based on the small black-and-white photos in the camp brochure. She sat at the window seat of the aircraft and waved to her parents as they watched from the hangar office. When the plane taxied to the runway, the roar of the engines made people put their fingers in their ears, and once again, the wind sent hats flying.

The adventure was harder on her parents than it was for Anne, and the promise of a phone call and a midsummer visit seemed hardly enough. Anne's mother held tightly to the small bouquet of daffodils Anne had picked that morning from their front yard garden to present to her after breakfast. It was Anne's way of saying good-bye in the calm and privacy of their home instead of publicly at the airport.

Anne's mother flashed back to tucking her daughter into bed when she was young, kissing her on the forehead, and wanting the moment to last forever. As she and her husband walked back to their car, with sounds of airplanes in the background, she knew those moments were behind her for good.

* * *

There was one more stop in Halifax, where four more students got on the plane, bringing the forty-passenger plane to full. Jamie read the sports section of *The Boston Globe*, occasionally nodding off for short naps. Up until now, he had only read about this much-anticipated summer adventure. Camp Montague was everything he had ever dreamed of. It was the kind of visual arts experience he had always wanted, along with classes in creative writing.

While government and foundation subsidies kept costs for families within reach, Jamie's tuition was being paid for by his grandparents, as well as a scholarship from the Irish American Club. In addition, Jamie had worked in a local grocery store all year to save money. He was expected to do well.

He began to write on the first page of the leather-covered journal his sisters had given him that morning before he left, to document the summer events. They had made him promise to write them each a letter weekly, and to read the journal entries when he returned.

The final leg to Charlottetown was a short hop over New Glasgow and across the Straits of Northumberland. From the air, Prince Edward Island looked like a fairyland with thousands of inlets leading to the lush green rolling landscape patched by farm fields and orchards. As the

DC-3 flew low over Hillsborough Bay, the passengers could see a fleet of fishing boats several miles off Pinette Point.

The plane descended, banked west, and Anne looked out her window at the hundreds of lobster buoys that peppered the Charlottetown Bay as the plane made ready to land. The sounds of the landing gear opening made a loud clunk, frightening some of the young passengers who had never been on an airplane. Once they'd landed safely, excitement and anticipation replaced the fear. The students exited the plane, looking for the camp bus that had been described in their letters.

The dark green vehicle was, indeed, unmistakable with MONTAGUE lettered in bold yellow along both sides.

"Everyone for camp over here!" shouted Jeremiah, the porter.

His small stepladder made it possible to lift and load luggage onto the top of the bus, where it would be restrained by a small rope fence. Jamie was the oldest, and his muscular frame was apparent. He helped by lifting the suitcases to Jeremiah, a fifty-year-old Jamaican man, who was working to keep his balance on the ladder.

"I can lift my own," said Anne.

Jamie stepped back as she struggled to lift both suitcases up to the porter. "You sure have a lot of clothes," he said. "Do you know we wear uniforms at Montague?"

Anne ignored the question, moved immediately to the door, and took her seat on the bus.

The bus ride through Charlottetown was an eyeful for the students. The air was fresh and smelled of saltwater and fishing gear. The sawdust from the meat shop spilled over onto the boardwalk and into the street. Most of the buildings in the town were made of white clapboard with long, low-set double-hung windows. The windows all sported flower boxes, and the selection of flowers in each box was a type of signature. The hand-painted signs were trimmed silver and gold, and old hitching posts along the storefront railings were remaining symbols of times gone by.

Montague was an hour's ride from the town, and the rolling red clay road gave everyone a tour of the picturesque countryside as they headed due east toward the coast. White picket fences surrounded the Elizabethan farmhouses, and there were rows and rows of orchard trees still clinging to an occasional late spring flower. As the bus finally rolled through the entrance, they could see small trails leading through pine-woods and over sandy mounds.

Half of the camp members had arrived the day before, and the sounds of French horns and flutes floated through the air as students practiced. Girls walked holding hands, wearing blue knickers and white short-sleeved blouses.

Students complained about the fact that they had to wear uniforms. They were, after all, artistic by nature and sought their individuality. But because there were so many visitors during the summer, the uniforms were designed so they could easily be recognized as Montague campers.

There was a large and colorful welcome sign that greeted the bus as it rolled to a stop in front of Panamure Center. Everyone unloaded and waited for Jeremiah to get their luggage. Jamie assisted him, along with two other boys, to make the job go quicker.

"Is it all right if I hand you down your suitcase?" Jamie asked Anne as she approached the ladder.

"The other brown suitcase is mine as well," she said, "Remember, I'm the one with too many clothes. In case you're interested, my instrument and music stuff are in one of the bags. What's your name?"

"Jamie McCloud from Boston," he said. "And you are?"

"Anne Marie Courtier. I got on the plane at Portland, but we actually live in Blue Hill, a small town on the way to Bar Harbor."

"Nice to meet you, Anne Marie Courtier," said Jamie, stepping away from the ladder. By then, the bus was unloaded, and everyone had dispersed for his or her locations. Dressed as modestly as possible, it was hard to hide Anne's natural beauty. Nearly five seven, her long, dark hair and full figure made even grown men turn their heads. On the plane, she had lightly put on some pink lipstick for the first time.

"Nice to meet you," Anne said as she turned to follow the other girls to the Panamure Center.

The girls' line stretched two blocks as they waited to confirm registration and be assigned to a cabin. Jamie, meanwhile, saw the boys' sign pointing to the Gasperaux Auditorium. The large wooden structure was Gothic in design and seated five hundred people for concerts and theater productions. It resembled Shakespeare's Globe Theatre, except with a roof. The boys' line was about half as long as the girls', and most of the boys were sitting on the edge of their suitcases, waiting for cabin assignments.

* * *

Sunday night was the first official dinner. Afterward, Dean Brewster approached the podium and made some introductory remarks to all the students. The dean was followed by the president of the board, who announced that the National Film Board of Canada was sponsoring a visiting film artist, Norman McLaren. He would be at the camp for four weeks teaching film animation techniques. After the announcement, the symphony began with Mozart's Symphony no. 25 in G Minor, and closed the performance with selections from *Don Giovanni*.

Spontaneous applause and cheers followed the performance, after which students were finally able to mingle. The excitement of having arrived at Camp Montague was contagious and spread through the performance hall like electricity as students connected and made friendships spontaneously. Jamie walked up the middle of the aisle with some of the guys from his cabin and noticed Anne getting up from her seat.

"How did you like the concert?" he asked.

Anne pretended not to hear him.

Jamie waved a hand in front of her face. "Remember me? I helped you with your suitcases."

By now, Anne was well aware of who Jamie McCloud was, but she decided to hold her cards close for a while.

"Oh," she said, as if she'd just realized he was there. "I liked the concert, especially *Don Giovanni*. How about you?"

"I loved the Beethoven," said Jamie.

"You mean the Mozart?"

"Uh, yeah. The Mozart."

"Gotta go," Anne said, and moved up the aisle with her cabin mates, leaving Jamie stuck in a long line of people.

Maybe I'll see her tomorrow, he thought.

* * *

The next morning, after cereal and juice at the Panamure Center, Jamie's first class was ceramics. The ceramics studio held twenty large wooden kick wheels. Students were already seated, centering their clay. At the rear of the studio, a woman in her late thirties was pulling sixteen-inch cylinders, only to cut them with a wire and throw them into a bucket of used clay. She repeated the process until she finally stopped and announced that the class and her lecture were about to begin.

Anne skipped breakfast and went directly to her solo and ensemble class, where students were already warming up on their woodwinds. She unpacked her clarinet and felt the cold instrument, wondering how it was going to sound. With two reeds soaking in her mouth, she watched through the window as her teacher approached the practice hall. He was a very short European-looking man with jet-black hair combed straight back and with round eyeglasses, white shirt, and black pants. He entered the building and immediately passed out the sheet music. He spoke briefly about the rigorous schedule. His Italian accent made it difficult to understand what he was saying. One girl's music stand fell, and she scrambled to pick up her sheet music. The teacher ignored it, but everyone sensed he was annoyed.

Anne sat on the cold metal chair and turned the practice pages. She was the last to play. Her sight reading was extraordinary, better than anyone's in the class. The other clarinetists were awed by her playing.

She lowered her instrument and wondered, *How did I end up sleeping in the upper bunk?* She was afraid of heights.

* * *

The camp experience was beyond imagination for the young people that summer. There were trips to Panmure Island to visit the famous lighthouse and walk the sandy beaches. There was a national wildlife preserve on the island where hundreds of great blue heron waded through a salt marsh.

The ocean water was warm to the north because of the currents in the Saint Lawrence Seaway. Students pushed up their knickers and ran along the beaches. Along these shores, poems were written and drawings made. There were dances at sunset and sonatas by moonlight. Students snuck out after hours and smoked cigarettes in the practice cabins in the dark, discussing modern art and jazz music. Letters flowed to and from the mailroom, while the infirmary was busy treating asthma, insect bites, and occasional dysentery. The concerts were continuous, as were the dance recitals, art exhibitions, and poetry readings.

As the weeks passed, the students built allegiances around their individual disciplines and with their cabin mates. The cabins competed for points by successful cleaning checks, being on time for meals, attendance to the Monday-night lectures, and community service. Jamie's cabin was leading with two hundred points when something was stolen from his counselor's locker.

Randy Denoted was from Toronto. He had just received his teaching degree from McGill University. He had attended Montague between junior and senior year of high school. When he was asked to be a cabin counselor at Montague, he agreed enthusiastically. It was a common practice to recruit former students who went on to college in Canada. Randy owned a gold pocket watch that had been given to him by his grandfather. As he reached for it one morning to check the time, he could not find it. He searched his room without any results, and then recruited his cabin mates to help him look for the watch. After going through everything in the cabin, the watch was found in the pocket of Jamie's sweater hanging outside the bathroom.

"I didn't put it there," said Jamie. "Honest, Randy, I would never touch anything of yours."

All the campers quickly left the cabin, leaving the two of them alone. There was silence, and then Randy spoke.

"Trust is the most important thing we have here. We cannot tolerate stealing. I want you to stay in the cabin until I talk to the dean. Understood?"

"Understood," said Jamie.

Randy grabbed his bag and left the cabin, leaving Jamie sitting on the edge of his bed, staring out at the woods. *I don't even remember wearing the sweater*, thought Jamie.

At the breakfast table, there was plenty of buzz. The guys in Jamie's cabin were all talking about the missing watch and finding it in Jamie's sweater as Randy approached the table.

"I don't want this discussed outside our cabin until I have a chance to talk to the dean. Is that clear? For now, get to your classes, and not a word. Jamie is confined to the cabin. I'll get back with all of you at lunch and let you know what's going to happen to Jamie." He started to walk away, then turned back. "Did any of you know about this?"

He was met with blank stares until Sean spoke up. "Jamie's a good guy, Randy. I don't think he would steal from you."

"Well, it looks as if he did, Sean."

With that, Randy returned to the cabin to speak to Jamie one more time before he went to the dean's office.

"I have an appointment with the dean. If you confess to this, it may make a difference. If not, you'll be sent home. Maybe you should start getting your things in order. For now, I don't want you to leave the cabin. Someone will bring you lunch. I will be in contact with your parents. Understood?"

The whole conversation lasted thirty seconds before Randy closed the cabin door behind him.

Jamie sat on the edge of his bunk bed, stunned by Randy's remarks. He reached under his bed and opened a small box that had come in the mail from his grandfather. The box contained all the parts for a crystal radio kit. Some copper magnet wire, two capacitors, a germanium diode, and a small earphone were all accompanied by a sheet of instructions and diagrams. Within an hour, he was getting a signal from Charlottetown that served as a convenient distraction.

The camp was flooded with students going to and from class. In the Panamure Center, Randy saw his friend Mary at a table working on her schedule. He sat next to her. Mary Donahue was another counselor who came from McGill. She and Randy had dated a few times earlier that spring, and he needed someone he could trust to talk to about the incident with Jamie. When Mary looked up at him, she read his expression instantly.

"What is it? You look upset."

"Something happened in the cabin this morning, and I had to ground one of the guys. He stole my watch, and we found it in his sweater. It's pretty obvious what happened. I may have to call his parents and have him sent home. I'm going to meet with the dean this afternoon."

Mary had looked puzzled throughout Randy's explanation. Finally she said, "Randy, do you remember the other night when I was over to see you at the cabin and I was cold? You put a sweater around my shoulders, and as it got to be late, I asked you what time it was?"

"I do remember that, yeah," said Randy.

"I looked at your watch, and I think I may have put it into the pocket of the sweater."

"Are you kidding?"

"I'm sure of it. I remember it was getting close to curfew and I needed to be back in my cabin, so I asked you for the time, and I was interested in looking at the beautiful gold watch. Then you were called away to help with the cabin lantern, and I must have put the watch in the pocket of the sweater. Poor kid, I don't think he stole it. It was me. You better get back to the cabin and talk to him."

Randy headed straight for the cabin trying to think of what to say. *The truth is the best*, he thought. He found Jamie lying in his bunk, writing in his journal.

"Jamie, the watch was placed in your sweater by my friend Mary the other night. You didn't steal it. I am so sorry."

"Wow, are you kidding? I was really worried! I couldn't even remember wearing that sweater," said Jamie, jumping up from his bunk.

Randy walked over to where Jamie was standing and hugged him. "All the guys in the cabin said it wasn't you, and they were right. I was completely mistaken." Looking at the now infamous watch, he said, "I think you can still make your writing class. I owe you a public apology, Jamie. Let's eat together with the rest of the cabin, and I'll tell everyone what happened."

With that, Jamie ran out of the cabin and lifted off into the air, gliding over the steps. Randy stared at his watch and realized there were challenges to being a counselor, and it had been a mistake on his part to rush to judgment. Right now, it was important to talk with everyone about what had occurred.

* * *

Anne had finished practicing scale runs on her clarinet and gazed out of the practice room window, where she saw Jamie running through campus at lightning speed. She wondered, *What's the rush?*

She and Jamie had become close friends over the course of the summer, and he was always interested in walking her back to her cabin after evening concerts. It was just a few nights ago that after saying good night, he kissed her on the cheek, the very first sign of his romantic interest. Anne remembered being caught by surprise and wanting more as he stepped back and asked, "Can I see you tomorrow?"

"Of course. I'd like that," she said.

Anne recalled turning slowly as he made his exit, only to see most of her cabin mates' faces pressed up against the small pane of window as if they were watching a love scene in a movie. As soon as their eyes met, they dispersed, falling over each other.

Anne pushed open the screen door and found everyone picking themselves up from the floor. "You guys, can't I have a second of privacy?"

Midway through camp, Anne was scheduled to challenge another girl for first chair in the student symphony. Her teacher had selected a Beethoven Sonata in A Minor, and both girls were scheduled to sight read the piece in the presence of two teachers. She practiced for two hours the night before and felt confident she had a chance to advance. If Anne became first chair, she would be in charge of the clarinet section. It was an opportunity to gain leadership experience. Her parents would be proud of her, as well as her high school teacher, who had tutored her throughout her youth.

At 9:00 a.m., both girls entered the large practice room followed by the two woodwind teachers. Sin Yoo Lee, the girl playing first chair, was difficult at best, and everyone in the clarinet section disliked her. She was constantly critical of the second- and third-part clarinets, but avoided Anne, as she knew she was an excellent player. Sin Yoo Lee would play first, since she currently held the position. She was handed a single piece of sheet music and placed it on the chrome music stand. Her playing was impeccable, with only one minor flaw playing a B-flat in the neutral position. If Anne could execute and perform without a mistake, the position would be hers.

She opened her clarinet case and looked inside, only to find the mouthpiece was missing. As she looked in the case, it seemed as though the blood left her head, and she was slightly dizzy. After much ado, the teachers offered her a school practice instrument. Then a very young girl from Australia stepped forward and offered her instrument, a Buffet Tosca clarinet. Anne had only read about such instruments. She slipped her own reed into the clarinet and played some scales. The performance was impeccable. Even Sin felt happy for her.

When the points were counted, it was a dead tie for first chair. It would be left to another challenge to change the position. But what remained was that someone had sabotaged her instrument. When she returned to the cabin, the piece was sitting on the floor next to her bed, as if she had mistakenly left it there. She knew she had put the instrument away after her last practice and not opened it since. Her clarinet sat on the shelf for several hours while she was at dinner and then later as she attended a dance recital. Anyone could have accessed her cabin during the evening hours.

When word got to Jamie, he was upset. It was the kind of story that moved through the gossip channel at lightning speed. Most people thought it was Sin, but not Anne. Sin was unpleasant at times, but not unfair. At dinner, Jamie sat with Anne and got the story firsthand.

"I went in prepared for the challenge, and when I opened the case, the mouthpiece was missing. Whoever did this didn't take out the whole instrument because then I would have noticed the change in the weight of the case. When I got back to the cabin, the mouthpiece was at the edge of the bed."

"Who would do something like that?" he asked.

"It might have been one of my cabin mates. Not all is perfect in cabin twelve. I think Dena resented me getting the upper bunk. She is so stuck up, from the Manhattan Conservatory of Music and all. What about your problem?" asked Anne.

"It was all a mistake. It was my counselor's friend who put the watch in my sweater. I'm cleared," said Jamie.

"And to think they were ready to send you home," said Anne.

"Hey, I'm starving. Let's eat."

Jamie grabbed Anne's hand, and it felt good to her. They walked up to the cafeteria-style food line as many campers watched. The two events had captivated everyone's attention in the small world of Prince Edward Island. At Camp Montague, everyone was connected.

After dinner, Jamie asked Anne about her other classes.

"How is your creative writing class? You haven't said much about it."

"I love it. The teacher is so motivating. She reveals herself to all of us, in her talks and in her work. Would you like to hear something I wrote?"

"Sure," Jamie said.

"It's a short poem I wrote a few nights ago. It's called 'Chilmark.'"

Chilmark

There is a winding stone fence
surrounding the house in Chilmark.
Large red rose bushes spread out
beneath the two bay windows.

The sheep are grazing across the road
at the edge of a small salt pond.
Wildflowers trim its border,
as time is slow.

Not far away, tall grass cliffs
look out onto the Atlantic Ocean.
Suddenly they rise to meet the horizon
against the silhouette of a lighthouse.

Wood rail fences join in
outlines against the yellow moon sunset.
Seagulls soar upward, lifted
by a warm summer breeze.

A door closes to the Chilmark house,
the fireplace already in use.
I walk through the kitchen,
wondering if you'll hold me tonight.

Jamie was spellbound. He didn't know what to say. He had been to readings all summer and listened to poets recite their work, but Anne's poem moved him and felt personal. *Could this be real?* he wondered.

* * *

The concerts, exhibitions, and performances continued, and the days of summer flew by as the young people bonded in the spirit of art. There were occasional parent visits, a few illnesses, and a few sprained ankles, but they all knew this was something they would never forget. Now, in mid-August, the final concert came after Sunday dinner. The performances were stunning, full of emotion that would leave a mark on those in attendance. A tall young woman with long, dark hair finished the student performances with her heartfelt poem. Dean Brewster made his way to the microphone.

"Each year and summer, I am so incredibly moved by your work and accomplishments. Tonight's performance is a good example of what motivates us all to be here. All of us who work here are privileged, as we get to reconvene for each summer camp session and get to know some of the most talented young people in the world. The teachers and counselors…we see the effervescent energy in your eyes. We sense your dreams through the art you express. We become the audiences for your exhibitions and performances. And now you leave us to go back to your homes knowing that we are linked by these experiences. I wish you all a safe trip home, and as alumni of Montague, you are always welcome guests."

* * *

At the airport, Anne took one long last look at the silhouette of Charlottetown on the horizon, wondering if she would ever be back this way again. The weather was clear as the DC-3's engines sputtered black smoke and kick-started to a roar. Jamie looked at the ground crew as the wind from the engines blew their clothes tightly against their bodies. It reminded him of the departure from Boston just eight weeks earlier.

Anne sat one row in front of Jamie, next to a flute player from Halifax. The plane slowly taxied down the runway and pointed its nose south into the warm wind. Within seconds, the plane lifted off the runway on its way toward Boston.

An hour into the flight, the captain's voice crackled over the speaker. "At this time, we are told there is some weather moving in from the northeast, but we should be able to fly above any storm activity. I'll keep you posted."

"Can these planes do that?" Jamie asked the boy sitting next to him.

The pilot took the airplane up to an altitude of ten thousand feet and cruised there for about a half hour before preparing for the first decent to Halifax. The sky to the north was pitch-black, and it was beginning to rain. The landing was smooth at the Halifax field, and students greeted their families on the tarmac in the rain. Soon the plane lifted off once again, heading east for Saint John. Anne heard the thunder and could see rain pellets bouncing off the wing. Fear knotted her stomach.

The half-hour jump, and landing in Saint John, were normal, and more passengers, including the stewardesses, left the aircraft, leaving only the crew, Anne, and Jamie left on board for the flight on to Portland and, finally, Boston. Jamie slid up to the seat in front of his to sit with Anne.

"Can I sit here?" he asked.

She looked at him and thought, *Why haven't you been here all along?*

"Please" she said. "I'm nervous and not feeling well." Anne grasped Jamie's hand more tightly than usual.

By the time the plane refueled and left Saint John, they could see lightning in the clouds on the horizon. Within ten minutes, the storm was upon them, and the plane bounced in the turbulence. Jamie looked out the small window, noticing the engine prop moving ever so slightly in the wrong direction.

Anne held on to Jamie with both hands. "This doesn't feel right," she said.

The PA crackled as the pilot announced, "We have lost power to one of the engines, and we may be forced to land before the Portland airport. Please make sure your seat belt is fastened."

The plane began to descend as the storm raged on with winds clocking in at fifty miles per hour. Finally, the word came from the captain that he was landing the aircraft near a string of islands off the coast of Maine. The DC-3 rolled and descended dramatically. The pilot was familiar with Whitehead Island, and set a course to land on an open area located at the north end of the island.

At that moment, lightning hit the tail of the plane, and more control was lost as the pilot attempted to find the grassy field without lights. Instead, the plane rolled left, missed the landing area, and headed downward toward the beach. With the electrical systems knocked out, the pilot prepared to land the plane in the water, as close to the beach as possible.

The bottom of the aircraft skipped along the water like a stone, until the right wing went under, causing the plane to flip upside down in five feet of water, partially broken in half. The nose lay in the deepest water, leaving the crew submerged and unconscious. They did not survive. Jamie and Anne were also unconscious, but they were above the waterline. The storm raged on as high winds and hard rain continued throughout the night.

By morning, the violent storm was over. The water off the north beach of Whitehead Island was calm. Seagulls fed on dead fish swept ashore from the incoming tide as the sun gradually rose. Only part of the DC-3 fuselage and tail could be seen protruding from the water. Jamie opened his eyes and took a breath, still buckled into his seat. His face was cut, and his collarbone may have been fractured, but he was alive. He quickly glanced over and saw Anne's head lying against the window bay. Her eyes were closed. He managed to reach down and unbuckle his belt, allowing him to reach over and touch her. She was alive.

"Anne," he said quietly.

There was no answer. He could tell she had taken a blow to the head, as her forehead was cut, and there was some swelling. Jamie looked forward, wondering if there could be someone else alive on the plane, but the door to the cabin was completely submerged. Jamie unbuckled Anne's safety belt and held her hand tightly.

"Anne, can you hear me?"

Her eyes opened slowly, and she moved her head toward the sound of his voice.

"What happened?"

Jamie felt tremendous relief. He talked to her in a whisper.

"The last thing I remember is hitting the water and flipping over. My head hit the ceiling, and I was out." He touched her forehead lightly. "You must have collided with the luggage rack and cut your head. You've lost some blood, but the cut isn't too deep."

"What about the crew?" asked Anne.

Jamie just shook his head grimly. "We're really lucky." Jamie eyed the side exit door. "We have to get out of here. Can you move?"

"I think so," she said. "My head really hurts, and my wrist is swollen."

He helped her out of the seat. Carefully, Jamie moved her down the aisle through the warm salt water that filled the bottom half of the cabin. Progress was very slow, but eventually Jamie and Anne reached the exit door. He grabbed the door latch and moved it downward, releasing its lock and forcing it open into the sea.

It was early morning, and he could see seagulls on the beach, not more than a hundred yards away. They both made their way out of the aircraft, and Jamie held her next to him as he paddled toward the shore until they reached shallow water. Once on the beach, he carried her fifty feet or so, up onto the pristine white sand, and laid her down. They were exhausted and fell asleep.

Though it was late August, the air temperature was still unusually warm. Whitehead Island consisted of six square miles and had been used by the navy for bombing practice. Fortunately, the navy was off on maneuvers in the Caribbean Sea and not practicing its bombing runs.

When Jamie woke, he saw Anne sitting up with her hand over her face.

"What's going to happen to us?" she said.

"How long have you been awake?" Jamie asked.

"Not long. They must know the plane went down, and someone will be looking for us, won't they?"

"Of course," said Jamie. He stood up and looked out at the plane in the bay. "Have you seen any search planes or boats?"

Anne stood up and began looking around. "No, I haven't seen anything."

Jamie was trying his best to reassure Anne that everything was going to be all right. "Listen, I'm going back out to the plane to see what I can find. I think I saw a first aid kit. Will you be all right until I get back?"

She nodded, and watched from the shore as he swam out to the plane and disappeared through the same exit door they'd opened earlier.

The tide was going out, making it easier to move around inside the plane. Jamie found Anne's small suitcase and clarinet case. Tucked at the back of the rear luggage rack, he could see his backpack. Next to the rear seats was a first aid kit attached to the wall of the plane. Jamie tied everything together and was grateful to find that the suitcase floated. He headed back to shore with everything in tow.

The sky grew overcast, causing darkness to come earlier. Using debris from the crash and some tree limbs, Jamie built a lean-to under a sand embankment. He built a small driftwood fire using matches he'd found in the first aid kit. Anne returned from a short walk along the beach.

"No sign of life," she said. "I walked about a half mile, and all I saw was sand and these small scrub pines and a US Navy 'No Trespassing' sign. That was about it."

"Tomorrow we'll look around the island. There might be somebody else here. We should see a rescue plane pretty soon." He peered closely at the cut on her forehead. "How's your head?"

"Better, thanks. I keep thinking about the people in the cockpit of the plane. Is there anything we can do?" asked Anne.

Jamie had been thinking of that, too. "When I went back to the plane, I tried to open the door to the cabin, but it was locked from the inside. When we're rescued, they'll be able to reclaim the bodies. Right now, we need to take care of ourselves."

Anne sat next to Jamie and hugged him. "We're lucky, Jamie. We made it. And you're right. We'll be fine."

The moon rose, bathing the island in muted light. The crickets were unusually loud. Small crabs were out on the beach soon after dark. A flight of pelicans were reflected on the water's smooth, moonlit surface. Jamie and Anne could see the tops of the tall grass sway in the breeze like feathers. One by one, the constellations premiered themselves against the dark eastern sky.

Not more than a hundred yards away, in the opposite direction of Anne's walk, stood two five-foot poles placed about ten feet apart. The poles were eight inches in diameter, like clothesline poles, and color coded with stripes. They were connected at the top by wire with a small white ball at the center.

"Look, Anne, do you see that light reflecting off that round ball?"

Anne stood and walked closer. "It looks like a clothesline or something. But what is that round thing?"

As they moved closer, Jamie could hear garbled sound coming from the suspended ball. The closer he got, the more it sounded like a radio transmission. When he was only three feet away, he reached out to touch it. A small electric charge jumped to his hand with enough force to knock him on his rear.

Anne stifled a scream.

Jamie got up, brushed the sand off his pants, and edged carefully closer to the structure again.

"What are you doing?" asked Anne. "Stay back. It already shocked you once."

Again, Jamie heard the radio sounds coming from the ball, sounding now like a technical message or weather information for captains or pilots. He listened closely from about five feet away. Anne took hold of his arm, worried he'd try to go closer. The ball glowed slightly, like a Christmas light, and vibrated on the tightly strung copper wire. Jamie began to speak.

"This is James McCloud, and this is an emergency. I am calling from the crash site of a DC-three headed for Boston. We're on a small island. This is an SOS. Can anyone hear me?"

The only response was a burst of light that generated static electricity before the object dimmed and went silent.

"I think it's some kind of radio transmitter."

Anne was now actively pulling him away from the structure. "Well, I'm not sure what that thing is, and we don't need any more problems. Let's wait until the morning and come back for a closer look."

Jamie kept looking at the ball and wondered what it was he was looking at. "OK, maybe you're right."

Hand in hand, they walked back to the lean-to, where the fire was almost out. Jamie lay down in the lean-to and pulled Anne along. They were hungry and tired.

"Do you really think it's some kind of radio?" Anne whispered.

"Whatever it is, it's beyond my understanding," Jamie said softly.

Suddenly Anne had an idea. She grabbed her clarinet case that Jamie had rescued from the plane and opened it. She put the pieces of it together and warmed up with a few scales. Then, for the first time in many years, she played a piece she had learned in her youth. It was a simple Mozart melody that had been used by her first teacher as a lesson. Its beauty was unmistakable as she repeated the refrain several times before putting the clarinet back into its case. Jamie listened and watched her intently, realizing how much he cared about her.

She turned to Jamie. "Let's get some sleep. Tomorrow will be a better day."

The crickets quieted when clouds obscured the moon, and the only sound was the tide coming ashore. Close to each other, with jackets covering their bodies, they fell sound asleep.

* * *

Jamie woke up early and realized they were into their second day on the beach. So far they were surviving off some crackers and snacks Jamie had in his backpack, but he knew they needed to find a source of freshwater. He was still thinking about last night's experience as he got up and walked in the direction of the structure. Nothing had changed as he walked by at some distance.

Beyond the dunes, he spotted some pines and tall grass and headed for them. There he found a small natural pond, and with his fingers, he tasted the water to make sure it was fresh. Surrounded by tall silky grass, the pond was fed by a fresh spring. Jamie knelt down to drink from the crystal-clear water. *I"ll bring Anne back here*, he thought.

On his way back to the beach, he ventured closer to the two poles and stopped in front of the ball less than twenty feet away. He looked at the sand directly below the ball and noticed small animal skeleton remains. *How strange*, he thought.

"Jamie!" He heard the sound of Anne's voice calling from the lean-to. With that, he quickly made his way back to the beach.

She stood up and stretched. "Where did you go?"

"I found some freshwater over there, just beyond those pines," he said.

"Great," she said. "I could really use a drink of water."

They walked in the direction of the pond, carrying some small containers to hold extra water. When Anne saw the pond, she couldn't believe Jamie had found it so easily. The surface rippled from the force of the spring pushing up from below, causing the water to sparkle in the morning sunlight.

"How did you find this?" she asked. She kneeled, cupped her hands, and washed her face after taking a long drink. "Did you go back to the structure?"

"No," said Jamie. "I was waiting for you so we could go together. If you're finished, let's go take a closer look."

As they approached, they noticed the poles had bands of primary colors around the middle sections. The ten-foot wire was stretched as tight as possible, and the ball resembled a ping-pong ball, except it was nearly as big as a soccer ball. As they got closer, they could make out a transparent beam of light projecting from the ball into the sky. They stared in wonderment.

"What could that be?" asked Jamie. He grabbed a small handful of sand and tossed it directly into the stream of light, causing an array of sparks, as if the small grains of sand were disintegrated by the energy of the light. The beam disappeared.

"Look, Jamie. Small skeletons." Anne pointed to the small bones lying along the sand beneath the wire.

"Yeah, I saw these earlier. I think they're from birds. See the feathers?" They both moved in closer. "Maybe the birds flew into the stream of light or hit the wire?"

For no apparent reason, they heard some of the same radio sounds they had heard the night before. It sounded like a two-way radio with static, unusual audio distortions, and unrecognizable languages.

"It sounds like radio communication, but distorted," said Jamie.

They looked closer at the round semitransparent object connected to the wire and noticed that it was attached on each side by two small metal electrodes. The object had displayed various levels of luminance, but at the moment, it was a dull white. On a hunch, Anne began to whistle a continuous monotone. The ball responded with a display of low-level light.

"Wow, did you see that?" said Jamie in amazement. "It's responding to your tone."

Anne increased the volume of her tone, and the light level responded. Jamie began to repeat what he had said the night before.

"This is James McCloud, and we are at the crash site of a DC-three somewhere off the coast of Maine. This is an SOS. Please respond."

But there was no response. They sat down on a small rise and stared at the structure, wondering what it was and whether it could help them be found. For the longest time, the structure did nothing.

Then, for no apparent reason, they saw the ball begin to glow, and the intensity increased until the globe was bright, even on this sunny day. At the height of its intensity, they could hear audio signals of a mixed origin and a variety of languages. Anne could see a group of seagulls landing on the beach just beyond the structure. One of the birds flew toward the structure's wire as if it were going to land and perch. Before it reached its landing point, the gull entered the electromagnetic field. Sparks covered the bird's body, and it dropped straight to the sand, lifeless. The gull didn't know what hit it. There was no sign of struggle, no marks left on the bird.

Anne grabbed Jamie's arm and said, "Did you see that? There is some kind of electric field around the ball."

"Yeah, I saw it. And I felt it. Remember?" said Jamie.

Jamie walked slowly toward the unit, Anne trailing behind him. From a distance of about ten feet, he threw some sand into the air in an attempt to figure out where the boundaries were. He was close enough. Again, he spoke loudly in another attempt to communicate.

"This is Jamie McCloud. We survived the crash, and we are on an island off the coast of Maine. I am here with Anne Marie Courtier on a return flight from PEI to Portland. This is an SOS."

"Do you think they heard you, Jamie?" said Anne, staring at the dead seagull.

"I don't know, but it's our only hope," said Jamie, backing away as the ball started to dim.

"Do you know how a radio works?" she asked.

"Yeah, a little. My science teacher said that the sound signal comes from our vocal cords vibrating. Through a microphone, the sound produces an electric signal that varies the voltage. Feeding the electrical signal to a transmitter produces the radio waves, and the electrons in the atom of the metal change the energy and emits the actual radio waves. This wave has a frequency that can be measured. I hope this structure is some kind of transmitter."

After a long walk and a trip back to the freshwater pond, the evening was upon them for a second night. The southerly breeze kept the air temperature warm. Anne sat by the driftwood fire, staring out at the silhouette of the DC-3's fuselage. She opened her clarinet case for the second time since she left camp and assembled the instrument while Jamie watched.

"Will you play for me?" he asked.

After some scales, she began with Mozart's Sonata in G Minor. The music was soft and lush with feeling. The notes seemed to float. Jamie closed his eyes and listened to her rendition while thoughts of his family drifted inevitably through his head. When he opened his eyes, he looked beyond the fire. In the distance, he could see the ball on the wire beginning to glow as if it were responding to the clarinet music. *How strange,* he thought.

Anne finished playing, and the glow from the ball was gone.

"Let's take a swim," said Jamie, standing up and reaching for her hand.

Their clothing was sparse, but they could both use a dip and wash off from their two days on the island. They walked slowly to the water's edge, hand in hand, both a little nervous. Gradually they waded into warm salt water waist high.

"Can you swim?" asked Jamie.

"I learned one summer in junior high, and I've always loved the water," she said. "I'm surprised how warm it is."

Jamie submerged himself completely and came up, pushing his long, sandy hair out of his face.

She looked at him and remembered the time they kissed outside her cabin. It was the only time that something like that had ever happened. She submerged her head and came back up wiping her eyes. Now, the light from the moon reflected off her wet hair as Jamie reached for her. After a moment of pause, she took hold of his hand as they both pulled closer together, bringing their foreheads to rest against each other. Then, very slowly and very softly, they kissed. The sky cleared, and the night's stars traversed the sky. The tide was in, and there was little to no breeze. Only a pelican, flying low to the water, watched while Jamie and Anne kissed and comforted each other in the shallow part of what Indians had once called Moonlight Beach.

* * *

The roar of an airplane engine woke them the following morning. Jamie jumped to his feet, waving his arms back and forth.

"We're here!" he yelled. The C-7 coast guard pontoon plane banked west and circled the crash site.

"They heard your transmission, Jamie!" said Anne.

The pontoon plane made its final approach and landed gracefully on the water, coming to rest about five hundred yards offshore. As they gave each other a hug, Jamie looked over her shoulder in the direction of the structure.

"Look, it's gone. The structure is gone."

"It was there last night," she said as they walked in the direction of where the two poles had once stood.

The white sand looked undisturbed. There were no signs of poles, wire, or the round glass globe. The animal remains were gone, and even their footprints in the sand from the day before were missing. It was as if the structure had never existed. Jamie and Anne stood frozen, looking at the area that may have saved their lives. In the distance, a small dinghy had been launched from the coast guard plane and was headed for shore.

Anne kneeled and looked closely at the sand, running the white grains through her fingers. "There is nothing here," she said. "Everything is absolutely gone. Do you think they'll believe us when we tell them about it?"

"It'll be hard to explain without any evidence," said Jamie, watching the boat approach.

Anne continued to rake her fingers through the sand. "Look," she said, pulling a tiny breastbone out of the sand. "This is all that's left."

Jamie peered at the small piece of bone between her fingers. "That's not exactly convincing evidence. That could have come from any dead bird. Let's keep this to ourselves for a while."

Anne rose, brushed the sand from her knees, and slid the small Y-shaped bone into her pocket.

The rescue boat was close to shore, and although both Jamie and Anne were thinking about their families, they both knew that they had less than a few minutes alone before the dinghy reached shore.

Rather rushed, Anne said, "Thank you for everything. You saved our lives, building the shelter, finding freshwater, and sending that SOS. Thank you so much for everything."

Jamie could not take his eyes away from hers. "I think it was your tone that made the ball respond. And last night was nothing less than the most beautiful event of my life. I will always be connected to you and this summer." With that, Jamie held up his palm, facing upward, and she did the same. They pressed them tightly together.

The rubber dinghy had reached shore, and two young coast guard officers jumped out. Jamie and Anne went to meet them.

* * *

The moments, minutes, and hours that followed were routine. There were questions and more questions, mostly regarding the crash and the people who were still inside the plane. They gathered up the few things they had salvaged from the DC-3 and eventually boarded the coast guard plane.

Inside the cabin, wrapped in two army blankets, they began to share the details of the event, leaving out any information about the structure. Two officers stayed behind at the crash site as the pontoon plane lifted off the water, heading due west toward the Portland airport. Jamie gazed out the window of the twin C-7 and saw the DC-3 tail fuselage protruding from the water, and a small lean-to just a hundred yards back from the shore. He could see the small pond where they'd found their freshwater, surrounded by pines and tall grass. The area of the beach where they'd encountered the poles, wire, and ball looked pristine as if it were just a dream.

"How did you find us?" asked Anne.

"We had a transmission from a fishing boat nearby," said the coast guard yeoman. "There was an SOS sometime late yesterday, which allowed us to lock in on these coordinates. We were searching south of here when the plane went missing. It managed to go much farther than we first believed based on our radio contact. You two are really lucky that you survived the crash and there are so many of these small islands along this part of the coast."

"Who was on the fishing boat?" asked Anne.

"We lost contact with the boat, but I think his name was James. We're not sure where he was transmitting from, as there were several boats helping with the search in the area."

Jamie and Anne both sensed it was better to hold back and not talk about the SOS Jamie had transmitted. It would be impossible to explain.

It would be hard to imagine how happy the families were when the two of them stepped off the plane in Portland. Families, parents, brothers, sisters, and friends ran to greet them. Both families had feared the worst, yet here they were, kissing and hugging their loved ones. Jamie, with his backpack, and Anne, with her clarinet case, spent precious moments embracing each other in tears of joy and relief.

As each family finally gathered around their vehicles to make their separate journeys to their respective homes, Anne asked her mom if she could have a few minutes of privacy with Jamie, and simultaneously, Jamie did the same thing.

"I'll miss your music," said Jamie.

"But we'll see each other again, won't we?" asked Anne.

"Of course we will. I'll come up to Blue Hill for one of your performances," said Jamie, avoiding her eyes.

"Jamie, I feel close to you. I want us to see each other."

"Me too. Maybe you'll need another swimming lesson sometime."

"Yeah, I'd like that."

Jamie leaned down and kissed Anne on the forehead. "Take care of yourself. After all this, I don't want you to fall off one of your fancy horses."

They knew their parents were monitoring the conversation, but Anne was caught up in the emotion of the moment and boldly kissed Jamie on the mouth before she turned and ran to her family. Jamie's heart dropped as she got into the back of the car.

* * *

Their lives had converged that summer of 1938 at Camp Montague along the east coast of Prince Edward Island. The classes, experiences, and events were glorious, but paled in comparison to what came afterward. Autumn and the return to school came quickly. Their schedules were busy. Jamie was back working in the grocery store, and Anne was playing first chair in the high school orchestra.

It was early October when Jamie came home from school and found a small package wrapped in blue paper on the table in the foyer. He immediately noticed the Blue Hill return address on the package and ran upstairs to his bedroom. Lying on his bed, he carefully unwrapped the package and opened a small white box where he found a small Y-shaped breastbone. The delicate bone lay on a piece of cotton padding. Beneath that was a handwritten note.

> *Dear Jamie,*
> *This is for you. It represents our time in camp, on the beach, and how I have come to feel about you. I miss you, and I love you.*
> *Anne*

The small breastbone would get sent back and forth between Boston and Blue Hill for weeks to come, each time with a letter. Eventually, one thing would lead to another.

All the Right Moves

Ever since he was very young, Vern loved to dance. It came naturally, and the talent started to display itself around the age of seven, when he would dance to his father's violin playing. In those days, the house on Hill Street was home to Vern and his brother, Walter, and their parents, Harry and Ada, two musicians, who had traveled throughout the countryside playing multiple instruments at parties and weddings. Now married and raising two boys, music was a pastime, not a vocation.

Young Vern would try every step imaginable as he danced to the classical music his father played. He made his mother laugh as she accompanied them on piano. Vern would slip step forward or sidestep backward, always aware of his audience's reaction. The more they responded, the harder he performed. He knew when to take it up a notch and make his parents laugh.

"What the heck makes him dance like that?" asked Harry. "He has some kind of natural-born rhythm, like a wind-up toy!"

Ada laughed. "He just loves to move to the music."

Although he was a toolmaker by trade, Harry had built the house on Hill Street entirely by himself. The two-story Cape Cod had an attached one-car garage with a small workshop in the rear. The backyard was large, with a garden, grapevines, and a chicken coop. The year was 1936, and the country was trying to come out of a depression. General Motors now employed Harry, and fortunately, they always had a paycheck. Ada raised the boys, took care of the housework, cared for the yard, and did all the domestic chores. She played piano accompaniment part-time for school plays and an occasional wedding, while Harry had just been inducted into the violin section of the General Motors Symphony.

"Can I take dance lessons, Mom?" asked Vern as he ate his pumpernickel and liverwurst sandwich.

"I don't think we can afford dance lessons right now. The country is in a depression, and we're lucky to have enough money to live. Is there something you can do at school, like a club?"

"I'll check." With that, Vern grabbed his schoolbooks and pushed open the screen door, forgetting to ease its closure.

* * *

The quiet Centerline neighborhood lay on the north edge of Detroit, Michigan. These small communities were mostly made up of autoworkers who had migrated from all parts of the country to find employment. At the corner of Nine Mile Road and Mound Road was one of the largest automotive plants in the country. The railway had several direct tracks into the massive complex of buildings that housed steel forges and blast furnaces. Iron ore and large deposits of nickel were transported by boxcar from faraway locations, and the high-rising smelting stacks plumed smoke continuously. The iron ore came from the mines of Northern Michigan and vast reserves of Canada. The raw nickel deposits came from quarries in North Dakota. The steel from the Mound Road plant provided enough raw materials to supply eleven regional stamping plants that created chassis for Chevrolet, Pontiac, and Buick.

Three shifts of soot-covered men, all dressed in gray overalls, lined up at exit gates to punch out before catching the bus home. At eight o'clock each morning, there were two lines, one made up of fresh workers entering the premises, and one line exiting from a shorter night shift, as there was some time needed for routine cleaning and maintenance. Many of them could not afford the cars they made.

The Hill Street house was less than ten blocks from the complex gate where acres of buildings supported the production lines of new cars. Harry was a professional toolmaker. He had been trained as an apprentice in Ann Arbor, working at the Willow Run aircraft factory. The precision lathes and drill presses that were used to build aircraft engines required the same skills needed in the automobile industry.

Shortly after Ada and Harry were married, Ada had seen the ads in *The Ann Arbor News* for precision toolmakers, and the salary ranges were higher than what he was currently making. Although Harry was comfortably employed, there was always a chance for improvement, so he decided to apply to General Motors.

He recalled his interview at the GM headquarters on Grand Boulevard. The historic building had been designed by the famous architect Albert Kahn, and was located just off Cadillac Square. The large, majestic lobby, with two-story arches and inlay tile designs, communicated an impression that was unmistakable: General Motors was the giant company in the auto industry. He entered the large revolving brass doors and went up to the reception desk, where he stood in line waiting for his turn to speak.

"Yes, how can I help you?" asked the young woman.

"I am here for an interview."

"Do you have an appointment?"

"Yes, with Mr. Barnard."

"And your name…?"

"Harold Dunstan. Harry."

"Please take a seat," she said, pointing to the modern brass chairs with black leather cushions located in the middle of the lobby.

This was the beginning of Harry's career with General Motors. The interview went well, and just as Ada had predicted, the job was at a higher salary.

Harry flourished as a tool and die maker in the GM machine shops. Clutch housings, water pump fixtures, and manifold details were all part of the model changeover and often required him to work overtime. Before long, he was supervising a mostly European-born group of men who handled the tools necessary to make the new automatic transmissions. But the real opportunity had come with his acceptance as the first chair violin for the company symphony.

Just as his son Vern had a natural talent at dancing, so had Harry a natural talent for music. Harry had been introduced to the violin at age six by his father, an Irish mill worker who played jigs passed down by several generations. Harry's talent consisted of more than the mechanical mastery of the fingering and note reading. He expressed himself emotionally through his playing. His interpretation was more original and heartfelt.

The standing ovation he received from the symphony audition committee was completely deserved, though Harry secretly felt he had more of an edge than the other players. The day of the audition, Harry had opened the bottom drawer in the oak chest of drawers in the bedroom and pulled out a small wooden box and unlocked the clasp. Inside, wrapped in a dark piece of blue velvet, was a necklace made of thin leather with a chicken wishbone suspended at the center. He opened the cloth and glanced at the small, delicate bone before wrapping it back up and placing it in his violin case. Just before the audition, he had put the necklace on and tucked the wishbone safely inside his shirt. It was this, he felt, that gave him the lucky edge to win.

* * *

It was late summer, and Walter and Vern were about to begin high school. Harry knew that it was time for him to pass on the necklace to one of his sons. When he was sixteen and living in rural Michigan, his father had given him the necklace after a long explanation of its origins. Harry was told to wear the necklace only on important occasions. It didn't grant special "wishes," as many liked to believe it did, but the necklace provided a lucky edge, or a piece of insight, that could give the wearer an advantage.

The evening sun was setting, and after dinner, Harry asked Vern to join him in the backyard for a talk. Ada and Walter looked at each other wondering what this could be about. Vern was a little worried. Had he done something wrong? Normally, Harry was very straightforward and direct with his thoughts and opinions. It was not like him to call for a special and private conversation.

Next to the pergola of grapes was a small chicken coop that provided eggs for the family. A small copper windmill perched on the roof peak was spinning slowly in the warm evening breeze. Harry sat on the handmade oak bench, watching his son walk slowly through the grass with his head down.

"Vern, I want to talk with you about something that has been passed down in my family for a few generations, something I want to pass on to you now. But it requires an explanation."

Vern was relieved at his father's tone. "What is it, Dad?"

"It's a necklace that was made from the breastbone of a male chicken, or rooster. Some people call it a wishbone, but this bone is a little different. My father's father made it years ago and coated the wishbone with shellac to preserve the structure. My father gave it to me when I was sixteen and told me to pass it on someday. Today is that day."

Vern reached out with his delicate hand as his father handed him a piece of dark blue velvet containing the leather-strapped necklace. He folded back the cloth and saw a thin piece of dark rawhide connected to a small bone by way of a brass ring.

"Why are you giving this to me?" Vern asked.

"Walter is interested in mechanical things. He likes athletics and the engineering aspects of life, but you are more interested in the arts and issues of the heart."

"Does it have a purpose, or meaning?"

Harry had rehearsed this conversation for years. There were times when he was alone on the beach and he would wear the necklace, devising the words and explanation for this event.

"My father told me the story just as his father told him. There was an unusual thunderstorm that rolled in after a scorching hot summer day. The lightning strikes on this small rural farm were continuous. Suddenly, several bolts of lightning converged on a small wooden chicken coop. The sound vibrated the ground for miles. There was a huge charge of electricity that consumed the small coop, and everything in it, except for this one bird that was airborne at the time and so was saved from the massive surge of high voltage. All in all, twelve chickens died, both hens and roosters, except for this one light golden-brown rooster who was shocked off its perch and suspended in flight, escaping the jolts of electricity. The storm raged on, and finally, when the clouds cleared, the family members emerged from their storm cellar to see fences moved, a farm wagon on its side, windows missing in the farmhouse, and the entire farmyard in disarray. One cow had been thrown nearly a quarter of a mile. When my grandfather saw the chicken coop, he couldn't believe the destruction. It had suffered multiple strikes of lightning. But as he stood amidst the debris, this one surviving chicken walked out through the coop's square opening... alone. There were no sounds coming from the usually noisy coop, and when he opened the door, the birds lay strewn on their sides, not moving."

"That's unbelievable, Dad," Vern said, his eyes shining with excitement. "Then what?"

"My grandfather thought there was something special about this bird. It may have been the color of its feathers, but most everyone knew it was because the chicken had survived the lightning strikes. He kept the bird alive to a ripe old age, and when the chicken finally passed on, he kept the breastbone on a piece of leather around his neck. Before my father was seventeen, he told him the story and implied there was something protective about wearing the necklace. My father kept it in his chest of drawers until I was about your age, and sat me down, told me this story, and gave the necklace to me."

"Did you ever use the necklace?"

"A few times. I wore it when I asked your mother to marry me. Your mom laughed when I wore it under my shirt before a formal performance, but it seemed to give me a feeling, something I can't describe," said Harry, looking carefully into Vern's eyes. "I want you to have this."

"What should I do with it? asked Vern, holding the velvet cloth in his lap. He held up the necklace and looked closely at the small, delicate bone. There was something beautiful about its design, a perfect arch, like a church lintel.

"That's up to you," said Harry. "You can try it out at times that seem important to you. The original idea was that it was protective, but there is a poem by Robert Frost called 'The Road Not Taken.' Two roads diverge in a wood. The poet took the road less traveled, and that made all the difference. So maybe it can be used to help you choose the right road. I don't really know, but I may need to borrow it sometime, if you don't mind. Is that OK?"

"Of course. Should I tell anyone?"

"I didn't share this with anyone, not even your mother, but that's up to you. She knows I have the necklace, and she thinks it's just something I wear for good luck. I just leave it at that. But it's yours now, your decision."

* * *

The boys had entered Centerline High School, and although they were very close siblings, their interests were very different. Walter was involved with sports, on the track team, and liked his math and science classes, while Vern took music, theater, and sang in the school choir. There were dances at the high school once a month, but he was shy and not yet sure of himself.

Vern practiced steps and moves to *The Big Band Show* sounds on the family radio. These bands had a jump beat. Tommy Dorsey, Woody Herman, and Glen Gray were the headliners in the big cities like Detroit and Chicago. Vern tuned the radio to shows that highlighted this new music.

He had traveled to Palmer Park with a friend's family for a picnic and by chance visited the pavilion. A band was performing the new jump music they called "swing," and he was beside himself. He was so excited he jumped the gate, slipped onto the floor, and danced with a girl he didn't even know, imitating the steps as he saw them. For Vern, it was as natural as walking. This experience launched a love that was already inside him, and occupied his thoughts night and day.

Vern memorized the steps he saw that night, and when at home, he cleared away the rugs in the living room and waited by the radio for *The Big Band Show*. All his life he had seen his parents practice their instruments, so the model for practice was something he knew. A subtler feel than the earlier forms of jazz distinguished the swing music. Harry told him they were putting the emphasis on the two and four beats, not the first beat.

"Vern, the family has been invited to a GM picnic at Walled Lake Casino next Saturday. Are you interested?"

Vern kept reading his English workbook, ignoring his mother's question.

She continued, "I heard Benny Goodman's orchestra will be playing. Does that ring a bell?"

Vern fell off the couch, slipped on the rug, and fell again on his way to the kitchen. "Are you kidding? Benny Goodman's big band? I'm definitely in."

While at Walled Lake Casino, Vern first saw the Lindy Hop backed up by the music of Benny Goodman playing "Stompin' at the Savoy." He was so excited he tried to teach his mom how to swing dance right there on the grass. Ada did her best, as she could see the enthusiasm in Vern's eyes. To learn all the moves of this new swing dancing became an obsession for him, and it was now clear what he needed: a partner.

* * *

Roxanne lived at the end of Hill Street, and she sat at the desk behind him in homeroom. She was the only girl Vern knew well enough to ask to dance. He had seen her dancing with her friends in the cafeteria. He wanted to jump in, but it was an all-girl thing as they danced to "In the Mood" played back on a 78-rpm record player. Vern watched the group dance and noticed carefully how Roxanne moved her hands, two fingers up high, swaying back and forth. She wore a pink sweater, a dark navy skirt, white saddle shoes, and pink socks. Her dark hair was held back with barrettes, and she wore a touch of lipstick and rouge. Vern could hardly stand still as he watched them dance. *She has to dance with me,* he thought. *She's my partner.*

* * *

Everyone was absolutely silent while Miss Murphy took attendance in homeroom, passed out emergency contact cards, and gave the morning announcements. After she finished, the students had ten minutes of free time before the first bell. Vern turned around and spoke softly to Roxanne as she worked on some homework.

"Hey, there's a dance this Friday night. Would you be interested in going together and doing some swing dancing?"

Roxanne continued with her homework and refused to make eye contact with Vern. Although she was extroverted on the dance floor, she was otherwise shy and quiet. She was completely caught off guard and needed some time to digest what was being proposed. Vern stepped up the pitch with some flattery and enthusiasm.

"I saw you dancing in the cafeteria the other day. You were great, and I think we would dance well together. What do you think?"

"My mom doesn't let me date yet, and besides, I don't really know you, Vern."

"It wouldn't really be a date, just dancing. We could practice."

"Practice? Where?"

"At my house, I guess. I live pretty close by, on Hill Street. I already practice to *The Big Band Show.* It's on at seven p.m. this Wednesday. I think you'd love it. I have some new Lindy moves," said Vern with an intoxicating smile and confidence that took Roxanne by surprise.

"Let me think about it. I'll let you know, OK?"

"You'll love this, Roxanne." The bell rang, and Vern was up and gone.

Roxanne sat in her chair in a daze. *He is cute*, she thought. *I wonder if he can dance?*

Roxanne and her best friend, Lynette, walked to their first class together. Lynette noticed Roxanne was in her own world. "What happened to you? Hello? Anyone home in there?"

Roxanne blushed. "I'm here, I guess. You know that guy who sits in front of me in homeroom? He just asked me on a date. I'm not even allowed to date yet, but I don't know. There's something about him."

Vern had never even thought about dating. He didn't even think about girls that much. All he could think about was dancing, and he knew Roxanne was the one he wanted to dance with. From the moment he saw her dancing, he knew she was the perfect partner. He grabbed his books from his locker and quickly navigated the crowded hall to his next class. *She'll say yes. She has to*, he thought.

* * *

As a tool and die maker, Harry was required to visit the production plant once a month and monitor the lathes and drill presses that used his measurements and configurations. For him, it was a ten-block walk to the GM facility that occupied twenty acres on the Eight Mile divide between Detroit and Centerline. A small portion of the complex, Plant Two, was separated from the main plant structures by railroad tracks. An underground tunnel ran under the tracks and connected the two areas. Harry never liked walking through this area. He was claustrophobic as a child, and even now, being closed in was very uncomfortable, especially if he was alone.

The rail access was important in that it allowed hundreds of boxcars to load door assemblies, stampings, tires from Goodyear, and wheels from the Budd Corporation. Harry showed his ID at the gate before passing drums of paint from Ditzler, sealers, glass, and coke to feed the gigantic boiler in the powerhouse. As he walked toward the plant, he could see finished cars being loaded on the haulaway trucks to be driven to the Great Lakes freighters on the nearby Detroit River.

Just as he entered Plant Two, he saw a worker walking counter-clockwise around a large steel lathe. *That's odd*, Harry thought. *Why is he doing that?* He watched from a distance as the man repeated the circular walk again and again. Harry had arrived early and had some extra time.

"Hello," Harry said. "How are you?"

The man was dressed in the standard gray overalls, which were open at the chest, disclosing a white T-shirt. He was wearing a set of heavy plastic work glasses, black work boots, and a gray cap that sat on the back of his head. Harry noticed a reverse swastika tattooed to his arm.

With a strong European accent, the man replied, "I good. Help you?"

"I was just wondering why you were walking around the lathe."

"It's a *withershin*. Lathe bad today. I walk around wrong way, fix problem," said the man in broken English, finally making some eye contact with Harry.

"Really? Have you thought about contacting the foreman?"

"I try this first, from Old Country. If it not work, I put in work order. Thank you."

"Good luck," said Harry.

As he moved on toward his plant, he glanced back and waved. The worker did another rotation, and Harry heard the lathe start up. It sounded like a sewing machine. He stopped and looked once again at the worker. Their eyes met, and the man put his hands up into the air as if to say, *Who knows what makes these machines work properly?* Harry scratched his head and continued on his way.

Chip turnings and debris from the machine shop littered the floor, along with cutting fluids and a fine black sand. Finally, he reached the heat treatment area where they tooled the transmission gears and rocker shafts for the V-8 engine. He signed in at the small office and talked to the supervisor about checking the tolerances on the new high-speed fastener lathe.

* * *

It was at school during lunch when Vern again approached Roxanne in the cafeteria. She noticed his white flannel shirt and dark pleated pants with approval. He was nice looking, or maybe it was just his hair. He had gorgeous long, dark hair that was combed back and high on his head. When Vern spoke, he looked into her eyes.

"Just walk home with me tomorrow. Let's just give it a try. You'll never be the same."

Roxanne laughed. *What is with this guy?* she thought. "OK. I'll try it, but I'm not promising anything."

The walk home was about a mile, and the students walked together in groups. Books in tow, Vern and Walter walked with the two boys who lived next door, and Roxanne walked with her best friends, but by the time they all got to Hill Street, there were only a few left. As soon as Lynette left the group, Vern caught up with Roxanne. This would be their first practice, the first time they ever danced together. Vern had prepared his mom for the practice, and Ada was waiting in the front yard, pruning some flowers, when they walked up.

"Hello. You must be Roxanne. Vern mentioned you might stop by. Come on in."

Walter headed upstairs to his bedroom, and Vern asked Roxanne to sit down while his mother got them a snack. The living room was warmly decorated with a stained glass lamp, some Persian throw rugs, a large stand-up RCA radio console, and a piano. The windows were adorned with fresh flowers, and an oil painting depicting a Southwest landscape hung over the couch. It was the home of a family that surrounded themselves with culture. Family pictures were framed, and a watercolor that had been a wedding gift stood out next to the piano. Vern opened up the top of radio console and warmed up the record player. Ada brought in a tray of grapes, crackers, and lemonade. Roxanne sat on a soft, plush overstuffed chair, taking it all in.

"Where do you live?" asked Ada.

"Just down the street, at the corner of Hill and Conner. We live in the white house with the big pine trees. Your home is beautiful. Does someone play the piano?"

"I play, and Harry, Vern's father, he can play a little, but he's a violinist. We used to play together at events before we were married, but he works at GM now, and I take care of things here. Do you dance?"

"Well, I like dancing, and…"

"Speaking of dancing, let's try this," said Vern enthusiastically as he pulled a 78 record out of its paper sleeve. "It's called the 'Jumpin' Jive.'"

Vern rolled back the rugs and moved the coffee table to the wall to make room. From the moment they stood up, clasped hands, and started with a simple shuffle, they were like two peas in a pod. The more they danced, the more they laughed. Vern had all the moves, and Roxanne picked them up quickly, adding a few of her own. Simply said, they could swing.

Ada had been watching them practice with delight for more than an hour, when Harry came home from work and walked into the living room. He sat down to watch, reserved at first, but unable to resist the excitement finally. It was contagious. He had thought this new big band sound was a passing fad, especially compared to his world of Mozart and Beethoven.

To the music of Cab Calloway, the two young kids started to match their moves identically with an intuition that seem to compound itself. He held her close as they matched steps, then slipped sideways with a jump, then came face-to-face with palms flat against each other's. It was so intoxicating. Harry and Ada laughed. By then, Walter sat on the top step of the stairway in total amazement. This first practice on that warm September afternoon would live in the hearts of everyone present for a long time to come.

Vern and Roxanne practiced once a week. Usually after school, on the way home, she would stop over for maybe an hour. Ada always had a snack for them, and having her there made it easy for Roxanne. She liked Ada, and if the truth be known, she wanted to dance as much as Vern. Before this, she had only danced with her girlfriends for fun, but this guy Vern, he was something else.

Centerline High School had dances on Friday nights, once a month, to raise money for the student council. The dance started at 8:00 p.m. and finished by 10:30. The students running the dance placed the microphone in front of the record player and projected the 78-rpm records over the public address system. Vern and Roxanne arrived separately just before eight and kept an eye on each other through the first two songs, ballads by Kay Starr and Duke Ellington. Vern was sitting on a wooden bench along the side of the gymnasium, waiting nervously with anticipation, when he heard "One O'Clock Jump" come over the speakers. Roxanne knew he would ask her to dance, and she could not wait. This would come as a surprise to all her friends. She had not shared a peep with anyone. Everyone noticed as Vern walked up to Roxanne, who stood with a group of her girlfriends.

"May I have this dance?"

"Well, I guess so," she said, trying to act surprised.

Her friends tightened up the huddle with their eyes pinned to the couple. They had no idea they even knew each other. *Where did this guy Vern come from?*

Their first steps were in close, hand in hand, a shuffle two-step to the beat, and then within a minute or two, they broke into a Lindy Hop jump step with a swing move no one had ever seen. Within seconds, a small circle formed around the couple, and everyone watched. The audience fueled their excitement as they held one hand, sometimes no hands, and displayed the routines they had practiced. The circle got bigger as the couple introduced the jitterbug to half the student body. It was like magic. Girls started to imitate Roxanne from the sidelines, and a few boys matched Vern's moves. When Roxanne left to use the bathroom and get a drink of water, four girls lined up to ask him to dance. The DJ spinning the 78s stayed with big band swing the rest of the night, and the gymnasium was electrified.

"Well that's about it for tonight. And what a night!" the DJ said. "We have to thank Vern and Roxanne for the new dance steps. I think everyone knows what I'm talking about. See you all next month."

It was the beginning of a new era, and everyone was talking, including the chaperones. Vern and Roxanne became the talk of the school, and their popularity changed overnight. When Vern came home, his mother stayed up to hear about the dance.

"How did the dance go?" asked Ada.

"It was amazing, Mom. We got the whole school into swing dancing. It was unbelievable. It spread like wildfire, and by the time the dance ended, the floor was full of jitterbugs."

"How did Roxanne do?"

"She was fantastic. Better than ever. When we moved into our Lindy Hop routine, they went wild. Didn't they, Walt?"

"You wouldn't have believed it. Vern was spectacular! They formed this circle that kept getting bigger and bigger around them. Even the teachers were watching."

"Did you dance with anyone else?" asked Ada.

"A little. Not much. Roxanne took a break for a few minutes, and all these girls wanted to dance. I was sweating so much, my shirt's still damp. It was incredible."

Ada was so happy for Vern. She had known for a long time that he had a special gift for rhythm, but she was never sure how it would display itself. Now she knew, and she could not wait to tell Harry, but it would have to wait until morning.

The family did not have a chance to come together until lunch the next day, when Harry opened the conversation.

"Your mom said you had a great time last night."

"The crowd went wild. They loved the swing dancing."

"What do you mean?" asked Harry.

"It was like nobody had ever seen swing. Or sometimes they call it jitterbug."

"That sounds like a fish lure," said Harry.

Walter could hardly hold back and finally stood up. "Dad, everyone in the whole gym went wild. Everyone at practice today was talking about it. They were all saying that Vern and Roxanne transformed the dance floor. It was like they were a match that lit a bonfire."

Ada was so happy to hear Walt talk about his brother. Up until now, it was Walt who got all the attention from his accomplishments on the various sport teams, but his comments were heartfelt. He was proud of Vern.

Never sure how his father would respond, Vern said, "We never expected that kind of reaction. It was a really incredible experience."

"Well, it's not my music, but I'm happy for you. What's next?"

Ada grabbed the newspaper and said, "Did you see this?. It's about a dance contest coming to Detroit. Maybe that's what's next."

After the dance that night, Roxanne had left with her friends in a rush as they all piled into a car belonging to one of the girl's parents, while Vern, Walt, and some friends walked home. There wasn't any time for them to talk with each other about what had happened. The weekend was a busy time for both families, and it wasn't until late Sunday afternoon that Vern started to think about Roxanne. Since her house was only about four blocks away, Vern decided to take a walk. Hill Street was a narrow gravel road that had not yet been paved and lacked sidewalks. Many of the homes were recently built, and hardwood trees spotted the landscape.

The sun was low in the west as he walked along, kicking stones, wondering if she would be home. He could see large pines swaying in the breeze as he approached the white house. He hoped there would be someone outside so he could appear to be stopping by casually. No such luck. He walked up to the door and knocked. A tall woman with dark hair and striking features came to the door.

"Can I help you?"

"Is Roxanne home? She's not expecting me. I'm a friend from school," Vern said with all the respect and dignity he could muster.

"I'll see if she's here. What's your name?"

"I'm Vern. How do you do, ma'am?"

"So *you're* Vern. We've heard a lot about you. Just a minute." The woman turned back into the house and called Roxanne's name repeatedly.

Vern sat down in the middle of the front porch steps and waited for what seemed like forever. Roxanne finally came out dressed in khaki shorts and a white blouse. Her hair was pulled back in a ponytail, and she was barefoot. She sat down one step above him and rested her leg lightly against his arm.

"What's going on?"

"We didn't get a chance to say much the other night. I was wondering what you thought of the dance?"

Roxanne laughed. She put her hand on Vern's head and ran her fingers through his thick hair.

"It was great. I had so much fun. Who would have thought?"

* * *

Although Ada was a trained musician, she also had a talent for sewing. She could recycle clothes, often expensive clothing, from the Salvation

212

Army. She made all of Walt and Vern's school clothes, and now she was working on some dance clothing for Vern. She would take a pair of used suit trousers, add pleats, and taper the leg. Sometimes she would find a dressy silk shirt that she could tailor to fit Vern. They used photos from *True Confessions* to find ideas and designs. Before long, she was making clothes for Roxanne. There was a dance competition scheduled at the high school, and Ada thought it would be special if they wore outfits that matched.

Vern and Roxanne had become close friends, and continued to practice as they prepared for the school's first dance contest. First prize was twenty-five dollars, and by now, the school had at least ten couples who were practicing their swing dancing on a regular basis. The school was abuzz with the new music and the new swing dancing. This new generation had something that was their own, a music and dance that differed greatly from their parents'.

Vern was saving his money for a pair of white-and-black wing tip shoes. He considered wearing the necklace his father had given him, but decided it was not yet the time or place to experiment. Ada had made Roxanne a short pleated skirt and a black-and-white striped blouse. The dance was that Friday, and everyone was excited. Many students and faculty planned to be there.

This time, Roxanne's father drove Vern and Roxanne to the dance.

"Are you ready for this?" asked Vern.

"I think so. How about you?"

"I just love to dance, so no matter who wins, this will be a blast. I just hope they play some of the music we really like. You look great, by the way."

The high school auditorium was decorated with posters of big band names, and streamers. One of the parents, who owned a club in Detroit, had donated a mirror ball for the evening. That, combined with a high-intensity spotlight, would spin a thousand points of light around the space. The DJ had just updated the record collection and planned to introduce some recently released music by Glen Miller.

Vern and Roxanne made their way to the registration table. Each participant in the competition was given a square board with a number attached by a string that went around their necks. Vern and Roxanne had drawn number seven, which they both felt was a lucky number.

Each team had a rooting section that sat in the bleachers surrounding the basketball court. In the end, there were twenty couples registered. One couple dropped out after extensive practice, while another couple formed spontaneously. Any student could dance, but the judges were watching the couples with numbers.

The dancers took their places. As the mirror ball started to turn, the first tune was "Wholly Cats" by Benny Goodman. An hour flew by as the young dancers gave their all, perspired buckets, and tried to grab a paper cup of water between songs. By ten thirty, there were two couples left. The last song, "Gone with What Wind" by Duke Ellington and Benny Goodman, would determine the winners.

"How do you feel?" Vern asked Roxanne.

"I feel great. Let's just have fun."

The music started, and both couples were in rare form. Vern and Roxanne had saved a couple of new swing moves, just in case they got into the finals. The judges' decision would have been extremely difficult, but for the fact that Roxanne slipped on the shiny wood floor and fell, spraining her foot. She lay on the floor, with Vern next to her on his knees.

"Don't move. Just wait until we get some help. You'll be fine." Vern looked towards the officials for help.

The winners were decided by default, and although there was a celebration, it was not heartfelt. One of the teachers brought out some crutches from the locker room, and Roxanne made her way to the bleachers as her foot continued to swell. Vern sat next to her, watching people congratulate the winning couple, trying to console Roxanne.

"It wasn't important to win," he said soothingly. "It was just important to dance."

"Easy for you to say," Roxanne said, her voice shaking. "I was the one who fell. I'm so sorry."

"Roxanne, dancing with you is my dream. You'll get better, and we'll be out there again in no time."

Roxanne was on crutches for a week. Slowly her foot returned to normal. When Vern's parents offered to pay the registration fee for a dance competition in Detroit at the end of the month, Vern and Roxanne jumped at the chance.

They started to practice, and slowly, Roxanne was back in the swing of things. The afternoon practice sessions at the house brought everyone closer together, and Ada worked hard sewing new costumes. Walt helped Vern pay for the shoes he wanted, and Harry bought some new records for their practice sessions. He pulled Vern aside while handing him the records.

"I'm sorry about what happened at the last dance. Perhaps the lucky necklace has worn out."

Vern lowered his head. "Dad...I didn't wear it. I forgot about it, actually. But you can bet I won't forget it about it next time." Their eyes came together and rested with an unspoken understanding.

Edgewater Park was hosting the big event, and competitors from three counties had entered, including the couple they lost to at the school dance.

The walk home from school was a special time for Vern and Roxanne. They were now a couple and would occasionally hold hands. All their friends understood, and gave them the privacy they sought.

"Vern, this dance competition...do you think we can compete?" asked Roxanne, feeling a little insecure.

"Absolutely. Anyway, it's a chance to dance to a live band. Just think of that and how much fun it will be. And, most important, I'll be with you."

On the way home from school, there was a spot where each went a different way. As they faced each other in the shade from a large chestnut tree that gave them some privacy, they stood close together, talking about the dance competition. Without warning, Roxanne moved up on her toes and kissed Vern on the mouth, their bodies close. It lasted three or four seconds and left lipstick on his lips. It was something he had wanted to do many times, but her initiating it made it special. They looked at each other for a minute without speaking before Roxanne turned and walked away. Vern watched her walk down the long sidewalk toward her house.

* * *

"What's wrong with the coffeepot?" asked Harry.

The secretary looked at him and shrugged her shoulders.

"It died a couple of days ago, and no one has been able to get it to work. You would think with all these engineers, someone could fix it. Why don't you try? I could use a cup right now."

Harry stared at the percolator, scratching his head. He pulled the plug and checked the connection. He looked inside to see if there were any signs of a problem. Everything seemed to be in order. He filled the vessel with cold water, added four tablespoons of coffee grounds to the aluminum strainer, and pressed the On button. The small light did not go on, and missing was the familiar sound of hot water.

"I'll ask the boss to buy a replacement," said the secretary as she looked over at Harry.

The heavyset woman worked for a group of sixty men, handled all the typing, dispensed the mail, and answered the phones. Her desk was a pile of memos so high Harry could only see her head and shoulders.

It seems odd this would just stop working, he thought. Harry started to slowly walk around the appliance in a counterclockwise direction, trying to be as discreet as possible, while keeping his eye on the light. He did this repeatedly. Nothing happened, and he decided to get back to his office, thinking, *What a silly idea*—until he heard a sound. He turned back, and the small red light was on, and a bubbling sound could be heard, reaching out into the office. The secretary was the first to say something.

"What did you do? It's working!"

"Really? What a mystery."

* * *

The day of the dance competition had arrived, and everyone was excited. Ada had worked hard on the new costumes, with little left to do except hem Roxanne's skirt. Vern and Roxanne had practiced whenever possible, while Walt made sure he got all the tickets to the dance competition. Ada walked into the bedroom while Harry stood in front of the mirror. He saw Ada's reflection.

"What are you wearing tonight?" she asked.

"Suit, white shirt, and tie. The usual. I can't believe they scheduled our string ensemble to play at the dinner."

"Who is it for?" asked Ada.

"It's the General Motors executive board dinner. The secretary of transportation arrived this morning from Washington, and he will be attending. At least you and Walt can join me. It's early enough. We should be finished by six thirty. Time enough to get over to the competition."

"It's an honor you were asked. Do you have a solo?" she asked him quietly.

"How did you know?" said Harry, picking up his violin case.

"You must have mentioned it to Vern…He told me."

"I didn't want to make a big deal out of it. They drink a little wine, and I play a little Bach. It's one of my favorites. Toccata and Fugue in D Minor."

The plan was set. Ada and Walt would attend Harry's performance, then catch a bus to the competition. Roxanne's father would take Roxanne and Vern to Edgewater Park and make sure they were there on time.

The gathering outside the pavilion was huge, as people from all parts of the city were attending. Families, friends, and dance enthusiasts gathered for the first event of its kind. Vern could hear the band tuning their instruments as Roxanne held tightly to his arm. As they made their way to the registration desk, they noticed many of the contestants were in their early twenties and thirties. There was a good chance they were one of the youngest couples.

Roxanne held back, her eyes sweeping the crowd nervously.

"Are you OK?" Vern asked, noticing the pale sheen of perspiration on her face.

"Everybody looks so much older. More experienced."

Vern smiled. "Don't think about them. Just think about how much we love to dance. Can you believe we're dancing to a live band? And Benny Goodman at that!"

They stood in line, waiting to register, until they got to the desk where a young lady sat issuing the numbers.

"What number would you like?" she asked. "We're letting contestants pick their own number, as long as it isn't taken."

Vern looked at Roxanne and shrugged his shoulders. Roxanne thought for a moment and said. "Is number seven available?"

"Yes. Is that what you'd like?"

"Sure," said Vern.

The girl handed the number to a young man working a machine that they had never seen. He punched in the numeral, pulled down on a large lever, and produced a square card with the number seven in the center. It looked so professional. There were small lines around the edge of the sign.

"What are the lines for?" asked Vern.

"They're for signatures afterward. You can keep the cards as a souvenir."

* * *

Harry was dressed and ready, waiting for Ada to put on her makeup, and Walt was waiting in the living room. It was late afternoon, and after a walk to the end of Hill Street, all three caught the bus to Grand River Boulevard. Ada kept thinking about Vern and Roxanne. *I hope the costumes hold together. I hope they're all right.*

There were thirty-six couples who had qualified for the competition, and the card numbers ranged from one to thirty-six. Couples of diverse race and age had gathered to dance to one of the most popular bandleaders in the country. The band played a light ballad in the background as the announcer gave instructions.

"In the competition tonight, there are two divisions: junior and youth. The band will perform three songs, and then there will be a break. The judges will eliminate half the field, and then the band will resume with two songs. After the second break, the judges will eliminate all but two couples left in each division. There will be one final song to determine the winners. Dancers, are you ready? Let's begin."

Vern and Roxanne took the floor in the large open-air pavilion with a band shell on the north side. Small lights were strung everywhere, and hundreds of spectators filled the bleachers. Many came just to hear the famous bandleader. The first song was "Bugle Call Rag," a favorite of Vern's. Roxanne had noticed where the judges were sitting and made sure they worked their way over to that area. On the other side of the floor, Vern noticed the competitors from their high school dressed in dark-blue outfits. He caught the couple's eye for a moment and gave them the thumbs-up. Vern wished everyone could win. He just loved to dance. Roxanne seemed at her best, and they made the first cut after the third song. Resting against the side rail, Vern put his arm around Roxanne as they shared a cup of water.

"Roxanne you were great out there, not to mention you look beautiful. And I love you."

* * *

When they arrived at the Fisher Theater, Harry made sure Ada and Walt had their seats, and then he quickly walked to the dressing room. When he opened the violin case, there was a note lying over the blue velvet cloth.

Dear Dad,
I know this performance is important to you, and the necklace will help you with your solo. Don't worry about us and the dance competition. We'll do just fine. Hope to see you there later.
Love, Vern

The string ensemble's performance started running late, and Ada decided she and Walt should slip out and catch a bus. Harry caught their exit from the corner of his eye, glanced at his watch, and felt the perspiration on his neck. With dinner starting late, and the remarks running over, there was a chance he would not make the competition.

* * *

More people had gathered at the Edgewater Park pavilion as they got closer to the final rounds. The other couple from Centerline High had been eliminated in the second round, but stayed to see the final winners. The band needed a longer break, and Vern kept his eye on Mr. Goodman, who stood talking to one of the band musicians.

Vern grabbed a pen and walked up to the band shell with Roxanne in tow. "Excuse me, Mr. Goodman. Would you mind signing our cards?" he asked.

Benny Goodman turned and looked at the two dancers, their clothing clinging to their thin bodies, and laughed. "Sure! Give me your pen and turn around."

Bending over, using their backs as a tabletop, Benny Goodman signed both dance cards and wished them luck.

"Seven? Sounds like a good number to me."

* * *

The last four couples waited nervously for the band members to find their seats. Vern and Roxanne were competing against a couple from the affluent Grosse Pointe High who were, from what they'd seen earlier, really good. Their outfits were coordinated in satin green, and they both wore white saddle shoes. By now, each couple had a cheering section that yelled out the numbers of their favored dancers. The standing crowd was jammed together like sardines, and each person was standing on their toes to view the competition.

Harry managed to hail a cab, but remained frantic as traffic choked the route. He didn't see how he could possibly get to the pavilion and get his son's attention. As the cab arrived and pulled up as far as possible, Harry threw a large bill into the front seat, jumped out, and made his way into a sea of people. Next to him was an unusually large man whose height was about a foot above everyone else. He looked down and spoke to Harry.

"Do you need to get to someone?"

"Yes! My son…he's one of the finalists."

"Hold on to the back of my belt. I'll get you there. Excuse me…" The booming voice scared most people as the huge man made his way through the crowd with Harry in tow.

Once he'd finally got next to the rail, Harry yelled out, "Roxanne!"

Roxanne heard the voice first and saw Harry's arm extended over the rail, the necklace dangling from his fingers. She bolted to the rail, swept up the necklace, got back to Vern, who wondered where his partner had gone, and slipped the leather around his neck. The band turned up the volume and started playing the final song, "One O'Clock Jump," which was one of the top songs in the country at that moment. The crowd bellowed its approval.

All the dancers in the finals were good and had something special, but Vern had been holding out. His plan all along was to hold back a move, something new the judges hadn't seen. It was even something Roxanne hadn't seen. About three-quarters through the song, at a special moment where they were both stretched out, their hands dropped, and Vern did a full flip in the air and landed without missing a beat. The crowd roared so loud Walt and Ada could hear them from where they were standing. Vern and Roxanne danced their hearts out, and when the song came to an end, the contestants stood in the middle of the floor, out of breath. Everyone could see the judges adding up their scores, until they finally passed the paper to the announcer.

"OK, everyone...quiet down...I am here to announce the winners. In the junior division, it's Jim and Lucille from Beverly Hills. In the youth division..."

Walt and Ada climbed onto a few fifty-gallon drums and held hands as they spotted Vern and Roxanne on the dance floor.

"Vern and Roxanne from Centerline."

The crowd roared louder than before. It shook the pavilion, and the announcer grabbed the rail to balance himself. The band used their instruments to make sounds, and a feeling of tremendous enthusiasm came over the audience. Harry stood next to the railing in shock, but was elated for his son. Vern grabbed Roxanne and spun her around until the pleated skirt did a pirouette, then kissed her for what seem like an eternity. They were the darlings of competition, and by the time this moment came around, they had won over the hearts of everyone. Even Benny Goodman applauded, remembering the couple who had asked for an autograph. Finally, the announcer walked over and handed Vern the envelope. They had completely forgotten about the prize. Vern handed the envelope to Roxanne.

"We won! Do you believe it? We won!"

Hundreds of people flooded the dance floor in search of autographs. Roxanne took a second to pull Vern close and whispered in his ear, "I love you, Vern. I'll never forget this."

By the time Harry and Ada reconnected and made their way to the pavilion, the crowd was beginning to disperse. Vern spotted his father helping his mother up the stairway next to the band shell. He ran to them and embraced them.

"I love you guys...and thanks...thanks for everything!"

Roxanne's parents had also been buried in the crowd and finally made their way onto the floor to embrace their daughter. Walt was busy telling anyone who would listen that the winner was his brother, Vern. It was a time for celebration, and everyone loaded into Roxanne's family's station wagon and headed for the most expensive restaurant they could find.

The days that followed were wonderful, including the arrival of photos that had been taken at the event with Benny Goodman, a trip to the bank to put the money into their savings accounts, and some special recognition at school. Neither family had experienced anything quite like this. Walt made jokes at dinner that Vern was now a "dance star." Ada and Harry were proud of their son and his commitment to something he wanted. Roxanne became one of the most popular girls in school, and her family continued to celebrate for days.

One evening, later that week, Vern stood alone in his bedroom. He had wrapped the necklace back in the blue velvet cloth and placed it in his drawer for safekeeping, thinking about what he would tell his son someday.

Mont-Saint-Michel

Although Tristan was only twelve years old, he was just tall enough to see over the stone turret wall and watch the sun set on the horizon of the Atlantic Ocean. He had just left his duties as an altar boy, where he had said an extra prayer for Bishop Gabriel LeFore. The bishop's health was failing. He had just turned eighty years old and had recently suffered several stokes.

The Monastic Community of Jerusalem monks and Sisters had raised Tristan in the monastery after finding him in a pew as an infant. There had been a note pinned to the infant's clothing from his father, explaining that the mother had died giving birth to twins, one of which had died with the mother. The father had taken ill and had no knowledge or means to raise a baby boy. Although they searched the island village that surrounded the abbey, and the nearby town of Avranches, there was no sign of the father. It was left to the clergy to raise the angelic boy. At twelve now, the boy's hair was long and glossy black and framed the child's somewhat delicate face.

Mont-Saint-Michel was built on a natural granite island nearly a kilometer out into the bay, where the Couesnon River emptied into the ocean. The tidal island was home to a medieval monastery, the beginnings of which could be traced back to the eighth century. It was the Romano-Breton culture that had begun building the structure when, as the story goes, the Archangel Michael appeared to St. Aubert and instructed the bishop to build a church on the rocky island off the coast of Normandy, France.

A warm summer wind came off the water, causing him to keep a hand on his hat for fear of losing it as he walked up behind Tristan and placed his hand on his shoulder. Father Bernard was dressed in his all-black tunic.

"Am I disturbing you, Tristan? The view is always breathtaking, isn't it?"

"No, Father. I often come here to pray for the bishop."

"I am afraid his time with us is short. I'll have to take him to the hospital on the mainland if he doesn't improve."

Father Bernard was the abbot of the monastery, and although it was the bishop who had given the boy his name and had once assumed most of the responsibilities for raising Tristan, it was Father Bernard who now looked after the boy, who slept on a small cot in the father's room. He was schooled and cared for by the abbey community.

Growing up, Tristan had had an extraordinary education. It was as if all the Sisters were his mother, and all the monks his father. They each had their own body of knowledge they wanted to pass on to him. Tristan was fluent in Latin, proficient in advanced mathematics, could cook and sew, and raised falcons that soared high above the abbey steeple. Tristan was taught to play the piano by Sister Mary from an early age, and Friar Thomas taught him how to sail in the bay. He was much loved in the small, tight-knit Catholic community of Mont-Saint-Michel.

"If you will excuse me, I need to return to my chores, Father."

"Be on your way, my son."

Tristan had a rigorous schedule, beginning in the early morning with Mass, followed by kitchen duties, studies during the day, afternoon cleaning, late-afternoon Mass, and kitchen cleanup after supper.

When he was sweeping the upper chamber hallway that afternoon, he noticed a large stone block slightly recessed into the wall. It seemed odd. He had cleaned the hallway once a week for more than a year and had never noticed the recessed block in the wall. He propped his broom against the wall and got down on his knees to investigate. When he touched the rectangular stone, it moved inward with ease, as if it were gliding on a friction-free surface. He pushed again, and the block moved farther back into the opening that now cast light into a rectangular space. When Tristan pushed his head through the opening, he could see that the open chamber led to a room that was lit with natural light. The opening he had created was easily large enough for his whole body to pass through. Without hesitation, he entered the space.

He found himself in an eight-by-twelve-foot room lit by a single window made of beveled leaded glass. Tristan looked around. There was no doorway. Perhaps it had been mistakenly covered over during some remodeling construction.

His thoughts were suddenly disrupted by what he could only describe as a presence. He had never experienced anything like it. He was relaxed in a way that reminded him of prayer or meditation, only much deeper and more welcoming. It felt like an extrasensory perception that was reaching out to comfort him.

"Welcome, Tristan. I have been waiting for you."

Tristan turned around to find the source of the voice, only to realize that it had seemed to come from inside his head.

He stood quietly for several minutes, waiting to see if he heard the voice again, but nothing happened. Eventually he got down on his belly and crawled back into the hallway. By the time he stood up and dusted himself off, the large stone was back in place as if it had never moved. His broom and dustpan were right were he'd left them. Tristan shook his head and continued on with his duties. Still, he could not wait to find Father Bernard and tell him of his experience. Surely, he would know of the room.

* * *

The dining hall was an open space, with long tables made of oak with benches attached. Meals were served cafeteria style. The Sisters went first, followed by the monks and then the priests. Stained glass windows and frescoes that glorified the saints and their famous acts of sacrifice illuminated the room.

Tristan was late, but as soon as he entered the room, he looked for Father Bernard, who was deep in conversation with several friars. After Tristan filled his tray, he made a beeline to Father Bernard's table. He began to eat, waiting patiently for an opportunity to tell his story. But the conversation was focused heatedly on the French government, which had threatened to raise taxes on the monastery holdings.

"I don't understand how they can arbitrarily raise these taxes, especially on churches that have very little income. We barely make ends meet as it is, and with our bishop in poor health, there is very little we can do," Father Bernard concluded as he picked up his tray and headed off toward the busing station.

"Father!" said Tristan, running to catch up. "Can I speak to you?"

"What is it, Tristan? Nothing about the tax debt, I hope?"

"No, Father. It's just…something happened today. I would like to tell you about it."

"Something's always happening to twelve-year-old boys. That's what we love about you." Father Bernard noticed the frown on the boy's face and relented. "Sorry, I'm teasing. What happened today?"

"I was cleaning in the upper hallway, and I saw a block in the wall that opened onto a secret room. I'm sure you know about it, right?"

"There aren't any secret rooms that I know about. But come. Show me the place."

Father Bernard followed Tristan to the second floor, where the balconies to the abbey connected together via a hallway. When they approached the spot where Tristan was earlier, he pointed to the block beside his broom and dustpan, which he'd left as a marker.

"It was that block, Father. It moves inward and opens onto a small room behind the wall. I'll show you."

Tristan got down on his knees and pushed at the block with his finger. When nothing happened, he applied pressure with his whole hand, but the block didn't budge. Once again, he pushed harder with all his strength, but the large stone block remained in place.

Tristan sat back on his heels and scratched his head. "All I did was touch it with my fingertip before, and it moved easily. Honest, Father. It moved inward, and I crawled into a small secret room. Now, it's not moving at all."

Father Bernard cleared his throat. "This wall was constructed of limestone in the thirteenth century, Tristan. Each block is two by three by four feet and had to be levered into place by many strong men." He cleared his throat again. "Sister Juliana tells me you are very creative. There are times when we confuse our imaginations with reality. But don't let it bother you. It's normal for a boy your age. Are you OK with that?"

Tristan blinked rapidly several times, and his face turned deep red. "Yes, Father."

Father Bernard patting the boy on the head. "I need to be off and give the bishop his medicine. Don't forget to return that broom and dustpan and tend to your kitchen chores."

Tristan did not even get a chance to explain what happened in the room. It probably would have diminished his credibility even further. Still, he thought, *I know what happened today. But since I can't prove it, it's probably better to let it go, at least for now.*

* * *

Bishop LeFore had been hospitalized twice in recent months and was now slipping in and out of consciousness when Father Bernard got to his room, where two Sisters kneeled beside the bed, praying the rosary.

"How is he doing?" he whispered.

"I am afraid he is preparing for his last journey, Father," Sister Mary said. "His breathing has become weak, and he has a slight temperature."

Father Bernard touched the bishop's hand. "Bishop, can you hear me? I am going to take you to the hospital."

The bishop regained consciousness momentarily and looked at him. "As you wish, Father. I am ready to give myself to the kingdom of God."

* * *

Bishop Gabriel LeFore had been assigned to Mont-Saint-Michel twelve years earlier after serving ten years in Paris at the thirteenth-century Gothic cathedral of Sainte-Chapelle. He had worked hard at bringing together the diverse neighborhoods of Île de la Cité,which defined the medieval borders of early Paris. He had just moved into his new home when, on a wet, chilly morning, one of the Sisters came to him with a car seat wrapped in a blanket.

"Your Excellency, I found this in one of the pews this morning when I was setting up for Mass. It's a baby boy. This envelope was inside the seat."

The bishop was not amused. He peeked briefly under the blanket, where he saw a baby boy who was less than six weeks old, sleeping with a pacifier still in his mouth. He took the envelope and opened it.

>*Dear Bishop LeFore,*
>
>*My sister died giving birth to twins, and only this baby boy survived. She and the other twin died during childbirth and are now in heaven. I named this little boy Tristan. I have found myself unable to raise and provide for him, so I leave him in your care. I pray that you find a good Catholic home for him.*
>
>*In God I trust.*
>*Jerome Felur*

The bishop sat down and placed his hands over his face and did not speak for some time. Finally, he turned to the Sister and said, "People cannot just abandon their children. I want you to try to find the child's uncle or, better yet, his father. Search the village and nearby towns. Get help if you need it. Here is the note with the uncle's name."

"Yes, Your Excellency. As you wish."

The Sister picked up the car seat and was headed toward the door when the Bishop added, "You might also inquire as to who would want to adopt a child. Do you understand?"

"Yes, Your Excellency."

With the help of several monks and Sisters, they scoured the village and nearby towns, but no one had heard of the man or his sister and her twins. They could only assume the family lived in rural Servonor Beauvoir. They posted a notice in the local papers asking the father to collect his child, promising the church would help with his financial condition. After two weeks without finding a place for the child, LeFore called his most senior priest, Father Bernard, to his chamber.

"Father, as you probably know, we have had a child here whose family we have been unable to find. I would like for you to care for the baby until we can find an adoption service that will take him and find a suitable home. The closest one I know of is in Paris, so this could take a while. Do you understand?"

"Yes, Your Excellency. We need to baptize the baby. Is there a name you suggest?"

"Baptize him Tristan LeFore until we find someone, and Father Bernard, can you find some space in your room for his crib?"

"But Your Excellency, don't you think a Sister would be better?"

"No, I need for this to be under my control, at least for now. Thank you, Father."

Over the next year, there were many parents who came to be interviewed for the young boy, but each time the bishop found a reason to reject the couple. As time passed, everyone in the abbey shared in the raising of Tristan. The bishop took him everywhere he went, including vacations to his parents' home. Eventually there were rumors that the young boy was his child, but he paid no attention.

As each year passed, he grew to be more a part of the monastery community, and the thought of him leaving was not even discussed. Eventually, Tristan began to ask questions about his birth, and Bishop LeFore insisted that he know the truth. Around age seven, as he finished telling Tristan the circumstances of his birth, he finished by showing the boy the note left by Jerome Felur.

"Who knows, Tristan? Someday your father may return and claim you for his own, but until he does, I am your father, and we are your family."

* * *

The next morning Tristan watched from the bedroom window as the ambulance arrived in the courtyard at Mont-Saint-Michel and paramedics carried the bishop on a stretcher to the waiting vehicle. Father Bernard accompanied the bishop, carrying a bag of medicine. Before breakfast was served, the bishop had left the island.

Word spread, and the mood in the abbey was solemn. There was a special prayer said at morning Mass, and afterward, the Benedictine Sisters gathered to deliver a Lectio Divina. It was their way of coping with the bishop's condition.

Tristan decided the best way to deal with the weight of the situation was to do his best to continue with his studies and chores. When it came time to do his afternoon chores, he was scheduled to clean windows, but before he reached his destination, he made a detour and returned to the second-floor hallway, to the spot where he and Father Bernard had stood just ten hours ago.

His thoughts jumped back to Father Bernard's comments about having an active imagination, but once there, he saw immediately that the stone was now recessed. He rubbed his eyes in disbelief. When he kneeled to touch the stone with his index finger, it moved inward without effort. With a little more pressure, the stone moved in farther until the opening was cleared for passage. Tristan wished he had a camera.

He took a deep breath and pulled himself into the room. Nothing had changed. Suddenly, he felt the presence, followed by a soft, gentle voice.

"Don't be afraid, Tristan. There's something you need to know."

Although a thread of fear wove its way through him, Tristan had hoped for another encounter with the presence.

"Are you going to hurt me?" he asked.

"No. You will return to the church in what will seem like a few minutes."

Tristan could tell it was the voice of a girl his own age. "Your voice sounds familiar. Do I know you?"

"Yes...and no. We have not met, but in a sense, I am part of you. You have heard the story about how your mother died giving birth to twins and only you survived?"

"Yes, from the bishop. It was written on a piece of paper he found when I was left on a church pew."

"Yes, that is right. Well...I am the spirit and the soul of your twin. I am here to tell you that your life will be enriched if we can be together, but you need get the blessing of the bishop. Only then can I join you in spirit and we can be one."

Tristan was surprised by the revelation and could never imagine such a thing. "The bishop has been taken to the hospital. Why is this happening now?"

"You had to be old enough to understand without being afraid or confused. That's why you are here now. You need to go to the hospital and ask the bishop for his blessing. You won't need to explain anything about this secret room or me. Just ask him for a blessing, and he will understand."

Tristan became anxious and worried. "I don't know where they have taken him."

"You must find out. Get his blessing, and return to me. If he should perish without the blessing, then we cannot be certain of what will happen. Go to him before it is too late. There is little time."

With that, the presence was gone. He felt the difference clearly.

He wasted no time crawling out of the room, and once again, the stone returned to its original position in the wall without any evidence. He walked quickly in the direction of the convent part of the abbey, where the Sisters resided. He knew that Sister Mary did the shopping for the abbey and had access to a small car. She would be his only hope of getting to the local hospital and finding the bishop.

He searched the chapel and the bedrooms without any success. His excitement turned to fear. Sister Mary did not work in the kitchen. It could be her day off. The only place left was the laundry room, where the Sisters washed clothes and bedding daily. When he entered the large room, the vats were bubbling with boiling water, and he could now see Sister Mary adding soap to the copper vat.

"Tristan," she said, mildly surprised, "how are you this morning? Can you hand me that rod?"

"Good morning, Sister Mary. Could you take me to the hospital where they took the bishop? I must speak with him as soon as possible."

Sister Mary was very well disciplined and proper in her manner. She knew the rules and could not see any way to grant Tristan his request.

"You know Father Bernard accompanied the bishop, and I am sure he is getting the best of care. Don't worry, Tristan. He will be fixed up and back here in no time."

Tristan grew more agitated. Sister Mary was his only hope, and time was short. As he thought about a way to rephrase his request, he felt the presence enter his being, and he calmed immediately.

"Sister Mary, the bishop is my father and my mother. He is all I have. I know his condition is grave, and I need to see him before his passes on. Please, Sister. You may not know how much I love him... please?"

Sister Mary was moved by the young boy's request.

"Well, I do need to get some groceries. I could stop by the hospital and drop you off for a visit." Sister Mary chewed her lip for what seemed an eternity before she made her decision. "Get your jacket. I'll be finished here in just a few minutes."

Tristan threw his arms around Sister Mary. At first, it was awkward for her, and then she found herself embracing him in return.

"Run off now and get your jacket. We'll leave shortly."

* * *

The small community hospital was set back from the main road on a lush, ornately landscaped campus. The long driveway was bordered by high, thin evergreens. Where they pulled up at the front entrance, there was a statue of the Mother Mary in a marble fountain.

Sister Mary took hold of Tristan's chin and made him look directly at her. "I am going to pick up some groceries. I will pick you up in about an hour. OK?"

Tristan was anxious to get out of the car. "Thank you, Sister. I'll wait here for you."

As she pulled away slowly, Tristan made his way through large glass double doors and into a waiting room. As he approached the reception desk, he could see the silhouette of Father Bernard at the end of a long hallway, walking slowly in his direction. He waited for Father Bernard, who would surely have the most recent information about the bishop's condition. But as he approached and saw Tristan, the look on his face was solemn.

232

"Tristan, how did you get here?"

"Sister Mary had to do some grocery shopping, so I asked if I could stop by the hospital and see the bishop."

Father Bernard pulled the boy to him. "Bishop LeFore passed away just minutes ago. He is with our Holy Father. It was a final stroke that took him in his sleep. I was there with him when he died. I'm sorry, Tristan. I know he meant a lot to you."

They both sat down on a soft couch that faced a marble table with a large flower arrangement, and neither of them said anything for a long time. Finally, Tristan broke the silence.

"I didn't think he could die. He was always there for me. He always told me the same thing…that he loved me…more than anything. He was my father and my mother. Now I feel empty and alone."

Father Bernard held Tristan in his arms as he cried. When the boy seemed to recover a bit, Father Bernard reached into his jacket pocket and pulled out a thin gold chain with an ancient and worn crucifix.

"The bishop asked me to give you this. It is his crucifix. Do you recognize it?" Father Bernard held it out to Tristan. "It is his most precious gift. He told me he wore it for more than sixty years, and he wanted you to have it."

Tristan held it in his hand. It was an old-style crucifix that was worn smooth in places. He closed his burning eyes and held the necklace to his chest as he whispered, "The most precious gift he gave me was his love, and that will be with me forever."

* * *

Father Bernard and Tristan rode back to the abbey with Sister Mary. Very little was said. By the time they returned to the island, all the flags were at half-mast, and messages were coming in from all parts of Europe. Everyone, including the forty residents from the island village, came to Mass that evening, and funeral arrangements were announced.

After dinner, Tristan slipped out of the dining room and headed for the second-floor hallway. He knew the stone would be recessed.

As before, he kneeled, and pushed lightly on the stone. It moved backward without resistance. He crawled through the opening and entered the secret room. Nothing had changed. Evening light pushed through the window. The beveled cut glass cast designs against the far wall. Without warning, he felt the presence and began to hear the young girl's voice.

"Hello, Tristan."

Tristan turned in the direction of the voice and saw the image of a young girl his age. It was like looking into a mirror, but her hair was long, down to her waist, and the image was transparent. He spoke in a soft and apologetic voice.

"The bishop passed away before I could reach him, so I was unable to ask him for a blessing. He left a necklace for me." Tristan reached into his pants pocket and pulled out the ancient crucifix dangling from its thin gold chain. The presence smiled.

"That will do," she said.

"What does that mean?"

"It means everything. Hand me the necklace, Tristan."

He handed her the necklace, which she held up at each end with her delicate fingers. She came forward and placed the crucifix around his neck. Now only inches away from his face, she began to whisper.

"This is all we need. In the name of the Father, the Son, and the Holy Spirit, may the grace of our Lord be with you always."

With that, she looked deep into his eyes and stepped forward into his physical being. It was as if Tristan's body absorbed her. She was both gone and part of him.

Sunlight illuminated his face. He touched the crucifix where it lay against his chest. It brought back memories of the Bishop LeFore.

When he crawled back into the hallway, he felt changed, more whole, and less afraid. Over just a period of days, something had transpired in the abbey that he could never discuss or explain. He went down to find Father Bernard where he was making plans for the funeral, and Tristan helped with a new sense of gratitude and dignity.

Eventually Tristan was educated by the Benedictine scholars and became a priest. After completing his work one evening at the Grand Séminaire di Rouen, he walked the halls looking at the rosters of previous graduating classes. He marveled at how different the priests looked over the years. He stopped abruptly when a familiar name caught his eye: Jerome Felur.

Tristan hurried to the media center, sat down at a computer workstation, and quickly accessed the Act Estela Civil database. The recently digitized records converged marriages, births, and death records in all of France. He entered the name that was so familiar to him, some approximate dates, and tracked the man to the town of Rouen. He cross-referenced the name with the local Catholic registry. Jerome Felur had been a local priest. When he searched the name using the local newspaper obituaries, there was evidence that he had a sister who died giving birth to twins in the year of Tristan's birth. Searching birth certificates, he found a record of his own birth that listed his father's name as Gabriel LeFore.

Over a period of years, there were many times when he needed help dealing with desperate and challenging circumstances. It was then he would feel a presence. Many men in the upper echelons of the Catholic Church said that someday in the near future, Father Tristan LeFore was destined to become the bishop of Mont-Saint-Michel.

Made in the USA
Charleston, SC
08 February 2013